Praise for The Gunn

The Otter of Death
The Fifth Gunn Zoo Mystery

"While examining some timely social issues, Webb also delivers lots of edifying information on the animal kingdom in an entry sure to please fans and newcomers alike."
—*Publishers Weekly*

"The best part here is watching Bentley's investigative juices start to flow (Webb's background as a reporter really comes to the fore here)... This one will satisfy multiple audiences."
—*Booklist*

The Puffin of Death
The Fourth Gunn Zoo Mystery

"Iceland's rugged and sometimes dangerous landscape provides atmosphere, while Magnus, the polar bear cub, appears just often enough to remind us why Teddy's in Iceland. Webb skillfully keeps the reader guessing right to the dramatic conclusion."
—*Publishers Weekly*

"The exotic locale, the animal lore, and a nice overlay of Icelandic culture and tradition provide an enticing frame story for this solid mystery."
—*Booklist*

"California zookeeper Theodora Bentley travels to Iceland to pick up animals for a new exhibit but must put her investigative skills to use when two American birdwatchers are killed. The fourth book in this charming series doesn't fail to please. Teddy is delightful as she copes with the Icelandic penchant for partying hard."

—*Library Journal*

"I finished *The Puffin of Death* with a feeling of regret that I have not been to Iceland… This book is the next best thing to a trip there. A good Christmas present for those friends who still suffer from itchy feet."

—*BookLoons*

The Llama of Death
The Third Gunn Zoo Mystery

"Animal lore and human foibles spiced with a hint of evil test Teddy's patience and crime solving in this appealing cozy."
—*Publishers Weekly*

"Webb's third zoo series entry winningly melds a strong animal story with an engaging cozy amateur sleuth tale. Set at a relaxed pace with abundant zoo filler, the title never strays into too-cute territory, instead presenting the real deal."
—*Library Journal*

"A Renaissance Faire provides both the setting and the weapon for a murder… Webb's zoo-based series is informative about the habits of the zoo denizens and often amusing."
—*Kirkus Reviews*

The Koala of Death
The Second Gunn Zoo Mystery

"Teddy's second adventure will appeal to animal lovers who enjoy a bit of social satire with their mystery. Pair this series with Ann Littlewood's Iris Oakley novels, also starring a zookeeper."
—*Booklist*

"The author of the edgy Lena Jones mysteries softens her touch in this second zoo mystery featuring an amateur sleuth with a wealthy background and a great deal of zoological knowledge and brain power... Teddy's adventures will appeal to fans of animal-themed cozies."
—*Library Journal*

"Teddy's second case showcases an engaging array of quirky characters, human and animal."
—*Kirkus Reviews*

The Anteater of Death
The First Gunn Zoo Mystery

2009 Winner of the Arizona Book Award for Mystery/Suspense

"I've been impressed with Betty Webb's edgy mysteries about the Southwest, so I was surprised to find she has a softer side and a wicked sense of humor in a book that can only be described as 'High Society meets Zoo Quest.' I've always been a sucker for zoos, so I also relished the animal details in this highly enjoyable read."
—Rhys Bowen, *New York Times* bestselling and award-winning author of the Molly Murphy and Royal Spyness mysteries

THE PANDA OF
DEATH

THE PANDA OF DEATH

A GUNN ZOO MYSTERY

BETTY WEBB

Poisoned Pen
PRESS

Sourcebooks, Poisoned Pen Press, and the colophon
are registered trademarks of Sourcebooks.

Published by Poisoned Pen Press, an imprint of Sourcebooks
P.O. Box 4410, Naperville, Illinois 60567-4410
(630) 961-3900
sourcebooks.com

Library of Congress Cataloging-in-Publication data is on file with the publisher.

Printed and bound in the United States of America.
SB 10 9 8 7 6 5 4 3 2 1

For my brother Ron Corbin,
one of the happiest DNA surprises ever.

Chapter One

I was at the Gunn Zoo doing a live TV interview with a seven-foot tall dinosaur when I received a text message telling me a dead man had been seen floating next to my boat.

Trying not to let my alarm show, I smiled at the dinosaur—a bright orange Tyrannosaurus rex named Tippy-Toe—and asked, "So all the other dinosaurs in Dino Dell are upset that a non-dinosaur is moving into the neighborhood?"

Tippy-Toe nodded his great head. "Dinosaurs are just like people, Teddy. They have their likes and dislikes."

While Tippy-Toe continued to explain why some of his dinosaur friends hated their new neighbor, I inched the mike over to Zorah Vega, the zoo's director, and whispered, "Gotta go. Explain later."

"But you can't…" she hissed.

"Bye."

With that, I gave the camera one more frozen smile, then vamoosed.

At first sight, Gunn Landing Harbor looks like any other California seaside town, but closer inspection reveals no houses and no apartment buildings or condos. That's because the only land in Gunn Harbor—population less than five hundred—is a narrow, semicircular spit of sand and rock that juts out into the Pacific, enclosing a natural bay. Anyone who lives here lives on a boat. I'd lived on my *Merilee* for years before marrying Joe, and I still missed waking to the sounds of gulls and the barks of sea lions.

Not today, though.

As my battered Nissan pickup sped into the harbor's parking lot, I saw a sea of red and blue lights, along with the white van with SAN SEBASTIAN COUNTY SHERIFF'S OFFICE emblazoned on its side, so the text hadn't been an ill-timed joke.

After parking behind the crime scene van, I hurried to the dock gate, ran my ID card through the digital lock, then started toward the *Merilee*. At first, I was surprised not to see any of Dock 4's other liveaboarders, but I quickly discovered the reason when Orville Thompson, Joe's new deputy, stepped out of the shadow of a large catamaran and stopped me.

"Access restricted."

"I need to get to my boat!"

"Crime scene." Orville was a man of few words.

"What do you mean, crime scene? I thought it was some sort of accident."

He crossed his arms over his spindly chest and looked down his long nose. "Access restricted."

"You said that before," I huffed.

"Needed to."

"Where's Joe?"

"Sheriff Rejas?"

"Yeah, that Joe. The one I'm married to."

"Scene of crime."

"Which you think means my *Merilee*, right? So now what? Are you guys going to haul my boat off to the impound lot?"

"The sheriff..."

"Listen, Deputy Thompson, you can't possibly believe..."

"What the hell's going on here?" said someone behind me.

I turned around to see firefighter Walt MacAdams, who lived on the *Running Wild*, moored two slips down from the *Merilee*. His chiseled face was soot-stained, probably because he'd just put out a fire somewhere. "I've worked back-to-back shifts," he said to the deputy, "and I need some sleep."

"Don't firemen bunk at the firehouse?" Deputy Thompson said, in an unexpected rush of words.

Walt flexed his powerful muscles, never a good sign. "Since when are my sleeping habits any of your business?"

Thompson, although irritating, was no wimp, which he proved by stepping forward, closing the distance between himself and a man almost twice his weight. "Since it became my duty to block anyone from approaching slips one through twenty on Dock 4. Now please, sir, you need to step back or I'll have to…"

"Teddy, what are you doing here?" a bass voice boomed. "Oh, never mind. One of the liveaboarders must have tipped you off." It was the San Sebastian County Sheriff Joseph Rejas, here to lay down the law. A touchy situation for both of us, considering I'd had the word "obey" scrubbed from our marriage vows.

Seeing the stubborn set to my jaw, my husband turned his attention to Walt, whom he guessed would be easier to push around. "Regardless of what you've been told, Mr. MacAdams, no one's taking the *Running Wild* to the county impound lot. Your boat, along with all the others on Dock 4, should be cleared within a few minutes. Until then, why don't you go over to Chowder 'N Cappuccino while we finish up? I hear the clam chowder's extra good today."

Walt unflexed. "Well, I am a bit hungry. You wanna come with, Teddy? Treat's on me."

Not yet ready to give up the fight, I said to Joe, "I take it there really is a dead man floating next to the *Merilee*. Anyone know who?"

"No comment, Teddy."

"But…"

"I *said*, no comment!"

If I could just get close enough to see… "Can't I make sure the *Merilee*'s all right?"

His blue eyes, gifts from his Dublin-born mother, narrowed. "Like I told Mr. MacAdams, the chowder's extra good today."

Recognizing an impasse, I followed Walt to Chowder 'N Cappuccino, where we found Linda Cushing, my tipster, slurping down chowder with the rest of Dock 4's year-round inhabitants. Emotions in the room ranged from miffed to resigned.

Chowder 'N Cappuccino had started life as a food truck, but several years ago put down roots in the guise of a small clapboard shack that offered both indoor and outdoor seating. It did a brisk business among the harbor's liveaboarders, but today, with the police-enforced closure of Dock 4, the place was packed. Too upset to be hungry, I ordered a latte from the barista.

"Thanks for the text," I told Linda, after carrying my latte over to her table where she sat with Lila Conyers, owner of *Just In Time*; Gail Bauer, *Fleet Foot*; and Kenny Norgaard, *High Life*.

"Just thought you should know." Linda had lived on her sailboat for years, and the rough mercies of Monterey Bay weather made her look eighty, although she was only sixty-five. "At least they let me feed my cats before they evicted me."

"How's Toby handling that?" Toby was an orphaned white-and-peach-colored Siamese who had chosen *Tea 4 Two* as his permanent home.

"Better than me. But you know Toby, king of all he surveys, even the cops. I saw your handsome hubby petting him."

My concern for Toby out of the way, I said, "Anyone know who's dead?"

"Cliff Flaherty," they chorused.

I blinked. Flaherty—I'd seen him only yesterday—was the writer and producer for *Tippy-Toe & Tinker*, the kiddie show that starred the very dinosaur I'd been interviewing only thirty minutes earlier. That certainly explained the lack of sorrow around the table. Flaherty had been universally loathed.

"Are you sure?" I asked, feeling vaguely guilty because I'd disliked Flaherty, too.

"Him or his twin brother, and I happen to know he didn't have one." This, from Gail. A grandmother six times over, she was older than Linda yet looked years younger. "I was the first to spot him in the wake of the *High and Mighty* when it went speeding by. The harbor master needs to do something about its owner, Jervis whatshisname, before he kills someone." At this she stopped, considered what she'd said, then cleared her throat and continued. "Anyway, the wake washed Flaherty out of the channel and down by our boats. He bumped up against the stern of my *Fleet Foot*, which, ah, flopped his head around so I got a good look at his face before he floated over to your *Merilee*. Then he got hung up on her rudder."

I winced.

"After calling 9-1-1," Gail continued, "I alerted Linda and Walt, and Linda texted you. Now we're all homeless. Oh. Not you, Teddy, you're living the high life inland these days with the guy who evicted everyone."

"Just the guys on Dock 4," I muttered.

"Behave yourself, Gail," Linda snapped. "Teddy's married now, with a husband, a mother-in-law, two stepchildren, and two dogs and a cat. Surely you don't think they could all live on a thirty-four-foot boat."

"It's been done."

"Where?"

"Up near San Francisco you see stuff like that all the time."

"Geriatric hippies," Linda snorted. "Those boats are health hazards."

"You need to stop criticizing what other people do with…"

They would have squabbled longer, but Walt shut them up

by asking, "Anyone know why the cops are proceeding as if Flaherty's death was murder instead of an accident?"

The ensuing silence continued until my cell began to play "The Irish Rover." As if she'd overheard us talking about her, my mother-in-law was on the line. When I picked up, she didn't even bother saying hello, just started right in, her Irish burr thicker than usual. "Teddy, since you're already down at the harbor..."

"How'd you know I'm at the harbor?"

"A newscaster broke into the *Law & Order* rerun I was watching, the one about the serial-killing priest, and reported that the scriptwriter on *Tippy-Toe & Tinker* was found floating right next to the *Merilee*. So where else would you be, luv, besides at the harbor?"

"At the zoo."

"With a murder investigation going on? I know you better than that."

So now Colleen was using the M-word, too.

"Anyway," she continued, "Since there's nothing you can do for that poor man, could you at least bring home a quart of clam chowder? I've been writing all morning and, what with everything, lost track of the time and forgot to start cooking that big roast, and you know how long those things take. But if you bring chowder, everyone'll have something to snack on until the roast's done."

After agreeing, I ended the call. Through the big Chowder 'N Cappuccino window I could see scene-of-crime specialists moving up and down Dock 4, most carrying plastic evidence bags. I shivered, even though the October day was warm.

The second Joe and his minions finished interviewing everyone and reopened Dock 4, I joined the herd of liveaboarders rushing toward the dock, anxious to see if rough-soled shoes had scarred prized teak decks. When we reached the gate to Dock 4, we briefly joined hands and recited a prayer for Cliff Flaherty. Although he'd always gone out of his way to be unpleasant to everyone, we gave his immortal soul the benefit of the doubt.

As it turned out, the *Merilee* hadn't suffered much damage. The slight scraping on the starboard gunwale had probably happened while the EMTs hauled Flaherty's body out of the water, but with a touch-up of varnish, my thirty-four-foot CHB trawler would be good as new.

Unlike Flaherty.

An odd thing happens when someone you dislike dies; you feel guilty because you don't feel grief. To atone, I stayed at the harbor long enough to watch the CSIs tape off Flaherty's *Scribbler*, then leave.

Chapter Two

When I arrived home in San Sebastian, the first thing I noticed was that the silver-blue Toyota hatchback with the DON'T BE AN ASS—VOTE GREEN PARTY bumper sticker was still parked a few yards from the edge of our property. It had been there three days, but since it had been moved a few feet a couple of times, it couldn't yet be considered abandoned.

Still, this was a semirural area, and our nearest neighbor was a quarter-mile away, so who...? Oh, well, not my problem. I parked my pickup in the driveway behind Colleen's red Mustang and went inside the house.

During my return from the harbor, the clam chowder had cooled, but a brief sojourn in the microwave made it palatable enough for ten-year-old Tonio and five-year-old Bridey. They had already been seated at the dining room table when I'd walked in, staring longingly back at the kitchen where their grandmother was putting the finishing touches on the pot roast. The entire house smelled delicious.

"Did you see the dead guy?" Tonio asked.

Having become used to this kind of conversation at Casa Rejas, I replied, "Sorry, he'd been fished out by the time I got there. How was school today?"

"There's no school on Saturday."

Before I could recover myself, innocent-faced Bridey piped up, "Was the *Merilee* all icky with blood?"

I called into the kitchen, "Colleen, maybe you shouldn't let these kids watch so much *Law & Order!*"

"They were watching a PBS documentary on the Vikings, which I thought was going to be harmless," she called back. "But then they started describing something called the Blood Eagle—don't ask—so I switched channels to KGNN, because they sometimes show *Tippy-Toe & Tinker* reruns. But..."

"Tippy-Toe didn't get murdered, did he?" Bridey again, sounding alarmed. She loved that orange T. rex.

"No, sweetheart. Tippy-Toe's fine. The victim was one of the humans you never see on camera. The show's scriptwriter."

Tonio, older and wiser, frowned. "Wait a minute. If the writer's dead, doesn't that mean there'll be no more Tippy-Toe? Or Rosie? Or Zip? Or even that new red panda character who made everyone so mad by moving into Dino Dell?"

"Don't worry about it, Tonio!" Colleen shouted again. "Tippy-Toe lives in California, where scriptwriters grow on trees!" A great rattling of pots and pans.

"But..."

Eager to change the direction of the conversation, I asked, "Isn't this chowder delicious?"

"Daddy won't be home tonight, will he?" Bridey, who recognized a deflection when she heard one.

Although I'd once been a schoolteacher and was adept at dealing with touchy questions from children, I'd discovered that home life was more of a free-for-all, so I rolled out my standard soliloquy about daddies, and even mommies, sometimes needing to work late. And that when they have super important jobs to do—like policing—daddies and mommies sometimes wind up spending entire nights at the office. Especially when the daddies were cops.

In the middle of my soliloquy, I heard the back door open and close.

"Colleen?"

No answer. Maybe she'd gone out to pick some fresh herbs from her kitchen garden.

Tonio leaned over the table and whispered, "She's been acting weird all day."

"She even called me 'Teddy' this morning," Bridey said.

The child didn't think I'd noticed her slipping clams to DJ Bonz, my three-legged terrier mix, and Fluffalooza, Joe's ancient bichon frise, who were hiding under the table. Ordinarily I would have warned Bridey against further spoiling our pets, but I was too concerned about Colleen's behavior. This morning my mother-in-law had called me 'Sonia,' which was the name of Joe's first wife, whose murder had never been solved.

"Don't worry about Grandma, sweetheart," I told Bridey. "She's probably changing a few characters' names in her new book. She did say something about using our names this time out, so naturally she's getting them confused."

A few months back, Joe's mother had sold her mystery novel for a goodly sum, then followed that triumph with an even larger movie sale. The woman who had begun her life in a run-down Belfast tenement was now wealthy, which could have made the cozy-but-inelegant granny cottage Joe had built for her in the backyard redundant. Yet, instead of moving to a mansion, Colleen had stayed put to help care for Bridey and Tonio, so as far as I was concerned, she was welcome to mix up names all she wanted.

As I sat there trying to convince myself Colleen was fine, Miss Priss, my one-eyed rescue cat, rubbed against my ankle. *Feed me*, she purred. Sighing, I obeyed her order, then returned to my chair to stare at my empty plate. Animals fed, humans starving.

In a couple of minutes we heard the back door open and

close again, and Colleen emerged from the kitchen carrying a large platter holding a parsley-sprinkled pot roast surrounded by plump onions, new potatoes, and carrots. The brisket had seemed much larger when I'd come across it in the refrigerator this morning while looking for soy milk for my granola, but since meat often shrinks when cooked, I thought no more about it.

A few hours later I was struggling through a nightmare-plagued sleep when Joe arrived home, but upon hearing the snickerty-click of the gun safe's door closing, I woke up.

"Sorry," Joe murmured, crawling into bed beside me. "I tried to be quiet."

"Did you catch whoever killed Cliff Flaherty?"

"What an optimist you are. Go back to sleep."

I slid into his warm arms, and a few seconds later, I was gone. This time my dreams weren't as dark.

Sunday morning at the zoo started with a visit to the cafeteria. Not the cafeteria for humans, but the one for the animals, where I loaded up my zebra-striped electric cart with monkey chow for the squirrel monkeys; a bucket full of freeze-dried termites for the anteaters, high-fiber pellets for Alejandro the llama, and a mixture of bamboo shoots, quail eggs, and dried fruit for the red panda. I topped it all off with enough food to feed the rest of my charges, then left for the animal enclosures.

My workplace, the three-hundred-acre Gunn Zoo, is divided into several specific "neighborhoods." They include California Habitat, populated by condors, coyotes, and otters; Tropics Trail, with the giant anteaters, spectacled bears, jaguars, and macaws; Africa Trail, roaringly alive with lions, rhinos, and other lethal beasts; Verdant Veldt, featuring less-lethal animals like giraffes, zebras, and ostriches; Down Under, with koalas, wallabies, and emus; Cooler Climes, which starred our one polar bear (but hoping for a second), several penguins, puffins, and an Arctic fox pair; Asia Trail, where Poonya—our new red panda—resided. Nearby was the Komodo dragon, several Japanese macaques, slow lories, Malayan tapirs, and two Bactrian camels (the double-humped kind); last is Friendly Farm, where Alejandro the llama hangs out with his goat, cow, and chicken friends.

If there really is an Eden, the Gunn Zoo is it.

Of great importance to any well-maintained zoo was the large veterinary complex located near the Admin building, and that's where I headed to check on Lucy, the giant anteater. Our head vet had amputated her infected talon this morning, and when I'd checked on her, she'd not yet woken from the anesthesia. Although the loss of a four-inch talon wouldn't present a problem in a zoo setting—and after all, Lucy still had three left on that paw—in the wild it could be life-threatening. The misnamed giant anteaters actually lived on the termites they dug out of rotting logs, and an infected paw could result in death by starvation.

On my way down the hill from Asia Trail, I passed the giant aviary, where Carlos, the Collie's magpie jay, spotted me and flew over to visit. He brought along a twig, and when I stuck a couple of fingers through the meshed enclosure, he deposited the twig into my hand. It was meant to be a wedding gift for our new nest, poor Carlos not yet having figured out we were physically incompatible.

"Oh, Carlos, you shouldn't have!" I trilled.

"*Sweet-sweet-sweet!*" he chirped, mimicking a yellow warbler.

"But I'm sure it will fit into the nest nicely." Do you go to Hell for lying to birds?

"*Whonk, whonk!*" Snow goose.

"Are you sure about that?"

"*Klee-tree-weo!*" Crested lark.

He nudged the twig further into my hand, cocked his dark blue-crested head, and looked at me hopefully.

There was no point in leading him on. "This thing between us, Carlos, it can never be."

Maybe it was the sad tone I inserted into my voice, maybe not, but he responded with an anguished "*Chizz-chizz-chizz!*" Trumpeter finch.

Leaving Carlos to his misery, I drove along the keepers' trail trying not to think about what had happened to Cliff Flaherty. Not that I'd held any affection for him. In fact, I'd always tried to stay out of his way. But there had been that unfortunate occurrence in the harbor's laundromat…

Then there had been his drunken behavior at my mother's house during one of her fundraisers for the Gunn Landing Otter Conservancy, where another zookeeper and I had been discussing the recent murder of a local college professor. The solution to the case had revealed a veritable stink-pile of academic corruption.

We hadn't realized we were being listened to until Flaherty crossed the living room and broke into our conversation.

"We're all thieves and killers under the skin," he'd said, after belting back a rather large drink. With his aquiline nose and piercing blue eyes, he had probably once been handsome, but at the age of fifty-something his jawline had softened and the scar near his receding hairline grew redder the more he drank. I wondered if someone had smacked him.

"Aren't you rather overstating the case?" I'd asked.

He shook his head. "That, coming from a former gunshot victim?"

I'd started to rub my still-sore shoulder, then caught myself. "What happened to me was an exception."

He sneered. "You're a hopeless optimist, then. War could be raging all around, and people like you would all still be singing 'Whistle While You Work' with a hundred other elves."

"Dwarves, not elves, and there were only seven of them. And yes, they whistled because they liked their work, so guilty as charged. Don't you enjoy your job, Cliff? That *Tippy-Toe & Tinker* show is adorable, and your scripts urge children to behave with honesty and compassion. That's something to be proud of."

His laugh had a mean edge. "I doubt the little bastards pay attention to the messages. They just like watching the dinosaurs argue about who's going to go extinct next."

The room had breathed a group sigh of relief when he staggered out the door, smashing one of my mother's prized vases along the way.

He didn't stop to apologize.

"Watch yourself, Teddy!" Jack Spence's shouted warning jerked me out of memory and back to the present, so I was able to brake before my zebra cart had a head-on collision with the bear keeper's own cart.

"Sorry, Jack!"

"Better safe than sorry," he grumbled, steering around me. Jack had been in a bad mood ever since Robin Chase, the big cats keeper, had broken their engagement to take up with rhino keeper Buster Daltry.

But Jack's warning was a fair one, and I reminded myself to focus on the present instead of replaying memories of a dead man.

Poonya, the zoo's new red panda, was still sacked out when I entered her enclosure. As red pandas are prone to do when sleeping, she lay along a mock tree branch, her little legs dangling. As I swept the floor around the adorable creature, she woke up, stretched, twittered at me, then began cleaning her fur like a cat. Once she decided she was clean enough, she jumped down and rubbed along my leg, marking me as part of her territory.

Here's what people never tell you about zookeepers: we often stink. You would, too, if you spent the day cleaning up animal droppings and, in the case of particularly friendly animals, allowed them to mark you. But Poonya's scent wasn't too bad, more of a musky odor with popcorn notes.

"Brought you some fresh bamboo," I told her. "And as a special treat, a lovely egg."

Twitter, twitter!

"You're welcome, sweetie."

Red pandas—also known as the lesser panda or "bearcat"—are members of the Mustelidae family, which includes the weasel, raccoon, and skunk families. And despite being more familiarly known as a "red panda," Poonya didn't look anything like the more famous black-and-white Ling-Ling. To my mind, however, this house cat–sized creature was much cuter, with her long red fur, fox-bushy tail, and reverse raccoon mask on her pointy little face. She was so adorable she made you want to pick her up and cuddle her.

So, once she was through eating, I did.

While it's not common for a zookeeper to cuddle an adult animal, in Poonya's case it was required. Raised by a wealthy woman in Singapore, she had been kissed and cuddled every day until her owner died of a sudden heart attack. Since the woman was a friend of Aster Edwina Gunn, the CEO of the Gunn Zoo, the woman's will bequeathed Poonya to us on the condition that the adorable little thing be cuddled daily. And since all zookeepers are cuddlers at heart, we were happy to oblige.

Somehow the late-departed but certainly not lamented screenwriter Cliff Flaherty had learned about Poonya and, upon seeing her adorable face, had written her into *Tippy-Toe & Tinker*. In the storyline, Poonya was a major cause of dissension when she—a non-dinosaur—moved into Dino Dell. Anyone who knew anything about the last few decades of twentieth-century social history could figure out where the storyline was headed, but that was the genius of the popular kiddie show, a contemporary take on *Aesop's Fables*.

As Poonya lay contentedly in my lap, I began to wonder what would happen to *Tippy-Toe & Tinker* and to Poonya's role in it now that Flaherty was dead. If the show survived, would the storyline starring the little red panda be dropped?

Poonya didn't seem to care. As I stroked her fluffy coat, she twittered her pleasure.

Twitter, tweet, twitter! Tweet, tweet!

A few minutes later, her need for cuddles sated, she climbed back into her tree, and with a final *twitter*, closed her eyes and went back to sleep.

I had just entered the wallaby enclosure in Down Under when my cell rang. What a coincidence. The caller was Jocelyn Ravel, the puppeteer who played the Poonya character on *Tippy-Toe & Tinker.*

"Teddy, I need your help," she piped, her voice high enough to break glass.

Jocelyn, who looked little more than a teenager, had moved to San Sebastian only months earlier, so I didn't know her well, and her request came as a surprise. Why come to me? I knew nothing about show business, and even less about children's puppet programs.

"What's wrong, Jocelyn?" I said, while doling out lettuce, carrots, and kangaroo biscuits to hungry little faces.

"Your husband thinks I killed Cliff Flaherty!"

If my mouth had fallen open any further, one of the finches passing by could have flown into it. "You should be telling this to an attorney, not me."

"I don't have the money for an attorney, but I ran into Lila Conyers at the farmer's market this morning and she told me how you kept her from winding up in prison."

No good deed goes unpunished, does it? I needed to have a talk with Lila about this, but one problem at a time. Keeping my voice steady so as not to disturb the feeding wallabies, I asked, "What makes you think you're a suspect?"

"Because Cliff and I had a big fight a couple of days ago and the whole world probably heard us… I said an awful thing."

Maybe I'm no expert on show business, but I knew enough about actors—and puppeteers did fall into that category—to be aware that acting was a volatile profession. Actors' emotions tended to be raw, but if someone got killed every time tempers flared on a film or stage set, there would be no actors left alive anywhere. Besides, I'd promised Joe not to meddle in any more homicide cases.

I remained silent, keeping my eyes on the wallabies in case a fight broke out over the chopped carrots—they were partial to them—while Jocelyn gave me the details about her disagreement with the show's writer. The argument had been over something called a "character arc," and she hadn't liked what was happening to Poonya's.

"When I complained," she said, "he told me I was too inexperienced to understand what he was doing with my character, so then I told him all about my degree in puppetry at the University of Connecticut and my internship with the Norwalk Players, and my…"

I cut her off. "Fast-forward to the point where you said the 'awful thing.' What'd you do? Threaten to kill him?" Considering the circumstances, it was a tasteless joke, but it did have the effect of silencing her for a moment.

After taking a few ragged breaths, she answered so loudly I had to hold my cell phone away from my ear. "But I did, Teddy! I threatened to kill him! And somebody… Somebody must have told the sheriff all about it because a little while ago he and some deputy showed up at my apartment, and he didn't look like he believed me and I just don't know what…"

"Hold on. Even if you did threaten to kill him, I doubt there's an actor anywhere who hasn't said the same thing at one point in his career. Um, how old are you, by the way, and is this your first professional job as a puppeteer?"

She informed me that she would turn twenty-one next month, and yes, *Tippy-Toe & Tinker* was her first paying job as a puppeteer. Yet she'd argued with a man who I'd heard had more than thirty years' experience in Hollywood and had written at least two blockbuster films. Granted, Cliff Flaherty's halcyon days were long gone, but still…

Several tugs on my socks told me that the wallabies had run out of chopped carrots and wanted more. Still holding the phone to my ear, I complied, then said, "Look, I really don't think there's anything to be worried about, and besides, I couldn't help you even if there were. Despite what Lila might have told you, I need to keep my nose out of this. The last time I tried to help someone I got shot for my trouble—did Lila mention that?—and I'm not anxious to get shot again. You wouldn't believe how much it hurts. But here's what I can do. First of all, I think you're worried over nothing. I happen to know that Joe is having his detectives interview everyone in the cast, and it was simply your turn. If something serious does come up, not that I think it will, I can hook you up with a good attorney." Meaning my new stepfather, Al Grissom.

"But Teddy…"

"Gotta go now, Jocelyn!"

"But…"

Feeling like a heel, I hung up.

Jocelyn wasn't the only person intimidated by the authorities showing up at her door. Detectives paid visits to my friends at the harbor, too, and one by one my old neighbors called to complain. I gave them pretty much the same speech I'd given Jocelyn but was no more successful than I'd been with her. Not that it mattered, because before the day was over, the police had zeroed in on a suspect, and it wasn't Jocelyn or any of my harbor friends.

It was big Gordon "Gordo" Walken, otherwise known as Tippy-Toe, Bridey's favorite dinosaur.

Chapter Three

When I arrived home late that evening—there'd been a last-minute zookeeper's meeting—I noticed that the silver-blue Toyota hatchback was still there. Someone living in their car, perhaps? If so, I'd discuss it with Joe, and he would do what he'd done countless times before: give them water and food and direct them to the nearest social service agency.

Putting the possible homelessness problem out of my mind, I walked into the house to find that I'd missed dinner. Colleen and the kids were planted in front of the television set with our pets, watching a news bulletin while the remnants of dinner sat warming for me on the stove.

KGNN newscaster Ariel Gonzales, hair perfectly styled as always, but face free of the makeup that sometimes covered the scar she'd received in Afghanistan, looked somber.

"We here at KGNN, your place for the latest news bulletins, are stunned to report that Gordon "Gordo" Walken, the puppeteer who portrays a dinosaur on a popular children's show, has been brought in for questioning. Our sources tell us that this police action is in relation to the murder of Cliff Flaherty, the show's writer and coproducer."

She took a deep breath and continued, "The same sources say

that Walken and Flaherty fell into a disagreement on the direction the show was taking, but as yet, KGNN does not have those details. However, our own research shows that the two shared a history dating back more than twenty years to Hollywood, when they worked together on the MGM film *Zombie Lust.* Their apparent bad blood began when Flaherty—a caution here to parents. If young children are in the room, you might want them to leave for this next bit…"

I looked at Colleen, expecting her to shoo the children away. She didn't.

Before I could do the shooing myself, Ariel continued, "According to our sources, the duo's bad blood began when Flaherty had an affair with Walken's then-wife, Sarah. The two never worked together again until last year, when Flaherty signed on to write and coproduce the then-new *Tippy-Toe & Tinker.*"

At that point, the camera panned to the back of the San Sebastian County Jail, where Gordon "Gordo" Walken was being helped out of a sheriff's cruiser. No handcuffs that I could see, not even the prerequisite jacket to drape over them.

"What's an 'affair'?" Bridey asked.

"A party," Colleen answered, still glued to the tube.

"Like a birthday party?"

"Something like that, but without the hats and cake. Most of the time. But every now and then…"

"Colleen!" I admonished.

She paid no attention to me.

Neither did the newscaster. "The same sources tell us that behind the scenes, the show has been fraught with strife."

"What does 'fraught with strife' mean?" This time the questioner was Tonio.

"Lots of infighting," I told him. To Colleen I said, "This isn't news; it's gossip."

Her reply surprised me. "If the kids want to know what's

happening in the world, who am I to stop them? Anyway, I started watching because I once dated Bruce, Gordon's father."

I stared at her. "You what!?"

"Oh, it never went anywhere, Bruce being too old for me, forty to my nineteen. We had nothing in common."

"You dated...?"

"That was before I moved up to San Sebastian and met Joe's father." A dreamy smile crept across her pink-cheeked face. "He was just a deputy at the time—the first Hispanic deputy in the county, believe it or not—and he gave me a speeding ticket over on Live Oak Boulevard. Talk about handsome!"

"Colleen. Back up to where you said you actually dated Gordon Walken!"

"Not *Gordon*, Teddy. Weren't you listening? Gordon was only ten then, and it was his *father* I dated, not him. Come to think of it, he and I did speak once when I was over at their house. Little Gordon—I guess they call him Gordo now—was a sweet boy, and I doubt he killed that nasty Flaherty."

"I've seen the program, Colleen. Sweet little Gordo is all grown up, now, and he's huge, more than capable of killing someone with his bare hands." I felt guilty saying that, but truth was truth.

She sniffed. "I stand by my statement."

Here's the thing about grandmothers and mothers-in-law: we forget they once had lives separate from ours. "Okay, where and how did you meet Gordo Senior? Uh, Bruce."

As the children listened in awe, Colleen told us about coming to America to be with her earlier-immigrated family, and getting a job as hostess at a Hollywood restaurant.

"Mickey Chow, the owner, didn't see anything weird about an eighteen-year-old redhead with a thick Irish brogue working in a Chinese restaurant and hired me on the spot. At the time, I had some fuzzy notion of being a movie star, and since the restaurant was on Hollywood Boulevard only a few blocks away from Paramount Studios, I thought maybe one of the big producers might see me and..." She flushed. "Well, you know how it is when you're young. Everything looks possible, even the impossible."

"Not impossible," I corrected, having seen pictures of a younger Colleen. She had been an Irish beauty, with flaming red hair, blue eyes, and a face and body as flawless as a young Maureen O'Hara's. As far as I was concerned, her earlier dreams of stardom hadn't been too unrealistic.

"Bruce Walken was a regular customer at the restaurant, and a couple of months after I met him, he asked me to come to a party at his house. Me, being a total innocent, said yes." She looked at my face and laughed. "Don't worry. You know what they say, 'God protects drunks and fools.' Nothing bad happened. It was an actual party, and everyone who was anyone in Hollywood was there. The Fondas, Warren Beatty, Gene Hackman, Sally Field... I was so impressed I could barely speak, but Bruce behaved like a gentleman and introduced me around anyway." Then the bliss of memory faded from her face. "But by the end of the evening, I realized that almost everyone I met was still acting. I mean, acting *all* the time. Except for Little Gordon, of course. Like his father, he was a gentleman. Most of the actors, though, couldn't let go and be themselves. All that artifice..."

She shook her head. "Despite what you may have heard, they weren't bad people at all, no worse nor better than the rest of us. They just appeared to live their entire lives acting as something other than who they were. I mentioned this when Bruce took me out on our second dinner date—he had a regular table at Musso & Frank Grill and he treated the waiters with all the courtesy he'd treated the Fondas—and he said that was just the way Hollywood was. I did a lot of thinking that night after he took me home. I thought about Bruce being more than twice my age and about all those Hollywood people who made up his entire world. By the next morning, before I made any rash decisions about my future, I decided to visit my parents, who'd just relocated to San Sebastian. As I drove into town, I wasn't paying as much attention to the street signs as I should have, and..." A beatific smile. "Joe's father gave me a speeding ticket, and that was that. Love at first sight."

Then she turned to me and said, "Little Gordon is no murderer, Teddy. We have to help him."

"*We?*"

"Well, you know what I mean." She looked at her watch. "We'll get started tomorrow, but for now, I, uh, I need to..."

She jumped up and rushed into the kitchen. From my vantage point at the end of the sofa, it looked like she was piling leftovers from dinner onto a plate. I'd wanted to eat them myself, so I called out, "Colleen? I was going to..."

"Sorry, but I'm still hungry," she called back, and with that, headed for the back door. Before opening it, she yelled over her shoulder, "There's enough left for you!" then slammed the door and hurried across the yard to her granny cottage.

"See?" Tonio observed. "Even weirder than yesterday."

I'd planned on spending the evening typing up a Public Service Announcement for the zoo, but as soon as Microsoft greeted me with its signature chimes, the phone rang. It was Jocelyn Ravel again. This time she said she needed to tell me something important, but couldn't tell me over the phone, and I had to come and see her right now before something awful happened. She sounded more distraught than yesterday. Despite the young woman's annoying, off-the-scale voice, I couldn't help but feel pity for her. And after all, did I really want to write that stupid PR piece?

After getting her address, I told her I'd be right over.

Rents in San Sebastian being extraordinarily high, Jocelyn lived in a two-bedroom apartment she shared with three other girls. When I arrived, Heather, an overly made-up brunette, answered the door and told me Jocelyn wasn't there.

"But she said she was desperate to see me about something," I said, flabbergasted.

"Whatever." Heather shrugged her narrow shoulders. "Once the entitled bitch got that call from the tournament saying she'd made the finals, she was outta here."

"*What tournament?*"

"You know, the pinball thing."

No, I didn't know, so I slogged on. "Then if you wouldn't mind telling me which pinball 'thing' that would be, and where it is?"

"PinCon, at Pinball Wizardess. Where'd you expect?"

She closed the door in my face.

Beyond irritated, I took my smartphone out of my pocket. It proved more helpful than Heather, informing me that Pinball Wizardess was a gaming arcade located in a strip mall not far from the apartment. Sighing, I returned to my pickup and set off again.

I arrived at Pinball Wizardess ten minutes later, the short drive having given my temper time to cool. It being late, most of the stores in the strip mall had closed for the day, but at least twenty cars were parked in front of the arcade. One of them was the greenish Kia Soul I'd seen Jocelyn driving. The arcade's door was open, and the chimes and dings of various machines floated out into the cool evening air. Since the area wasn't zoned residential, the noise presented no problem. Once inside, though, the din proved excruciating to my ears. The arcade was also dark, lit only by the machines themselves, so it took a few moments for my eyes to adjust. When they did, I looked around in astonishment.

Upward of forty pinball machines—I'd stopped counting at that point—stood jammed side by side in three rows, operated by straddle-legged gamers ranging in age from teens to folks in their sixties. Their faces were rendered technicolor by the machines' colorful arrays, making the gamers look like visiting space aliens.

As I walked the noisy aisles hunting for my quarry, I passed pinball machines named *Genie, Eight Ball Deluxe, Black Knight, Gorgar, The Haunted House,* and a host of others, some with a mystical flavor, some sci-fi, and others as wicked-looking as a Mickey Spillane noir. One of the black-clad players, walking away from a machine named *Ninja Vengeance,* finally pointed Jocelyn out to me.

Spoiled though she might be, Jocelyn was extraordinarily pretty, although not quite beautiful. Her sandy-blonde bangs and pigtails framed a perfectly oval face and a rosebud mouth that needed no lipstick. She exhibited no trace of her earlier panic, when she'd believed the detectives were zeroing in on her. If anything, she looked cranky.

Spotting me, she grumped, "What are you doing here?"

"Waiting for you to tell me what was so serious that you needed to see me immediately."

Her face blanked for a moment, then lit in recognition. "Oh, yeah. Sorry about that. Something came up."

"You made the pinball finals."

"Yeah." Her childlike voice seemed at odds with her sneering, rosebud mouth. She might have been twenty, but she sounded like a tween.

"Why don't we go outside before my ears start bleeding?" I asked.

"Might as well, since everything's turned to shit in here. Two biffs, one kick-out hole, then I drained out. I'm done for the night."

I wished I liked her more, but I didn't. Her roommate was right: Jocelyn came across as one of those entitled, self-indulgent girls I'd always avoided, but since I was here, I might as well find out what was so important that she'd lured me away from the house.

Once outside, Jocelyn's own bad temper leveled off. "So okay, here it is. Just before Flaherty got himself murdered, he told me he was changing my character's story arc, but wouldn't say how or why, just that I'd find out soon enough. Well, I don't do 'soon enough,' which is just another way of saying 'none of your business,' so I told him I needed to know right now so I could make some plans."

"What kind of plans?"

"Not to renew the lease on my apartment, for starters. I hate my roommates. They're witches."

"Witches, as in the Wicca kind?" I knew a couple of Wiccans, and they both seemed pleasant enough.

"Huh?"

"Never mind. So you want to find new digs, I get that, but it seems like a pretty flimsy excuse to threaten someone's life."

Puffing herself up with self-pity, she whined, "You don't understand. Nobody does."

"Try me."

"Then here goes nothing. When I met with Flaherty at that dinky office he shares with Donaldson, he started saying all kinds of crazy stuff, like, 'big changes were in the works,' and I had to be patient, that a whole pile of new sponsors were climbing aboard, like Cheery Puffs and Gonzola Spread and all kinds of goofy-sounding companies. I kept trying to tell him that the other girls were on my ass to sign the rental contract this week or they were gonna go looking for someone else, and that the Cheery Puffs or whatever didn't mean crap to me. I was on a deadline, and didn't he understand what deadlines mean?"

Flaherty having been in the entertainment business for decades, I figured he did understand about deadlines, but I held myself back. No use arguing with Youth. "And then what happened?"

"And then he called me an ugly name. Wanna hear it?"

I shook my head. Given Flaherty's earlier behavior toward me, and the names I'd heard him call others, I could easily imagine his sobriquet for Jocelyn. "So what did you do?"

"I told him if he didn't take it back I'd bash him over the head with that paperweight on his desk. It was one of those tarantulas in glass. Nasty-looking thing."

Poor tarantula. "Was there anyone else around when you said that?"

"Donaldson was there, but he didn't say a word. Anyway, Old Fart Flaherty told me to lower my voice or leave. So I did. Left, I mean." She looked down and shuffled her feet on the asphalt. "Dumb thing to do, huh?"

In spite of her entitled attitude she wasn't life-savvy, but at least she'd begun to develop some insight. "Well, it wasn't smart, that's for sure. Jobs probably aren't plentiful in the puppeteer industry."

"Tell me about it. Anyway, on the way back to my apartment I started thinking the exact same thing." She bent down and picked up a plastic disc that had been lying there. "Free Coke medallion. Whoop-de-do. Things are really looking up." She overhanded the coin into the lot, where I heard it hit a car.

I bit back my irritation. "Before making your unfortunate death threat, what exactly did Flaherty say about big changes being in the works?"

"Just that things were going to be all peachy and shit, nothing else. He was lying, 'cause I know there's nothing big going on." She vented a victimized smile. "People are always lying to me."

"Who else?"

"Who else, what?"

Patience, Teddy. She's young, and just "drained" out of a pinball tournament. "Who else has been lying to you?"

"Just about everybody on the show. But especially Old Fart Flaherty and Dead Fish Donaldson."

It was becoming increasingly difficult to envision this girl—I couldn't call her a woman—as the sweet-tempered red panda in the TV show, but that's acting for you. "After your performance in the office, do you think you still have a job?"

Her *whatever* shrug mirrored that of her roommate's. "Nobody's told me anything different."

"Have the police been back to talk to you again?"

"Dunno. I've been trying to stay away from the apartment as much as possible, so maybe they stopped by while I was gone. You think?"

"I think if the authorities want to talk to you again, they'll have no trouble tracking you down. So what are you going to do now?"

"I already did it."

"Did what?"

"Tore up the damn lease. I'm through living with those bitches."

Since Mondays are my day off, I'd planned to sleep in, but Joe woke me with a goodbye kiss.

"What time did you come in last night?" I asked, my brain still fuzzy.

"I tiptoed in at two."

Looking at the bedside clock I saw that it was only a quarter to five. "You're taking off after only three hours' sleep?"

He straightened his belt over his flat stomach and gave me a lopsided grin. "Duty calls."

My brain was clearing, at least enough to remember last night's conversation with Colleen. "Is it true you're going to charge Gordon Walken with homicide?"

He actually laughed. "You need to stop watching KGNN. No, it's not true. He answered my detectives' questions satisfactorily—gave us lots of info we didn't know about the victim—and was released forthwith. He's probably home sleeping like a baby."

"I take it he had an alibi?"

"Yup, a doozy." After giving me a peck on the cheek, he left.

Regardless of my relief at Gordo being released from custody, I had trouble going back to sleep. After an hour of fruitless tossing and turning, I gave up and stared at the ceiling, remembering how the tide had lapped against the *Merilee*'s sides, lulling me to sleep. The tide would be going out now, gently tugging her seaward, while I lay here making a mental list of all the people who might want to kill Cliff Flaherty.

I was on that list, too.

Later, as I sat at the breakfast table waiting for the coffee maker to do its life-saving stuff, I looked out the kitchen window toward the granny cottage, where a light had just winked on in the kitchenette. Apparently, I hadn't been the only person having trouble sleeping. Remembering that Colleen's old Mr. Coffee was on the fritz and she hadn't yet replaced it, I decided to take her a fresh cup: one shot of half-and-half, one teaspoon sugar. The kids rarely awoke before six, so after pouring the fresh brew into a large go-cup and doctoring it to Colleen's taste, I crossed the yard to the granny cottage and walked in...

...to find a bronze, Apollo-esque young man dressed only in a towel, attempting to fix Colleen's Mr. Coffee.

"Honey, that coffee maker's broken, so don't bother..." Colleen, emerging from the bedroom, stopped short when she saw me. "Oh, crap."

I set the go-cup down on the counter while leaning as far away from the young man as I could without toppling over backward. "I just, ah, I just wanted to... Um, see ya later!"

After that bumbling speech, I headed for the door. Whatever was going on in here was none of my business. Colleen was an adult, and after all she'd been through in life, she had the right to privacy, but geez, she was in her sixties, and that guy looked so young...

Before I could make it out the door, a strong hand snatched me back.

"Wait! We can explain." Male. So Cal accent.

"Let her go, Dylan! Can't you see you're scaring her?" Irish brogue.

The hand dropped. "Sorry," *Dylan* muttered.

To me, Colleen said, "I'm sorry you had to find out this way, Teddy. I was going to…"

Mortified by the situation, I responded, "Let's pretend this never happened. Don't worry, I won't tell Joe, but, ah, I've got to get back to the house before the kids wake up, and since this is my day off, I was gonna make breakfast for them, and uh…" I couldn't stop babbling. "Bacon and eggs, I think, but maybe some pancakes for Bridey because she really loves…"

"Oh, hush, Teddy. The kids won't be up for another hour, and since you're already here, you might as well sit down and, as Dylan said, let us explain."

Explain? Did she think I was five years old? I knew exactly what was going on here, and if she preferred to pick her boyfriends from some Chippendales revue, it was her business, not mine. I just hoped for her own sake that Mr. Handsome had reached the age of legal consent. "Later would be better," I told her. "But right now…"

I never made it out the door. Colleen enveloped me in a big hug, which she used to frog-march me to her rose-patterned chintz sofa. "Sit," she commanded. Then, to Mr. Handsome she said, "Get dressed before Teddy has a heart attack, but be quick about it because I don't want to be the only one doing the explaining."

The young man shuffled off to the bedroom, where he tactfully shut the door.

"Feel less scandalized now?" Colleen asked. "And by the way, haven't you noticed something?"

Stung by her use of the word, "scandalized," I answered, "Yeah, you've got a resident stud muffin."

A smile tugged at the corner of her mouth. "Take a closer look at the sofa you're sitting on, Teddy."

Willing to do anything to keep from goggling at that closed bedroom door, I looked down to see white sheets and a blue comforter covering the sofa's floral print. Propped against the sofa's arm was a white bed pillow.

"He slept on the sofa?"

"Yes, oh you of the dirty mind."

I had the grace to blush. "Then what...?"

She took a deep breath. "Dylan is my grandson, Teddy."

"But you don't..." I stopped, finally putting two and two together. She'd been so young when she arrived in the States, and so innocent and easy to impress during her Los Angeles years. My heart went out to her. "I get it. Gordo's father got you pregnant and you gave up the baby for adoption and she—or he—had a baby and now you feel guilty and want to help Gordo's half brother and..." I stopped, having had trouble making the ages work.

Colleen exploded into laughter. When she calmed enough to speak, she said, "Oh, Teddy, you really are the most precious thing! You see so much, but yet you're blind."

"What are you talking about?" I said, crankily.

Before she could answer, the bedroom door opened and Dylan emerged, his bronze skin now completely clothed in fashionably tattered jeans the same color as his eyes, his six-pack abs encased in a tight-fitting, black-on-black *Game of Thrones* tee shirt.

The humor left Colleen's face, replaced by glowing, grandmotherly pride. "Look at that beautiful boy, Teddy. Look closely."

I did.

And I saw Joe.

Chapter Four

"Remember that new book I've been working on?" Colleen asked.

I had just taken a gigantic swallow from the glass of water Mr. Handsome/Dylan/my stepson handed me, so all I could do was nod. Now I knew who owned the silver-blue hatchback that had been parked near the house for the past few days.

"New book?" I squeaked, having trouble following her.

"Yes, Teddy. The book I'm writing. You do know what a book is, don't you?"

Dumbly, I nodded my head.

"Well, in the book there's a subplot about a girl who finds out through DNA testing that she's adopted, and she causes a family crisis when she decides to find her birth parents. You know how much I love research, so I decided to see what the testing entailed, and I…"

With the water safely down my gullet, I interjected, "You had your own DNA tested."

She waved her hand at Dylan, who had taken a seat across from us. "And got a wonderful surprise."

Dylan finally spoke up. "I'd done the test myself a couple of months earlier, just after my eighteenth birthday. When

Kinship.com matched us, I emailed her, she emailed me back, and I told her about Mom and Jon..."

"Who's Jon?" I asked.

"My stepfather. Mom's—her name's Lauren—been married to him since I was ten. Great guy, in case you're wondering."

I hadn't been, having other fish to fry. "Did your mother ever live in San Sebastian?" I asked, impressed at how calm I sounded.

He nodded. "Sure. She's always talked about it a lot, how pretty it was with all the farmland and trees and flowers and stuff. Not like where we live now in LA, with high-rises and freeways everywhere you look, but at least the neighborhood around our house is quiet 'cause it's on the edge of Griffith Park and all those hiking and riding trails. Some people even have horses in their backyards. Jon's been working for the same insurance company since I can remember, so he's doing pretty well. Mom, too. She did some acting when she was younger, then did a stint teaching drama at Hollywood High School."

High school. That must have been where... "Did your mother attend San Sebastian High?"

"Yep, just like my biological father did." A hint of defiance there.

Colleen leaned forward. "Dylan arrived three days ago, Teddy. He left a note for his mother, but I made him call home to let her know exactly where he is. Because we'd been emailing back and forth, he already knows Joe is the county sheriff, and all about Tonio and Bridey. And about you, of course."

Dylan smiled at me, his defiance vanishing.

I was still having trouble believing all this. "Colleen, are you *sure* you didn't know anything about this before Dylan contacted you?"

"Of course I didn't. And I can't believe Joe did, either." She crossed her arms across her ample bosom. "He'd never be able to keep a secret like this from me."

She was probably right. You'd think a man like Joe, who'd been in law enforcement for more than a decade, would be expert at hiding things, but I'd found that had never been the case. If Joe had a bad day at the office, it showed. If he was worried about one of the kids, it showed. The love on his face when we made love, it showed.

Come to think of it, why hadn't *I* known about Dylan? I'd known Joe since I was a child, had gone to grade school with him, and even part of high school. He'd been the love of my young life, and I would have known if...

On second thought, no, I wouldn't. My own mother, correctly guessing about my feelings for Joe, and not wanting to have the grandson of a Hispanic migrant worker for a son-in-law, had shipped me off to a finishing school in Virginia for the remainder of my high school years. When I'd returned home two years later, he was engaged to Sonia. Afterward, I'd soothed my broken heart in college, where I'd met Michael and moved to San Francisco. But after only two years of marriage, Michael left me for another woman, and my only partially healed heart had broken all over again. That time, though, I'd returned to my original home at Gunn Landing and found the *Merilee* waiting for me.

And Joe.

"Who's going to be the one to tell Joe?" I asked Colleen. "You? Dylan? My God, all he has to do is walk into our house and say, 'Hi, Dad,' and the resemblance alone..."

Colleen didn't let me finish. "You could do it. This evening, after Joe gets home from work."

The breath whooshed out of my lungs. As soon as I could speak, I said, "Me? You're kidding, right?"

"At the very least you could act as a go-between." She'd read my face and knew her first suggestion was a no-go.

"Okay, I'll try to make a few inroads, but since you're the one who started this, *you* should be the one to tell him." Then to Dylan, "Let your grandmother do all the talking, okay?"

He nodded. "Sounds good to me."

Now that the shock had begun to wear off, I stood up and gave the kid a big hug. "Welcome to the family, Dylan."

During lunchtime, Joe called to tell me that KGNN was retracting yesterday's story about Gordon "Gordo" Walken being a suspect in the Cliff Flaherty homicide. Apparently, Gordo and his roommate, Ansel "Bird" Yates, had been surfing twenty miles down the coast at the time Flaherty died, afterward joining a beach party of surfers who drank until dawn and then did whatever surfers usually did. My concerns now lay closer to home. As long as Joe was on the phone, I decided to ask the question that had had my mind awhirl all morning.

"Joe, how many different girlfriends did you have back in high school? Besides me. And Sonia, the kids' mother, of course."

"Huh?"

Remembering Dylan's earnest face, I soldiered on. "The high school years can be pretty hectic, what with all the stresses, you know, raging hormones, algebra tests, and…"

"Is there going to be a tie-in to something in there? I mean, first we're talking about how happy you are that Gordo's been released, and now you want to discuss raging hormones?"

Time for a little white lie. "Oh, while I was scrolling through the TV looking for *Animal Planet*, I accidentally landed on a *Jerry Springer Show*, and he was doing that who's-your-daddy thing and…"

Joe's laughter on the other end of the line sounded reassuring. "Teddy, you never cease to amaze me. Didn't Springer go into politics? Run for mayor or something?"

"Yeah, of Chicago."

"Good for him, maybe not so good for Chicago." He vented another laugh. "Well, here's the real reason I called. Surprise, surprise, I'll actually be home in time for dinner tonight."

I managed a smile even though he couldn't see it. His on-time-for-dinner arrival wouldn't be the only surprise around Casa Rejas today.

Neither Tonio nor Bridey liked the sandwiches I'd made. Their elementary school was playing host to a two-day teachers' conference, and they were bored.

"I hate peanut butter!" Bridey wailed.

"But peanut butter and jelly is all you would eat last week," I pointed out.

"I changed my mind! I want pizza!"

"Me, too," Tonio said. "I'm sick of peanut butter."

Giving up—someday I'll grow a spine, but not today—I called Matteo's Magnifico Mangia and ordered a large half-vegetarian, half-pepperoni-mushroom-and-ham pizza, plus a double order of stuffed cheesy bread. If the little kids didn't eat them, I would take them over to the big kid hiding out in the granny cottage.

"Where's Grandma?" Tonio asked twenty minutes later, after taking his first bite of the steaming pizza. "She usually eats with us. And she really, really likes pizza."

"She's busy," I told him.

"Busy doing what?"

"Housework and stuff." Not quite a lie, since hiding your eighteen-year-old grandson could fall under the heading of "housework" as long as you hid him in the house.

"Soon as I finish my pizza, I'm gonna go see her," Bridey piped up.

"Oh, ah, I was thinking about going over to the...the..." I thought hard, trying to come up with something that the two children would both like. "Going to the *Merilee* to do a little work on her. Maybe you'd like to help out?"

You've never seen children chow down pizza so fast, and within minutes, the only leftovers included two slices of vege-tarian, and one half-loaf of cheesy bread. Excusing myself for a minute, I walked the leftovers over to the granny cottage, where Colleen and Dylan were engaged in a game of *Monopoly* on Colleen's ancient board. Things looked fraught for Dylan's top hat game piece, since Colleen's battleship ruled most of the board. I'd forgotten to warn him about her.

"I'm taking the kids to the *Merilee*," I announced, as Dylan's dice roll landed his tiny hat on Boardwalk, which boasted one of Colleen's many hotels. For the first time I noticed his knuckles were scabbed over.

"Your boat's been cleared?" Colleen asked.

"Yes, I…"

Perhaps to avoid surveying the carnage on the board, Dylan looked up. "What do you mean, 'cleared'?"

"A dead man was found floating next to my boat a couple days ago," I answered.

Dylan's beautiful complexion suddenly looked much less bronze. "*Dead man?*"

"A guy named Flaherty," Colleen clarified. He's, well, *was* the writer on a local TV show, *Tippy-Toe & Tinker*. The authorities—" I noticed she didn't say *your father*—"thought they had someone, but now they admit they don't."

My cue. "By the way, I just got a call from Joe. He said the news story about Gordo Walken being arrested was overblown. The detectives merely wanted to question him, and they found his answers satisfactory enough to let him go. Apparently, he was at some surfer party when it happened." To Dylan, I said, "We're talking about the puppeteer who handles Tippy-Toe, the T. rex on the local kiddie show. You know, where they use string-controlled marionettes instead of hand puppets."

Dylan hadn't said anything for a while, but when I glanced at him, I saw that his face had gone white. "Are you talking about *Cliff* Flaherty?"

As rocky as I'd felt all morning, there was no missing Dylan's usage of Flaherty's first name. Colleen and I both stared at him.

"You knew Cliff Flaherty?" Colleen asked, the worry lines on her forehead prominent.

Dylan looked back down at the *Monopoly* board. "Um, those hotels'll cost me two thousand each, which I don't have, so it looks like you won, Grandma. Again." He snatched up the top hat and began collecting the bank's play money. "Three games in a row. If I didn't know you better, I'd think you cheated."

Colleen frowned at Dylan, and I doubted it was because she'd almost been called a cheat. As for me, my feelings had plunged from mere rockiness to dread. "You *did* know him, didn't you?"

Without looking up, he muttered, "Say, you know what? I'm getting superstitious about this stupid hat, so I think I'll exchange it." He rattled the pieces around where they'd been left in the box, and pulled out the little metal dog. "We had a Scottie once, so maybe he'll bring me luck."

Slick deflection, but it didn't fool me. "Dylan, when and where did you meet Cliff Flaherty?" *And did you hate him as much as everyone else did?*

Dylan returned the metal dog to the box. "Actually, giving in to superstition is a sign of weakness, isn't it? So I'll just stay with the top hat."

"Answer me, Dylan."

When he looked up, his blue eyes were fierce. "What is this? The third degree? Look, Teddy, you may be my stepmom and you may be married to my biological dad, but I don't need to tell you who I know and why I know them. Okay?"

With that he overturned the *Monopoly* board, sending dice and deeds flying, then stalked out.

Into the backyard.

"Oh, hell!" Colleen yelped, rushing after him. "The kids will see him!"

Too late. Tonio was already out the door racing toward Dylan, with Bridey right behind.

"Who're you?" Bridey piped. Her innocent face grew solemn as she stared at him in confusion.

Dylan froze.

Tonio was staring at him, too. "What were you doing in my Grandma's house?" He clenched his small fists and started toward Dylan.

Colleen, who usually had something to say about everything, remained silent, so the job of defending my new stepson fell to me. I clapped my hands and pasted a big smile on my face, hoping it didn't look too phony.

"Hey, kids! Let's all go into Grandma's house for a little talk!"

Chapter Five

If the day had been difficult, it was a walk in the park compared to that evening.

Since Colleen and I had decided it would be best to deliver the facts of Dylan's existence in easily digestible bits, I made certain Tonio and Bridey—whose excitement couldn't be contained—were stashed in the granny cottage when Joe arrived home. To further soften things, I'd roasted a small turkey and put together a Thanksgiving-style dressing, with all the usual side dishes: mashed potatoes and gravy, green bean casserole, yams, and cranberry sauce. Gaining a new family member was a Thanksgiving of a sort, wasn't it?

I'd envisioned a one-person-larger family dinner in the living room, filled with happy smiles and overflowing hearts. Real Hallmark Channel stuff.

It didn't work out that way.

The first thing Joe said when he came through the door was, "Sure smells great in here, but where are the kids?" DJ Bonz and Fluffalooza danced around him. Miss Priss ignored him, as usual.

Hoping that my smile didn't look as strained as it felt, I answered, "They're over at Colleen's. Uh, by the way, she has some, ah, news for you." I examined that clumsy sentence for a moment, then stretched my grin wider and added, "Some really, really exciting news!"

"She must have received another big royalty check for... what's her book's title again?"

"*Murder at the Zoo.*"

He sniggered. "Oh, yeah, the amazing adventures of Lettie Hently, the detecting zookeeper. Gosh, I wonder who she reminds me of."

For once I was happy to be teased about Colleen's new mystery series, which she claimed—despite its sound alike protagonist—wasn't based on me. But tell that to Joe and my fellow zookeepers, who every now and then "mistakenly" addressed me as "Lettie," then sniggered like Joe was doing now. But what the heck, his teasing put off the dreaded encounter.

"Forget something?" I asked.

"What, Lettie?"

"You forgot to kiss me."

He remedied that omission right away. "Better now?" Then he turned and started toward the bedroom where he kept the gun safe.

While he disarmed himself and changed into jeans and a Cal State Monterey sweatshirt, I went back into the kitchen and turned all the burners down to warm. When he emerged from the bedroom, he was rubbing his hands in anticipation. He hadn't noticed that the dining room table was set for six, not five.

"Had to work through lunch, so I'm starved. Want me to round up the kids?"

"Hmm, about that. Like I said, they're at Colleen's, and she wanted to talk to you about something before we all sit down to dinner."

"Can't she tell me while we eat?"

"Not really. We have, um, a guest, and she wants you to meet him."

A slight frown marred his face. "A 'him,' you say? For dinner? Please don't tell me my mother has a boyfriend, and that it's serious enough for a dinner invite." Joe might have been a grown man in his mid thirties, but in his own way he was still a mama's boy. Overprotective to a fault, he'd always viewed Colleen's prospective suitors—and she'd had at least two that I knew of—with deep suspicion.

"Nothing like that." I held out my hand. "Well, c'mon, let's go."

Time to get it over with.

As earlier agreed upon, Colleen had stashed Dylan, Tonio, and Bridey in her bedroom to watch a rerun of *Tippy-Toe & Tinker,* leaving the door ajar just enough to hear the children's laughter. No basso laughs, though. Dylan was probably too nervous to find any pleasure in old school marionettes.

Colleen was nervous herself, and tried to stall the proceedings with an offer of hot tea. "Chamomile. Very soothing."

"I don't need soothing," Joe said, ignoring my efforts to lead him to the sofa. "I'm starved. Just go ahead and introduce me to this mystery guest of yours so we can go back to the house and eat."

"All in good time. But first, let me explain."

Ever notice that when someone says, "Let me explain," the temperature in the room tends to drop? That's what happened now.

"What's going on, Mom?" Joe asked, sounding more cop than son.

Colleen was saved from answering when the bedroom door flew open and Bridey ran out and flung herself at him. "I knew I heard you, Daddy! I knew it was you! And guess what? I've got a brand new *brother*!"

Realizing our more measured plan was blown, Dylan

emerged from the bedroom holding Tonio's hand. He didn't say a word, just stared at Joe.

Joe stared back.

Colleen rushed into the silence. "Joe, I took this DNA test because of the book I'm writing and I…and I… Well, I got this match I didn't expect, and uh, and I…"

Still staring at Dylan, Joe barked, "Who the hell are you?"

I had to admire Dylan's aplomb. "My name's Dylan Ellis. You knew my mother. *Lauren Ellis.*"

Joe's mouth gaped.

Despite the grown-ups' discomfort, Bridey's joy was not to be contained. She danced in a circle around Dylan and Tonio, chanting, "Got a brand new brother! Got a brand new brother!"

I plucked at Joe's sleeve. "Dylan's very nice, and he's…"

Joe jerked his arm away and hurried out the door, not bothering to close it. Seconds later, I heard his cruiser's door slam, the roar of its big Charger engine, then the screech of wheels as it turned sharply into the street. A loud *vroom*, and Joe was gone.

It was all so shocking that even giddy Bridey shut up.

After a moment, Colleen said, "Chamomile tea for everyone!"

Two hours later, after we'd eaten what little dinner we could stomach, Joe returned.

We'd gone back to the granny cottage and were sitting on Colleen's flowery sofa, trying to comfort a morose Dylan, when Joe walked through the door. His eyes were red. They were dry, though, and his face was all hard lines. Regardless of whatever emotional upheaval he'd gone through, he'd reverted to his in-control self.

He addressed Dylan in the abbreviated manner he so often used in his job. "Went to the office. Ran a search on your mother. Too easy. Listed phone number, not smart. Called. Let her know you were safe."

"Am I?" Dylan responded warily.

Joe's face softened. "Don't be a snot, kid. Come here."

Dylan rose from the sofa and moved hesitantly toward his father.

While he was still several steps away, Joe rushed forward and enveloped him in his arms.

Chapter Six

The next morning, after taking a shower and putting on a freshly pressed zoo uniform, I wandered into the living room to see if any further drama had erupted overnight. All appeared calm. Dylan had slept on our convertible sofa, and bless his heart, had already folded up the bedding into a neat stack and returned the sofa to its usual shape. From the voices that emanated from the kitchen, I realized he was helping Colleen prepare breakfast. Giving a silent thanks to his absent mother for raising him so well, I found Joe, Bridey, and Tonio sitting at the breakfast table, watching the young man as if he were a god recently descended from Olympus.

"Sausages and pancakes, my favorites," I said, breaking into the awe-fest.

"Mine, too, Stepmom."

His wide grin revealed perfect teeth.

Stepmom. Not being a formal kind of gal, I suggested he call me "Teddy." After all, that's what everyone else, including Tonio and Bridey, called me when they weren't snickering and calling me "Lettie."

He gratefully complied, handing me a small stack of pancakes. "Blueberry syrup or maple, Teddy?"

"I'm feeling daring, so let's go with blueberry."

A bow. "Excellent choice, m'lady."

Breakfast progressed without a hitch. In between bites, Dylan gave us a quick account of his childhood. "When I was younger, Mom did a little acting, mainly commercials and stuff, but the only thing I can remember about that time is all her crazy actor friends showing up at our house for parties. You'd think she would wind up with one of them, but she met Jon, who's in insurance, and they got married when I was around ten." For a moment he looked wistful. "Things got calmer, but less fun, so not much to tell after that. As soon as I graduated from high school, I took a couple of drama classes at Burbank Community College. I was thinking about transferring over to USC, and I still may. But as soon as I turned eighteen, I sent off my DNA, and well, here I am."

"Girlfriend?" Joe asked.

"No one in particular."

Of course not. Given Dylan's spectacular looks, he probably had dozens of girls vying for the honors. But I wasn't as interested in his love life as I was in the material he'd edited out of that abbreviated biography. "How did you and your mom wind up in Los Angeles in the first place?" I asked.

"From what I've heard, my grandmother..." He shot a look at Colleen, then started again. "My *maternal* grandmother had a sister, Jeanette, in Glendale, so after she learned about the, ah, accidental, ah, pregnancy, she drove Mom down there to stay with Jeanette for the duration. The original idea was to adopt me out, but after I was born, Mom reneged on the agreement— she'd turned eighteen by then—and refused to give me up. There was a big family breach that's lasted for years, and in the end, Aunt Jeanette let Mom and me stay there until Mom got enough work to rent her own apartment."

"Enough work? For actors, that usually takes years," I pointed out.

He didn't blink. "Sure. That's why she signed on with one of those temp agencies, but Mom was beautiful, still is, and she started getting modeling and walk-on parts right away. A few good speaking roles, too, and when they were released on VHS, then DVD, she started getting residuals, and that added up. Somewhere along the way she got her AFTRA card and wound up snagging that series of commercials for the GoForth Insurance Company. Which is how she met Jon Overholdt. He's the vice president of GoForth."

Ah, Hollywood. Rags to almost riches, if you were lucky. And apparently, Lauren Ellis had been lucky as well as beautiful.

Throughout the rest of breakfast, I tried to ignore the jealousy chewing at my heart.

Although it was Tuesday, the day KGNN usually aired my live TV show, *Anteaters to Zebras*, I discovered the feature had been postponed. Instead, the station was running live coverage of the Miss San Sebastian County Beauty Contest (Miss Artichoke Farm seemed to be ahead in points, due to her archery skills). Thus freed, I was able to work a normal shift at the zoo.

While I laid out fresh bamboo shoots for the red panda, Lex Yarnell, one of the Gunn Zoo's park rangers, rolled up in his leopard-spotted golf cart. Normally a relaxed kind of guy, his handsome face looked tense.

"Did you hear about that big Gordo guy who works the T. rex marionette on that kiddie show?" he asked, after taking a sip from his still-steaming to-go cup. Suddenly his face relaxed into a grin. "Oh, look! Poonya's doing her 'Eek' thing again!"

I turned around to see the red panda standing on her hind legs, her forelegs raised high in the air. "You scared her so she's trying to look big and dangerous."

"As if. Talk about a cutie."

"No argument there. But back to Gordo Walken. Yeah, the authorities picked him up, then let him go. Turned out he was at some sort of a surfer party with a bunch of other people when Flaherty was killed." The image of seeing six-and-a-half-foot Gordo on a surfboard was a bizarre one, but there were no height restrictions in surfing.

The tension returned to Lex's face. "Uh, yeah, but when I was having lunch in the employee lounge a few minutes ago, there was a follow-up bulletin on KGNN. Ariel Gonzales, you know, that newscaster who used to be a Marine, was standing in front of the jail announcing that the authorities were looking in a new direction and that an arrest was imminent."

Finally deciding Lex wasn't going to kill and eat her, Poonya dropped back down to all fours and began snuffling through the bamboo. Upon finding a stalk of particular interest, she sat back on her rump and began chewing.

"What did Joe have to say?" I asked. "He's usually good for a quote."

Lex gave me an odd look. "If I were you, I'd give him a call. In fact, I'm surprised he hasn't called you already."

Before I could ask why, my cell phone played the opening measure of "I'm Too Sexy for My Shirt," my husband's ringtone.

"Speak of the devil," I said, pulling the phone out of my pocket.

"I'd better be going," Lex said easing his cart forward. "Just dropped by to warn you in case…well, just in case." With that, he took another sip of his coffee, made certain the lid was on tight, then drove away.

"What's up, hon?" I asked Joe, holding the phone close.

"Heard the news yet?" His voice was solemn.

"Gordo Walken's suing KGNN for defamation?" I joked.

"Gordo's too nice a guy to pull a jerk move like that. I'm talking about the real news."

"Which is?"

He cleared his throat. "I recused myself from the Flaherty investigation and turned the case over to Chief Deputy Emilio Gutierrez."

"*What*?!" I yelped so loudly, Poonya reared back up on her

hind legs. Softening my voice for the red panda's sake, I said, "Why in the world would you even think of doing such a thing?" Then I remembered the usual reason law officers are usually pulled from a case. "Have you been accused of something?"

In a firmer voice, he answered, "Absolutely not. Look, the Cliff Flaherty case isn't something I feel comfortable discussing over the phone, so why don't we meet at the Nairobi Café in a few minutes? I'm already there, sitting at a corner table where it's nice and quiet."

As soon as I agreed, he killed the call.

Poonya was still standing in her *Eek!* position as I drove away in my zebra cart.

The Nairobi Café, an African-themed food stop at the end of Africa Trail, was nearly empty. Joe had sequestered himself in a dark booth furthest from the door, so at first I couldn't see him well. As I drew closer, the misery on his face alarmed me. The glass of water in front of him was still full, and he hadn't even obliged himself of the café's famous Botswana Burger.

"What's going on?" I asked, sliding into the booth. "And don't spare my feelings. Whatever it is, I can handle it."

"Dylan's about to be arrested."

Certain I hadn't heard him right, I shook my head. "Give that to me again."

"My biological son, Dylan Ellis, is going to be arrested for the murder of Cliff Flaherty. He was recorded on a 7–11 surveillance camera in a physical altercation with Flaherty the morning of Flaherty's death. The lip-reader we brought on board says that Dylan was shouting…" Here Joe spoke slowly, as if to a child— "*'I'll kill you, just see if I don't. For what you did, you deserve to die.'*" He resumed his normal speech pattern. "A witness, a woman getting gas, confirms what the lip-reader said. Along with that, there are, ah, other indications leading the detectives to believe Dylan was involved in the homicide." He took a few gulps of water, then cleared his throat "That clear enough for you, Teddy?"

I felt sick. "There has to be another explanation." Then a thought struck me. "Oh, my god. Colleen! You've got to call her and tell her..."

"Shhhh!" Joe clenched my hand so hard it hurt. "I can't interfere. Before I called you, I got a call from Gutierrez. He and the detectives are on their way to execute the arrest warrant. Heck, they're probably at the house already."

"But the kids! They're home today because of that teachers' conference, and they'll be..."

"The kids will be fine. You know how warm and fuzzy Gutierrez's become since he's a new dad. Bridey's probably already got a new teddy bear, and Tonio a shiny sheriff's badge."

I jerked my hand away. "I can't believe you're allowing this!"

His eyes were bleak. "I don't have the power to stop it, Teddy. Not if I want to continue functioning as the sheriff of San Sebastian County."

Despite my horror, I knew he was right. Still, it was the first time he'd ever had to hand over control of an investigation to someone else. No. That wasn't correct. A couple of years earlier, when Joe was attending a refresher course given by Homeland Security in Virginia, Deputy Elvin Dade—now forcibly retired—sat in for him. Dade's many missteps created an unholy mess, the results of which still reverberated around San Sebastian County. Gutierrez was smarter than Dade, and less ego-driven, but still...

"This is just awful," I mourned.

Joe looked down at his glass. "Yeah. It is."

Like Joe, I soon learned I had no power when I drove my cart over to Admin to ask Zorah if I could go home for the day to comfort Colleen and the kids. Just as the zoo director began to answer, Aster Edwina, who was sitting in the guest chair, stopped her cold.

"Personal problems are no excuse for missing work," the old harridan snapped. "I don't care what kind of hell has rained down on your family, you're completing your shift. Zorah was just telling me about three keepers being out sick, which means we're shorthanded, so you need to stay here and take care of those animals. And by the way, finding secret sons is no emergency, even when they get arrested for murder."

"How did you know?" I gulped, before I realized that of course she knew. Aster Edwina Gunn, matriarch of the uber-wealthy Gunn family and head of the trust that managed the Gunn Zoo, knew everything that happened in San Sebastian County. I had, however, expected more sympathy. After all, Aster Edwina had once found a daughter she'd thought lost, and therefore should have understood the emotional upheaval my own family was now experiencing. But the ultra rich don't live by the same rules as the rest of us, do they?

Biting back my disappointment, I continued on my rounds. For once my heart wasn't in it, and the animals could tell. Magnus, the polar bear cub, wouldn't come near me, and Lucy, the giant anteater, even took a swipe at me through the security fence with her bandaged paw. But at least her swipe startled me out of my fugue. Since a careless zookeeper could turn into a dead zookeeper, I forced myself to be present in the moment, as that old hippie Ram Dass once counseled. *Be here now.* Therefore, I finished my shift without disembowelment or losing a limb, and was able to hurry home to confront whatever hell awaited me there.

As I pulled my pickup into the driveway, Bridey ran out the door, hugging a new teddy bear, but with tears streaming down her face. "Mean men took my new brother away!" she howled.

Tonio was right behind her, snarling. "I hate Emilio! He dragged Dylan away in handcuffs!"

Colleen, usually the epitome of calm, was in even worse shape. Despite my earlier phone call assuring her everything would turn out all right, her fiery red hair was in disarray, her blue eyes were bloodshot, and her hands trembled. "This is my fault. If I hadn't invited him up here, this never would have hap-pened. Teddy, you've got to do something!"

"Like what?" I said, aghast. "You know I can't interfere in a police investigation."

Her voice, earlier thick with unshed tears, turned fierce. "You've done it before, and for less reason. This is my *grandson* we're talking about!"

How strange it was that the fate of a young man whose exis-tence we hadn't even suspected a few days earlier could have such an impact on us all. But this was no time to wax philosoph-ical. At the sound of an approaching motorized growl, I turned around to see a KGNN mobile news van pulling up at the curb.

"Let's finish this in the house," I called over my shoulder, as I hustled up our walk, leaving my distraught family to follow.

They did, but as soon as the door closed behind us, the beseeching started again.

"I want my brother back!"

"Me, too!"

"Don't just stand there, Teddy! You need to find out who's responsible for that man's death, and it wasn't my grandson!"

"I... I..."

"Teddy, *pleeeeeeze!*" Two young voices, screaming in unison.

To insert myself into a police investigation would be an act of madness, especially since it might set me against Joe, the man I loved so dearly. Only an idiot would act so irresponsibly.

"All right," I said. "I'll do it."

Chapter Seven

Joe was expected home any minute, so I had to act fast. Using my cell so there'd be no telltale record on the house's landline, I phoned defense attorney Albert Grissom, the only defense attorney I could afford, mainly because he was my stepfather.

"Lovely to hear from you, Teddy," he said, sounding suspicious. "Am I right in guessing that you have a personal interest in one of the new residents of the San Sebastian County Jail?"

How well he knew me. "Dylan Ellis needs a good attorney. Someone of your caliber."

"Dylan Ellis, eh? And you are interested in the fate of said Mr. Ellis because? Remember, I'm at the office and haven't had time to indulge in those delightful newsbreaks on KGNN."

When I told him the story—the DNA testing, the hiding out for days, the preemptory arrest—I could almost hear his eyebrows rise.

"You're kidding."

"Wish I was."

"And you're getting involved in this because…?"

Rather than tell the truth, that I was an idiot, I said, "What person, er, what *mother* wouldn't want to help her stepson in a time of need?" Just saying the word *stepson* gave me shivers. I'd never even been pregnant, yet here I was, with two young children and an adult son.

After a few seconds of muttering, Al said, "Well, since it's such a lovely October day, I think I might take a leisurely stroll over to the jail. Not that I'm promising anything, you understand."

"Thanks. And Al?"

"*Yeees*? He stretched out the word longer than I thought necessary.

"Maybe you could partner with me in this."

"*Partner?*"

"Say, share information?"

The expected yelp emerged forthwith. "You know better than that!"

"But this is a special case."

"They're all special cases, Teddy." Grumpy now.

"You know what I mean."

"Yes, I do, and the California State Bar looks quite dimly upon such behavior. Not to mention Caro."

Conversations with my stepfather never got very far before my mother's name was invoked. "You don't have to tell her."

"Oh, please. The CIA, Mossad, and the old KGB pale in comparison to your mother."

"Just talk to Dylan. Then let me know the lay of the land."

"Lay of the land, huh?"

"Something like that."

A deep sigh, then, "Talk to you later, Teddy. Maybe."

With that, he rang off.

Less than five minutes later, Joe walked through the front door carrying a Colonel Sanders bucket of chicken. The dinner conversation ranged from near-hysterics (the children) to stoic calm (Joe), with me somewhere in the middle. Bridey wept as she halfheartedly gnawed at a drumstick, while Tonio waved his around like it was a weapon, promising what he was going to do to the deputies who'd had the temerity to arrest his new brother.

Joe tried to soothe Bridey while at the same time reminding Tonio that although revenge may sound sweet, it was against the law. Colleen, usually talkative, said nothing, but from her expression, whatever was going on in her head wasn't pretty.

Strained dinner finished, we trooped into the kitchen with our dirty plates and took up our usual stations at the sink. Since the dishwasher was on the fritz again, Joe washed, I dried, and Colleen put away. The children wiped down the table, straightened the chairs, then vanished into their respective rooms.

When the last dish was put away, Colleen announced in what I thought was a needlessly loud voice, "The San Sebastian Library called earlier today and told me they'd just received the new Stephen King. My name turned out to be the first on the waiting list, so I'm driving over there. Teddy, you can come with if you want. They have the new Jodi Picoult, too."

Joe stared at her. "You're going to the library? At seven in the evening?"

She gave him a hard look. "Something wrong with reading?"

"I've always loved Jodi Picoult," I said, heading for the door.

"You realize we have to do something," Colleen asked, as we cruised away from the house in her new red Mustang. Not a grandmotherly car, but Colleen wasn't the standard-issue grandmother. I was well aware that while she did enjoy Stephen King's gore-athons, this impromptu library visit had nothing to do with books, and everything to do with getting away from Joe.

"I already called Al Grissom, and he promised to meet with Dylan," I told her, as we passed by a house with a sign in the front yard that read FRESH EGGS FROM FREE RANGE HENS. In front of it, a couple of Rhode Island reds searched through the grass for bugs. "He hasn't gotten back to me yet."

Since we lived in a semirural section of San Sebastian County, traffic was light. As we drove on through the twilight, all I could think about was how much our lives had changed. Within the space of a week, we'd swung from placidity to joy to terror. But neither Colleen nor I were the type to sit by passively while fate washed over us. We were both fighters.

"Al Grissom, good. What else?"

"What do you mean, what else?"

"I know you, Teddy, and I can't believe you're going to let the whole thing rest with Grissom."

I gave her a sidelong glance. "He's the best defense attorney in central California."

Her eyes narrowed and her chin jutted out pugnaciously. She looked so much like Tonio, I almost laughed. Good thing I didn't, because she was spoiling for a fight. "Sure, and your step-father would be brilliant at the trial, but it shouldn't go that far. Not if I have anything to do with it, it won't. Poor Dylan. Sitting there in a jail cell, when all he wanted to do was find his birth family. It infuriates me that my own son is just sitting around like a bump on a log."

I winced at that description of my husband, but mama bears are allowed to criticize their cubs. Still, I felt the necessity of defending my husband. "You know his hands are tied."

"Which is why *you* can't be a log bump!"

She had nothing to worry about there. I'd already put together a list of people to contact, the first of whom was Lauren Overholdt, Dylan's mother. Having known Dylan all his life, as opposed to our measly few days, she might know what linked him to Cliff Flaherty. Next, I planned to talk to puppeteer Gordon "Gordo" Walken, who might tell me why he'd originally fallen under suspicion. Then there was…

A sudden screech of brakes threw me forward.

With a shaky finger, Colleen pointed to the white Chevy that had just pulled out from an alley without looking in either direction. "I almost hit him!"

I eased back, allowing the seat belt to loosen. "But you didn't."

"If that damned fool had even dinged my Mustang, I'd have killed him." She quickly added, "Figure of speech."

Fifty years earlier, the single-level San Sebastian Public Library had been built on a slight rise overlooking what was now the San Sebastian Mall. The library might have looked attractive when new, but over time it had lost its luster. Composed mainly of red brick with accents of gray concrete around the doors and windows, the building needed a major overhaul. But it did have two dozen public-access computers, most of which were always occupied by computer-less San Sebastianites looking for jobs. Colleen bypassed them, making a beeline for the Pickup desk. As for me, I headed for the women's restroom in search of an area more appropriate for phone conversations. On the way, I bypassed a sign that read MEET THE *TIPPY-TOE & TINKER* CAST HERE AT 2 P.M. SATURDAY. FREE REFRESHMENTS!

I made a mental note to attend, but not for the refreshments.

The white-tile-and-chrome bathroom was as out of fashion as the library's exterior, but at least it was spotless. All the stalls were empty, so I made myself as comfortable as I could on a toilet seat and punched in Lauren Overholt's Burbank phone number. Braced for a tense conversation, I was almost relieved when, after identifying myself and the reason I'd called, a frazzled-sounding Jon Overholt informed me that his wife, upon receiving a call from Dylan, had packed some clothes and taken off for San Sebastian.

"Have you met up with Lauren yet? I'm... I'm so worried." His voice trembled. "I couldn't go with her because there's an emergency board meeting tomorrow, and I have to be there. If something h-happens to her, I'll never forgive myself."

His raw emotionality, no doubt a temporary state for an actuary, probably explained why he was being free with information, so I pressed him further. "Nope, haven't seen her yet. But Burbank's only four hundred miles from San Sebastian, so we're talking a short flight. What time did she leave?"

"As soon as Dylan called her from the jail. She rang me at the office and left a message with my assistant, but I was at lunch with one of the other board members, so it was probably around one. But about that so-called flight. Lauren's always had this fear of flying, so she's driving."

Given the traffic around LA County, that meant at least a six- or seven-hour trip. "Have you heard from her since she left?"

"I've warned her time and again not to use her phone while she's driving, but she never listens."

"So she did call."

His voice changed suddenly, sliding down the slopes of angst to an actuarial grumble. "Isn't that what I just said?"

Dylan had told us that his mother was still on the outs with her San Sebastian family, so since his stepfather appeared to be sobering up emotionally, I skipped to my final question. "Do you know where she's going to stay once she gets here? I need to talk to her."

Too late. "Sorry, Ms. Bentley-Rejas, but I suspect I've already said too much. If you want more information, you'll have to talk to our attorney. In the meantime, have a nice day."

He rang off.

There were only four motels in San Sebastian, two of them el cheapo chains no corporate vice president's wife would be caught dead in. The Hyatt was a mere five-minute drive from the library, and if I didn't luck out there, the Hilton Inn was located on the other end of town. I checked my watch: 7:32. I knew from experience that jail visitors were allowed to stay until 8:00, so what would be my wisest course of action? Wait until tomorrow, since Lauren was certain to be in a fraught state after seeing her son in lockup? Or take advantage of that very state by quizzing her like I had her husband? The first course was the most humane, but...

While I was trying to decide, two women entered the washroom, complaining about the decrepit condition of the children's section. I knew them. Sharon DelViccio and Maud

Reynolds, high-ranking members of the San Sebastian Women's Club. Last year, when a bill had been introduced that would grant the library funding for badly needed upgrades, they had campaigned against it on the basis that libraries made no money, and were nothing but a financial drain on already overburdened taxpayers. The bill lost, and so did the library. The children's section continued to deteriorate.

Ordinarily, I would have given the two hypocrites a piece of my mind, but I had more immediate concerns, so I stood up, flushed the toilet, and exited. I did, however, dart poisonous glances at them while washing my hands.

Now I faced another decision. Take Colleen with me while I searched for Lauren, or go it alone? I tried to put myself in Dylan's mother's place: exhausted from a long drive, heartbroken at seeing her son jailed, then having to deal with two strange women firing questions at her at the same time. The imagined scenario made me shiver in sympathy. Weighted against Lauren's misery was the fact that Dylan had reached out to his grandmother after getting his DNA results, and I was merely the woman who had married Lauren's ex-boyfriend.

When I emerged from the bathroom, I saw Colleen standing in front of the Pickup desk, holding the latest Stephen King and Jodi Picoult.

Colleen and I were waiting in the crowded lobby of the San Sebastian Hyatt—a grape-growers convention was in town—when Lauren Ellis Overholdt strode in. Every name tag-wearing man froze, which was only to be expected since even at thirty-six, she was almost preternaturally beautiful. Easily six feet tall, with flowing platinum hair, flawless cream-and-rosebud complexion, goddess-gray eyes, the woman looked like a Valkyrie about to claim a dead hero from the battlefield.

"Lauren?" Colleen said, approaching this vision of womanly

perfection with her hand out. "I'm Colleen Rejas, Dylan's paternal grandmother."

Bypassing Colleen's hand, Joe's ex-girlfriend grabbed her by the arm and said, "Let's get the hell out of here."

Ignoring the gaping men—she must have been used to that sort of thing—she hustled us to the elevator, where we rode up to the fifth floor. It was only while standing next to her that I noticed a small scar on her left cheek, and that her dazzling eyes were rimmed with pink. She might have been a knockout, but she was still a mother. Once in her beige-on-beige room, I saw a turquoise leather Delsey suitcase sitting unopened on the beige satin bedspread. With a sigh, she settled herself next to it, leaving the two club chairs to us.

She gave me a quizzical look. "Who are you?"

"Joe's cur..." I started to say *current* wife, but thought better of it. My hair might be frizzy, my chest might be flat, and my bumpy nose wasn't all it could be, but for some crazy reason the man had married me. "I'm Joe's wife."

A blink. "Okay, back to the matter at hand. I've heard Dylan's version. Care to tell me yours? I mean, what in the world is going on? Here's my baby accused of murdering my ex-boyfriend, and I..."

"What?!" Colleen's screech matched mine.

Even scowling, Lauren was beautiful. "What do you mean, *what*?"

"Cliff Flaherty was your *ex-boyfriend*?" I managed to say.

"Dylan didn't mention that?"

"The only thing Dylan told us about your life—other than the, ah, unplanned pregnancy thing—was that you'd once been an actress. Is that how you met Flaherty?"

She nodded that beautiful white-blond head. "I was new to the business, but Cliff had already made a name for himself, while I... Let's just say I was having trouble. This was before the MeToo movement, you understand, when Hollywood was filled with bigger creeps than it is now. Cliff came across as different." Raising a perfectly manicured hand to the scar on her cheek, she added, "But as it turned out, he all of a sudden developed anger issues."

"He was a batterer?"

She managed a wry smile. "This…" She tapped the scar. "This happened the night I told him to get out and not come back."

I winced in sympathy. "Did Dylan see or hear the incident?"

"I'd thought he was upstairs asleep, but when I turned around, there he was, in the hallway. His eyes…" She swallowed. "But that was years ago—he was only eight—and I figured he'd forgotten all about it."

Her pause signaled there was more to the story.

"But?" I prodded.

A flush rose in that beautiful face. "A few months ago, I was talking with my husband about maybe going back into the business. Thanks to the new crop of women directors, there've been some good parts for grown women lately. And I was wondering if I should have some work done on my cheek first. That led to a discussion of how I got the scar in the first place. Long story short, neither of us realized Dylan had come downstairs to ask if he could borrow my Lexus. That's before we bought him his hatchback. He made a few comments like it was too bad somebody hadn't killed him because Cliff was a monster, and…"

Another swallow. "So you see. I'm worried. Then Jon said how ironic it was that a man like Cliff was now writing for a kiddie show with someone else I'd once known, and then we were all three off and running, talking about Hollywood and some of the creeps therein."

"Wait a minute. You guys knew about *Tippy-Toe & Tinker*? That's a local show, runs only on KGNN."

She made a face. "Of course we knew. Thanks to the *Hollywood Reporter*, which I, like three-quarters of the people who've ever been in the business, still read. When the conversation first started, I'd mentioned how weird it was that two of my old boyfriends were working on the same kiddie show. And they'd never even liked each other."

I was struck by what she'd just said. "Two? Who is the other one?"

"Gordo Walken. And I didn't date them at the same time, of course. Gordo came first, and it didn't last long. He was just this big jolly guy, sweet as he could be, and not bad-looking, but in the end, he just wasn't right for the girl I was then. Nice, but dull. You know the kind. Then I met Cliff, and..." She shrugged those beautiful shoulders. "I was young and stupid. But back to what you were asking. Everyone knows everyone in Hollywood. It's an incestuous town. Hell, I once went out with a man who'd once dated Cher, and another guy who almost married Natalie Portman."

Colleen, who had been sitting quietly before this, spoke up. "I don't give a damn about your former love life. What I want to know is—when Dylan found out about Cliff Flaherty hitting you, did he threaten to do something to him?"

Lauren studied her manicure, which was French and flawless. "That defense attorney, Albert Grissom. Is he any good?"

"The best," I assured her, noticing she hadn't answered Colleen's question.

"Money's no issue, you understand."

"I'm sure Al will be happy to hear that."

"Al?"

"He's my stepfather."

"Small world. Speaking of, how's Joe?"

"Joe is, ah, confused." It was my turn to scowl. "Lauren, why in the world didn't you tell him you were pregnant with his child?"

She looked at her nails again. "At first it was because my parents hustled me off to my aunt's as soon as they found out, and then, after the hysteria calmed down..." A sigh. "Ever been seventeen, single, and pregnant? And suddenly living with an aunt you saw only on Christmas? Hormones are bad enough when you're a teenager, but during pregnancy they really go haywire. Everybody was telling me I had to give the baby away, that I was too young to be a mother, and I just... I just..." She shrugged and looked back up, meeting my eyes. "Look, I just couldn't cope, so for a while I simply did what everyone told me to do. Until Dylan was born. Then I took one look at him and everything changed."

Her movie-star face twisted, and I could see how hard she was trying to keep from crying.

Seeing Lauren's grief spurred me toward resolve. Regardless of what happened, I would find out who had really murdered Cliff Flaherty.

When Colleen and I returned to the house, she went straight to the granny cottage. She's always been smart like that.

Joe was sitting on the sofa with a copy of *Law Enforcement Monthly*, but he dropped it when I came in. "What...?"

"Why did you leave her in the lurch?"

"Left *who* in the lurch?"

"You know who. Lauren!"

A mixture of conflicting emotions crossed his face. "Teddy, where in the world is all this coming from?"

"Answer my question!"

"You didn't go to the library, did you?"

Instead of answering, I tossed the new Jodi Picoult onto the sofa next to him. It landed on top of *Law Enforcement Monthly*.

"Okay, so you went to the library. But then you went someplace else, didn't you?" He gestured at the mantle clock. "The library closes at eight, and it's almost ten. I was about to go looking for you two. Please don't tell me you..." An expression of horror crossed his face. "Did you actually call Lauren?"

"Didn't call. *Saw!*"

The horror increased. "She's in town? Here? In San Sebastian?"

"Well, *duh*, since her son's in the county jail! Where'd you think she would be? Back in Burbank, knitting doilies?"

With that, I burst into tears.

"As I told you the other night, I never knew she was pregnant," Joe said, for about the tenth time as we cuddled in bed. "There was just that one date, the prom, and then all of a sudden her parents hustled her out of town before I knew what was happening, let alone realized that she'd gotten pregnant the *one* time we, uh, had...had relations. Furthermore, she wasn't really my girlfriend. The only reason I took her to the prom in the first place was because she was my lab partner, and Wayne, her sleaze of a boyfriend, had just been arrested for joyriding in a 'borrowed' car, and her parents had already bought her prom dress. She begged me, as lab partner to lab partner, to be her emergency date, and since you'd already been packed off to that hoity-toity girl's school in Virginia, I thought why not?

"The girl I really loved—that's you, Ms. Suspicious—had left town but I could at least salvage my pride by showing up at the prom with Miss San Sebastian High School. How was I to know the punch would be spiked and we'd get drunk and..." He paused and held me tighter. "For your information, we spent more time throwing up than we did, well, you know."

I sniffled. "If you'd known she was pregnant, would you have married her?" That question had been torturing me.

He studied the ceiling for a few moments, and finally, with a gruff voice, said, "I was seventeen, and so was she. But, yeah, I probably would have married her if we could have found the right justice of the peace. It would have been the honorable thing to do."

His statement held the ring of truth. Joe was all about honor.

"Then there would have been no Sonia, no Tonio, no Bridey," I said, my voice quavering again. Thinking about Joe's dead wife always made me sad. And now there was poor Dylan, locked up in a jail cell…

"Stop crying, Teddy."

Only a man would be dumb enough to tell a woman something like that.

Breakfast the next morning was a miserable affair, with Joe attempting to change the subject every time someone mentioned Dylan. Poor little Bridey took the brunt of it, because her "new brother" was all she wanted to talk about.

"Daddy, when is Dyl…"

"There's a carnival coming to town next week," Joe said. "If you're good, I'll take you."

"Do they have elephants?"

Knowing that they didn't, California having outlawed circus elephants several years back, I almost answered, but then Bridey followed up with, "And can Dylan go with us?"

"We'll have to wait on that," Joe grumped.

Our pets, sensing trouble ahead, left their usual spot under the table and fled the room, Bonz leading the way, Fluffalooza and Miss Priss right behind him. I watched them go, wishing I were with them.

Bridey is nothing if not persistent. "Daddy, will Dylan…"

Tonio shot her a warning look, but Bridey, being five, didn't interpret it correctly. "Will Dylan go to the carnival with us?" To the ensuing silence, she continued. "I sure hope he's home tomorrow, 'cause I really miss him."

At the other end of the table, Colleen sniffled. "Darn cold," she muttered, getting up and rushing into the kitchen, where she thought no one could hear her cry.

"Dylan's staying someplace else for a while," Joe finally managed.

"But no, Daddy! He needs to stay with us! We're his family!"

"His mother's in town, so he's, ah, he's seeing her." I said, hoping to sidetrack the whole "arrested and jailed" issue.

It didn't work. *"I want my new brother!"* Bridey wailed.

She didn't stop crying until the school bus arrived.

Chapter Eight

The rest of the day was difficult, too. Taking care of the animals didn't erase the pain I felt over poor Dylan's situation, but at least they distracted me. After cleaning up the giant anteaters' large enclosure, I took a few minutes out of my schedule to watch Lucy and Little Ricky, her pup. They usually played Chase, running from one end of their large enclosure to the other, but today, given Lucy's sore paw, they lounged lazily in the sun, Little Ricky tucked under her almost nonexistent chin.

Life was no peppier at the Koala Encounter either, since koalas sleep seventy percent of the time. Careful not to wake Wanchu and her mate, Nyee, I filled their manger with fresh eucalyptus fronds to the tune of koala snores, then headed toward Wallaby Walkabout, where things were jumping. I've always liked the wallabies. They look like miniature kangaroos, but have gentler temperaments, which makes for an enjoyable cleanup. As I swept up their droppings, little noses poked at my boots and chinos, tweeting and chattering as they followed me around.

By the time I made it to the red panda enclosure with a cart full of bamboo shoots, it was nearing lunchtime, but Poonya made it clear her hunger came before mine; I could wait. The public had fallen in love with the furry little thing, although some people still confused her with a raccoon, and others, a fox or lemur. I spread the bamboo shoots throughout her area, which would force her to get some exercise as she partook of her moveable feast. While I was doing this, Poonya only once went into Eek! Mode, and that was when a child's Mylar balloon, borne on a westerly wind, sailed over her favorite sunning rock. Like most zoos, the Gunn Zoo does not sell balloons. The risk is too high. There are authenticated accounts of species as far apart as tigers, coyotes, and baboons choking on balloons that had drifted into their enclosures. This balloon was such a runaway. Helium-powered, silver, with the words HAPPY BIRTHDAY DEBBI! stenciled on it, the balloon cleared Poonya's enclosure and headed for Africa Trail. Concerned, I picked up my radio and alerted the park rangers of the balloon's direction.

"Poor Debbi, lost her balloon," said a young woman nearby, as she watched the thing sail away. She had her back to me, but that squeaky voice sounded familiar.

Jocelyn Ravel. Chewing what appeared to be bubble gum— another zoo no-no.

"No work at the studio today?" I asked her.

She acted surprised to see me. "Oh! Teddy! Didn't think I…" With a final snap of her gum, she dropped the act. "Nah, no new script yet, but we're getting there. In the meantime, I thought I'd come up here and watch the real red panda so I can mimic her movements. How's this?" Without further ado, she spread her legs, threw up her arms and screeched something that sounded like "*Snort-snort-chuckle-EEK!*"

Which threw the real Poonya into another "*Eek.*"

"Not bad," I commented, "but please don't do that again. As you can see, she's prone to panic attacks. And make sure you don't spit that gum out where an animal can get it. There are receptacles throughout the zoo where you can dispose of it safely."

That pretty rosebud mouth formed a pout. "Well, pardon me for living."

Bad Teddy felt like smacking her, but Good Teddy held off, deciding the entitled brat had just given me a chance to find out what would happen to the *Tippy-Toe & Tinker* show now that its writer/coproducer was dead. So I asked her.

"The show must go on." She snapped that damned gum again.

"Not close, were you?"

A shrug. "He was a shit, but so's everybody else, so no biggie."

Below us, Poonya was busy sorting through the bamboo fronds I'd scattered throughout her enclosure. Jocelyn pulled her iPhone from one of her many pockets and took several pictures. Although nasty and self-involved, she did seem to take her job seriously.

"Who's taking Flaherty's place?" I asked, keeping my irritation at bay. "I mean, how can you keep shooting without a script?"

Still snapping her gum, she answered. "Nestor Vanderman. He wrote most of our latest scripts, anyway. Oooh, ick! Did you see what Poonya did? I thought pandas were vegetarians."

I turned to see Poonya finish off a large beetle. "Red pandas are omnivorous. If something fits in their mouth, they'll eat it."

She screwed up her face. "Nasty!"

Forcing myself not to say, *Takes one to know one*, I said, "Most people are omnivorous, too. By the way, while you're here, maybe you could help me out with something. I remember you telling me that you and Cliff Flaherty were arguing about your character's story arc, that he was changing it over your objections. I've been wondering what exactly those changes were, and what they would mean to the program."

She gave me a blank look. "Changes? To my character arc?"

There was no way I could believe she was as dense as she acted, so I pressed on. "Yes, Jocelyn, changes to your character arc on *Tippy-Toe & Tinker*."

"I can't remember." She turned and pretended to be fascinated by the red panda. "Look at what she's doing now!"

"Eating a bamboo shoot. But back to that character arc..."

"Who do *you* think killed old Fart Flaherty?"

I was startled. "You're wanting me to guess?"

"You have before in other cases. You helped that woman Lila get out of jail."

"I got lucky." *But not so much with my own stepson.*

"But you must have some clues."

"No, I told you, I haven't been..."

Jocelyn suddenly made a big show of looking at her watchless wrist. "Oh, gosh, I'm about to be late for a...a *dentist's* appointment!"

Then she spit her gum out onto Asia Trail and hurried away.

After picking up the gum with a tissue, then depositing it in the proper trash bin, I spent the rest of the day doing what zookeepers do, while every now and then attempting to get in touch with the other members of the *Tippy-Toe & Tinker* production. In the end, I'd have had better luck trying to coax a Madagascar ringtail to sing the entire score of *La Traviata*.

Once home, I didn't see much of Colleen, either. After fixing us a stir-fry dinner, she went back to her granny cottage, muttering something about having to fix a problem with chapter sixteen, but I suspected she was merely attempting to write her way into emotional numbness. Tonio pretended stoicism re the Dylan situation, but Bridey wasn't so tough, and the sight of her trembling lower lip made me feel worse than I already did. As for Joe, we didn't expect him home anytime soon. There had been a crash on a feeder road to Highway One that had ended up fatal, and he had to oversee the investigation. The paperwork alone would take hours.

So the kids and I settled into the living room to watch a

Tippy-Toe & Tinker rerun I'd recorded earlier. I'd never seen the program in its entirety before, just snippets, so I was curious.

After opening on a small stage decorated to resemble a jungle, a voiceover began...

"Although the day was a fine one in Dino Dell—sun shining, flowers blooming, birds singing—Zip the Stegosaurus wasn't happy. He had just discovered that a red panda was moving into the neighborhood.

"I don't like her," Zip, who was turquoise, grumped to orange Tippy-Toe the T. rex. "She's the wrong color."

It took me a moment to get used to the old-fashioned marionettes and their bright color palettes, but once I did, I decided I liked them. After all, who knew what colors real dinosaurs really were? Yes, archaeologists had dug up pieces of skin along the years, but the wear and tear of time could have bleached out their remains.

Before Tippy-Toe could answer, Rosie, a bright pink triceratops huffed in irritation. "There's no such thing as a 'wrong' color. Inside, where it really counts, Poonya's just like us."

"No, she isn't," rumbled Randy, the lavender Brachiosaurus, bending down his long neck so Zip, who over the years had become slightly deaf, could hear. "That red panda's not a dinosaur. And instead of beautiful orange, turquoise, pink, or lavender skin, she's a nasty shade of red! Furthermore, she's not even extinct, and I don't want to be around anyone who refuses to follow the herd."

Tonio and I both laughed at that, but Bridey didn't get it.

"But Tinker's not like us and we like her," the T. rex pointed out, snapping his huge jaws.

"That doesn't count," Zip said. "Humans take care of us, and Tinker..."

Zip was interrupted by the arrival of Tinker, a human, looking especially pretty today in her khaki zoo uniform, twinkly blue eyes, and bouncy red curls. "Are you dinos arguing about Poonya again?"

"I don't like her," Zip muttered.

"How can you dislike someone you've never met?" Tinker asked him.

The stegosaurus shook his head in irritation. "Because people told me anything red is sneaky and can't be trusted."

I sat up a little straighter on the sofa. For a children's show, these brightly colored marionettes were entering some interesting territory.

At Zip's comment, Tinker's smile devolved into a frown. "I'm disappointed in you, Zip. I would have thought you had more sense than to let other folks make up your mind for you."

"Sense? From a turquoise stegosaurus?" snorted Rosie. "Zip's head is all bone and no brain."

Tippy-Toe stopped gnashing his huge teeth long enough to wail, "Can't we all just get along?"

After a commercial break, the show continued, with Poonya, the red panda who was causing all this disturbance, trotting onto the stage. Her coloration was realistic, a lovely rust-red body and a white face with a reverse raccoon mask. The marionette was almost as adorable as the real Poonya.

"I'm so happy to have all these new friends," the Poonya said, in a voice high enough to break glass. She was totally unaware her presence in Dino Dell had touched off a firestorm.

"And I'm sure they're all happy to have a new friend in you, too, Poonya," Tinker said.

As the show continued, I couldn't help but notice that ten-year-old Tonio appeared to be an even bigger fan of the puppet show than his five-year-old sister, but I soon figured out why.

Jocelyn Ravel, the gum-spitting puppeteer who played Poonya, was central to the show's let's-all-just-get-along plot. Because of the animal's sweet nature, even the obstreperous Zip eventually decided to live in peace and harmony together. As the show's credits rolled along the bottom of the screen, the puppeteers briefly appeared on-screen dressed in their public appearance animal costumes which perfectly matched their marionettes. When Jocelyn lifted the red panda's head off her shoulders to reveal her cute, pigtailed self, I heard Tonio sigh.

My stepson was suffering a serious attack of Puppy Love.

"Hi, boys and girls," Jocelyn/Poonya said, in her trademark squeak, "Always remember the lesson we learned today. Even though someone looks different than you, you can still like them. And that's a good thing, because the more different kinds of friends you have, the more you learn!"

When she batted her long, mascaraed eyelashes, Tonio did all but swoon.

He only stopped sighing when Tippy-Toe took off his own headpiece to reveal Gordon "Gordo" Walken. At least six-and-a-half feet tall and chunky around the middle, Walken's physique was perfect for his T. rex character, but it was hard to envision the gorgeous Lauren dating him. Maybe he'd been better looking when younger.

After smoothing back his thinning hair, Walken said, "Remember, kids, never get in a car with a stranger, even when he tells you your mommy sent him to pick you up. Always ask for the secret word! It's the word that only you and your mom and your dad know, the word that means a message really did come from them. Bad men can wear smiling masks, just like Tippy-Toe, but we know that Tippy-Toe is safe, don't we?"

Walken shook the big T. rex headpiece in his hands. "To learn more about dinosaurs, be sure and come to the San Sebastian Library on Saturday at two o'clock, and hear Tippy-Toe and Rosie the Triceratops talk about those exciting old days when dinosaurs like us roamed the earth. In the meantime, kids, stay safe! And study hard!"

"He sounds just like Daddy," Bridey said, between sniffles.

"This is kid stuff," Tonio sneered, now that his Lady Love had vanished from the screen. "I'm gonna go get some ice cream from the fridge. Sitting around moping about Dylan isn't going to change anything. You want some, Squirt?" This last to Bridey. With that, he took off, with Bridey trailing behind.

I continued watching while the rest of the *Tippy-Toe & Tinker* cast came from behind the stage, doffing their own costumes' headpieces. First out was Zip, the judgmental stegosaurus, played by Ansel "Bird" Yates, an ambidextrous puppeteer who also played Randy, the long-necked Brachiosaurus. The next out was Rosie the three-horned triceratops, played by Karla Dollar. Last to emerge was Bev Beaumont, who played Tinker the zookeeper, who at sixty-two—I'd read in a *San Sebastian Journal* article—was the oldest person in the cast. Being the only human in the dinosaur show, Bev had no headpiece to take off. After revealing themselves, each puppeteer voiced a message of bonhomie and optimism, leavened with the safety tips necessary for a world that appeared to be growing darker all the time.

I liked the show. The use of string-controlled marionettes may have lent the program a somewhat old-fashioned feel, but the floppy creatures were part of the show's charm. The unmasking bit at the end was clever, too, as was the four-puppet rephrasing of the plot's Aesopian moral. There was some good writing there, which begged the question: How could a lout like Cliff Flaherty write such a sweet morality play?

As Joe was getting ready for work the next morning—I knew better than to ask him how his night had been—I received a phone call from Al Grissom. My stepfather had made such a convincing argument to the court about Dylan's strong roots in the community—"His father's the sheriff, Judge!"—the judge set Dylan's bond at a manageable level. Well, reasonable, considering his mother and stepfather owned a large home in an exclusive section of Burbank, and a vacation home in Big Bear and were willing to use both as collateral. Dylan had to remain in San Sebastian County on his biological father's property, and wear an electronic ankle monitor to ensure his continued presence.

Bridey was so excited she threw up.

After the thrills on the home front, the zoo seemed relatively peaceful. True, the squirrel monkeys in Monkey Mania had suffered a few minor injuries overnight when unusually high winds brought down a small eucalyptus in their enclosure, but nothing serious. The brief storm had made Poonya jumpier than usual, and she went into *Eek!* mode twice during her morning feeding. Giant anteaters Lucy and Little Ricky remained unruffled, as did Magnus the polar bear cub, who was having fun with a downed palm frond that blew into his pool.

This was a day for the zoo's gardeners and grounds crews to shine, and they did, clearing the debris from the paths, lopping off low-lying and weakened branches that could lead to an animal's escape. The only near-disaster was when a careless grounds-crew member leaned too far over the edge of Koko's enclosure, causing the outraged Asian sun bear to take a territorial swipe at him. Zorah, the zoo director, promptly issued an order for a zookeeper—namely me—to accompany any grounds crew detailed to clean around the high security areas. After that, there were no more close calls.

When I broke for lunch in the staff lounge, a special report from KGNN-TV News was blaring from the room's small TV.

"In a new development in the Cliff Flaherty murder case, Dylan Ellis was granted bail this morning and is now at home with his grandmother, the famous mystery writer Colleen Rejas." Newscaster Ariel Gonzales took a deep breath, then continued, "Dylan Ellis, you'll remember, was recently revealed as the biological son of San Sebastian County Sheriff Joe Rejas, who reportedly didn't know of his existence until the young man, a resident of Burbank, showed up and announced himself.

Dylan's mother, former San Sebastian resident Lauren Ellis Overholdt, attended San Sebastian High School at the same time as Sheriff Rejas."

As she spoke, video footage showed Dylan being hustled to a waiting opalescent-white Lexus driven by Lauren, with my step-father bringing up the rear. All appeared to be saying unkind things to the mob of reporters.

"What an exciting life you lead, Teddy," said Jack Spence, the bear keeper, after finishing off what smelled like a pastrami sandwich.

"Thank you for pointing that out," I grumped.

"Oooh, touchy!" said Buster Daltry, rhinos.

"That Dylan guy's awfully good-looking," chimed Robin Chase, big cats.

"Yeah, well, Joe Rejas and that Lauren woman getting it on, geez. He's no dog, that's for sure, but did you see *her*? Talk about drop-dead gorgeous." Buster again. His one-time romance with Robin now a thing of the past, he felt free to admire other women.

"She's *old*!" Robin snarled at him. "Didn't you notice her crow's feet?"

Apparently, the fires of love were not as dead as I'd believed, so I excused myself from the table before I got hit by flying insults. Both Robin and Buster, while unfailingly tender with their animal charges, could be brutal with humans.

Out in the more peaceful air—the staff lounge was near the aviary, and the meadow lark was in fine voice today—I took a deep breath. This caused me to inhale several types of animal dung, offset with notes of eucalyptus and roses.

It was so pleasant that for a few minutes, I even forgot about awful Cliff Flaherty and the mess his murder had left behind.

When I walked into the house that evening, I found Dylan and Lauren sitting at the dining table. No crow's feet were in evidence, just a face that could have launched a thousand ships. Joe was sitting in his usual place at the head of the dining table, pointedly trying to keep his eyes off her. Bonz, Miss Priss, and Fluffalooza were nowhere in evidence. And some people don't think animals are smart.

Not bothering to change out of my zoo uniform, I moseyed into the kitchen, where Colleen was hiding out. "Why in the world did you invite Lauren here?" I hissed.

Hissing back, Colleen replied, "She won't let go of Dylan, he can't leave our property, and they're both starving. What was I going to do, feed them outside on the stoop like stray cats?"

"But Colleen, this…this…" My voice failed me.

"You'll just have to make the best of it, Teddy. Now help me carry out dinner. And by the way, you should have showered before you came home. You smell like a goat."

"Asiatic ibex from the Hindu-Kush," I snapped. "Her name's Donna and she turned up unexpectedly pregnant."

"Then mazel tov to Donna," she hissed, handing me a platter of pork chops.

Once I'd carried the food in, I sat my Goat Lady butt down. The only seat left was next to Bridey, who wrinkled her nose. This put me directly across from Lauren, sitting next to Dylan, so while I chewed on a chop, I had no choice but to stare at that Helen of Troy face.

"Mmmm, aren't these pork chops good?" I said.

"Delicious," Lauren agreed. "But what's that smell?"

"Ibex named Donna," offered Colleen. "She's pregnant."

"Good for Donna." Dylan.

"A baby? Somebody's gonna have a baby?" Bridey. "You, Teddy?"

"No, it's not me."

"But I wanna 'nother brother!"

"Maybe someday." Joe, turning red.

"Wanna 'nother brother *now*!"

"Oh, maybe there's more of them out there." Me, to Joe.

"These pork chops are terrific." Joe, through gritted teeth.

"Your stepfather is the greatest guy, Teddy." Dylan.

"Did you hear what Teddy said? Maybe I gots me *more* brothers!"

"Shut up, Squirt." Tonio, to Bridey.

Joe, to Tonio, "What did I say about talking to your sister like that?" Then, to me, "Pass me the peas, please."

"Here's your damn peas."

"No swearing at the dinner table." Colleen.

I thought about upping the ante by dropping the F-bomb, then decided against it because Colleen would probably send me to bed without my supper. "Don't you take all those peas." I sniped at Joe as he ladled a dozen out on his plate.

"Didn't I get you Chanel for your birthday?" Joe, sniffing the air.

The desire to use the F-bomb rose again, but I controlled myself.

"I use *L'Aire du Temps*, myself." Lauren. "It's flowery without being overly so."

"You *would*." Me.

Open mouth, no sound. Lauren.

"Daddy got me Princess Jasmine Bubble Bath for my birthday." Bridey.

"I apologize for causing so much trouble." Dylan, sniffling.

"*There's no trouble!!!*" Everyone except Bridey, who burst into tears.

Chapter Nine

My formerly happy home had turned into the seventh circle of Hell, with me dodging Joe, Joe dodging Lauren, and Colleen dodging me. Meanwhile, Tonio, Bridget, and Dylan dodged everyone but each other and squirreled themselves away in the enclosed back porch, playing video games. God only knows where DJ Bonz, Miss Priss, and Fluffalooza were—probably hitchhiking out of town.

So that morning I set off for work with more enthusiasm than usual, freshly showered and dressed, no longer the Goat Lady. The only downside was that on Fridays, the Gunn Zoo offered freebie tours for local elementary schools, and as much as I enjoy children, sharing space with several hundred of them at the same time can be difficult. Adding to the all-over chaos was the fact that the groundskeepers hadn't yet finished clearing away the storm damage from the other night. Tropics Trail had lost so many trees it even had to be temporarily closed to visitors.

Not to staff, however. No matter the mess, the animals needed to be cared for. Fortunately, the crews had already cleared the zookeeper trails in back of the giant anteaters' enclosure, so I was able to zip along in my zebra cart all the way to their night house, where I expected to find Lucy and Little Ricky waiting for me near the door. Not today. Instead, I found them hunched in the far corner, their long blue tongues slithering nervously back and forth. When I opened the holding pen gate, they refused to leave. Lucy even made a noise that sounded like a hiss.

Suspicious now, I shut the gate and patrolled the enclosure to see what was wrong. No snakes, no raccoons, no tarantulas— nothing on the ground to worry about, other than a few palm fronds blown in during the windstorm. Using a stick, I flipped the fronds over to check if any palm rats had ridden the fronds down, but they were clean. I took another tour around the enclosure, flipping over every piece of storm debris, but found nothing that could have spooked the anteaters.

Only when I looked at the thirty-foot-high eucalyptus near the edge of the enclosure did I discover the problem. A brown-and-green hairy thing was climbing up its trunk.

Seabiscuit.

The juvenile three-toed sloth had apparently escaped from his quarters by making his way along a large broken limb that had dipped down into his own enclosure, and he was now headed up the tree trunk with all due speed. For a three-toed sloth, that is. What he didn't know, but I did, was that several of the tree's upper limbs overhung the jaguar exhibit. By the sound of El Presidente's roar, he hadn't yet eaten breakfast. An adult sloth would have understood the danger and stayed on the ant-eater side of the tree trunk, but young Seabiscuit had never been known for his street smarts.

I radioed a Code Blue, the alert for the escape of a nonle-thal animal, but the longer I waited for the Animal Response Team, the more worried I became. Rather than climb straight up, the clueless critter was slowly corkscrewing his way around the trunk, a path that would shortly put him on the jaguar side of the tree. And if he slipped...

"Seabiscuit, you little jackass," I muttered, heading for the back of the giant anteaters' night house, where I'd spotted the ladder used while the zoo's carpenters were repairing the leaky roof. The ladder was aluminum, therefore not too heavy, so I soon had it braced against the eucalyptus. Five rungs up, I switched to the tree.

Climbing a eucalyptus without proper equipment isn't easy. Pre-storm visits by the grounds crews had kept the tree's lower limbs lopped off in order to prevent exactly what was happening now, but there was no way they could foretell a sudden storm taking down one of the tree's heavy upper limbs. The bark on a eucalyptus presents a problem, too. At the best of times, strips of eucalyptus bark are only loosely attached to the tree, so if you try to use them as handholds, you can find yourself tumbling to the ground amid a hail of menthol-smelling bark. Then there was the trunk itself, oily and glass-slick, so forget about wrapping your arms around it and shimmying up the thing. Mother Nature. Can't live with her, can't live without her.

Fortunately, there were enough short "nubs" left on the trunk from the groundskeepers' earlier efforts to keep the tree safe from slothful escapees, so I was able to wiggle my way upward using them as hand- and footholds.

As I neared Seabiscuit, he stopped and slowly turned his head as if to say, "Hey, Teddy, fancy meeting you here!" Then he stopped his crawl and smiled. Well, of course he smiled. Sloths always smiled, no matter what dumb thing they were in the middle of doing. Crawling. Climbing. Eating. Napping. Smile, smile, smile.

Catching him proved easy.

"Gotcha," I said, as I hooked my right arm around him, and pressed him to my chest. "You're going back where you belong."

Seabiscuit didn't struggle, not that it would have made any difference, the little runaway being only around sixteen inches long, and weighing less than eight pounds. He did, however, issue a slow, frightened "*Aaawk!*"

He didn't smell so great, either. Since sloths have such long hair and move around so sloooowly, algae grows along their backs, lending the grayish-brown coat a greenish tint. Nasty, yes, but algae helps camouflage the witless creatures, and moving as slowly as they do, a sloth's near-invisibility does help deter predators. Another interesting thing about sloths is that they only defecate once a week, climbing slooowly down from their arboreal homes to do their business on the forest floor.

Usually, that is.

Seabiscuit's rattled nerves—caused by the broken eucalyptus limb, his near-escape from a hungry jaguar, and his subsequent capture by a mean old zookeeper—resulted in a flood of hot, evil-smelling diarrhea as I hustled him down the tree to safety.

My clean khaki uniform was ruined, not to mention my mood. But not Seabiscuit's. As the semiliquid sloth feces ran down my chest, across my belly, and down my legs, he smiled and smiled and smiled.

When the zoo's Animal Response Team arrived with their nets and stun guns, they took a few minutes to laugh, then made a wide, upwind arc around me to tear the low-hanging limb away from the tree. I'd already carried Seabiscuit back to his enclosure with its own phony set of tree trunks and limbs, so now there was nothing left to do other than retreat to the showers. While walking my smelly self up the hill, I realized that because of the recent chaos in my life, I'd forgotten to bring in a spare uniform, so I placed an open radio call for anyone with a spare to please meet me there.

As luck would have it, the only person to answer my call was the big cat keeper, Robin Chase. Robin is almost six feet tall, and I'm not. I'm thin, and Robin's not. She is, as they say around the zoo, *robust*, but on Robin, the extra weight proved useful. The woman is a walking art canvas. Over the years, Robin has visited the local tattoo parlors to get portraits inked of all her charges, thus her arms are covered with lions, tigers, jaguars, etc.

Her legs are a symphony of less fierce animals: zebras, giraffes, orangutans, and several birds—thus her continued comeliness to all male zookeepers.

"It's old and not in great shape, but it'll do in an emergency," she said, handing me her spare uniform. My own clothes, including my favorite pair of lavender lace-trimmed panties and matching bra, were stowed in a sealed plastic bag, and on the way to a nearby landfill, so thanks to Seabiscuit, I was now going Commando.

Have you ever noticed you get some of your best ideas in the shower? You finally figure out why Bobby Sikkin slipped that frog down your dress in the third grade; or why Veronica Cameron started that rumor that you were adopted and your parents just hadn't told you. That's what happened to me in there while soaping away sloth shit. It suddenly became clear to me why Jocelyn Ravel had shown up at the red panda enclosure today. It wasn't because she wanted to work on her Poonya character; she wanted to find out how much I knew about Cliff Flaherty's murder.

What an interesting turnaround.

My don't-know-nothing answers had been a lie, too, because my shower had also washed away some fog in my brain—all Flaherty-related. He wrote like an angel, but behaved like the devil. People aren't usually that complicated, so it might be interesting to take a look-see into his past.

And to the other members of the *Tippy-Toe & Tinker* cast.

Clean again, I wandered into the staff room and poured myself a tepid cup of coffee. While sipping at the nasty stuff, I rummaged around the room until I found a half-used notebook and scraggly ballpoint to replace those on the way to the dump with my stinky clothes. Then I sat down at a table and made a list of everyone I knew who'd had trouble with Flaherty. It would be lengthy, since I needed to start my list on Dock 4, at Gunn Landing Harbor.

WALT MACADAMS—He'd almost had a fistfight after Flaherty shoved him so hard at a party on *Running Wild* that Walt fell into the harbor. As much as I liked Walt, his temper was infamous. As far as I knew, Walt's life was an open book, but a little research into his past wouldn't hurt.

LINDA CUSHING—She lived on *Tea 4 Two*, next door to Flaherty's *Scribbler*, and could have snuck over there during the night and done whatever. Motive? He'd once called her the c-word, too, and Linda didn't take insults lightly. But she rescued cats, otters, and damaged women, so if she turned out to be Flaherty's killer, I'd probably keep it secret.

The landlubber suspects included:

LAUREN ELLIS OVERHOLDT—Flaherty had left her permanently scarred, ending her acting career. Then again, I wondered, why had she dated such a creep in the first place? Maybe something needy and ugly was going on under that beautiful face.

DYLAN ELLIS—I hated putting my stepson on the list, but in all fairness, it was necessary. Besides, Dylan must have carried a grudge after seeing Flaherty beat up his beautiful mom. Had he ever committed any acts of violence down there in Burbank?

MARTIN "MARTY" DONALDSON—Flaherty's business partner and coproducer. I'd met him once at one of my mother's fund-raisers for the Otter Conservancy, and I knew nothing about him, but experience had proven that it was always wise to follow the money.

JOCELYN RAVEL—The young actress/puppeteer was a nasty piece of work, and was probably keeping all kinds of secrets. Like everyone else, she despised Flaherty, and made no secret of it.

ANSEL "BIRD" YATES—Ambidextrous, plays two characters on the show, other than that, a blank. But if a one-legged man could still surf, he'd probably have no trouble killing someone, either.

BEVERLY BEAUMONT—Actress playing Tinker, the puppet show's only human role. I knew nothing about her, either, other than she'd moved to San Sebastian when the show began.

GORDON "GORDO" WALKEN—He played Tippy-Toe, the gentle giant, which Walken supposedly was, too. Talk about someone too good to be true!

In all honesty, I should probably have included myself on the list, because I'd once been violent with Cliff Flaherty—the less said about that, the better. I certainly wasn't going to write what happened down on a piece of paper for a real cop to find...

Like the one I was married to.

I studied the list. Nine names and probably a host of unknowns. When my head began to hurt, I decided that tomorrow, Saturday, would be better for catching people off guard. I'd just have to wait until my zoo hours were over before I could begin.

Have you ever tried to get around while wearing a two-piece outfit four sizes too big for you? It's not easy. As the day dragged on, my pants kept slipping down, and the huge shirt flapped around me like a Fourth of July flag. I had cobbled together a belt from rope, but while I was attending to the squirrel monkeys, it gave way, allowing my drawers to drop all the way down, making me moon the monkeys and some middle-school kids on the viewing platform. One of the teachers even caught it on his iPhone.

As if that wasn't embarrassing enough, the accidental flashing made KGNN's noon news, so shortly thereafter, my mother showed up at the zoo to put the finishing touches to my humiliation. By then I had made my way to the large quarters of Magnus, our polar bear cub, in Cooler Climes, but Mother seemed to have an almost preternatural gift for knowing where I could be found.

"You are a disgrace, Theodora," Caroline Piper Bentley Huffgraf Petersen Grissom said, as she gave the bear a quick look in case he decided to splash water on her, but she was safe. I'd put Magnus in his holding pen while I cleaned up.

Today my clotheshorse mother wore a belted, Chinese red Stella McCartney pantsuit, its bias-cut top cunningly revealing one bare shoulder. As she teetered along on black Valentino stilettoes, I wondered how she could even walk at all.

"A disgrace?" I laughed. "You won't get any argument from me on that. By the way, did you think to bring me something more fitting to wear? I think there was an old uniform in the attic."

She sniffed. "I never go up there."

"Ah, well, it was just a thought."

"Do you realize everyone in San Sebastian County has now seen your rump?"

"Ass."

"Don't be crude, Theodora."

"I'm a zookeeper. If you expected delicacy, you've come to the wrong place."

After a final disapproving look at my baggy outfit, she revealed why she'd actually come, and it wasn't because I'd been flashing my naked butt.

"Promise me you're not going to play detective again," she demanded.

Caroline Piper Bentley Huffgraf Petersen Grissom believes she knows best for everyone, especially her only child. Every now and then she's right, which just encourages more interference. She has her reasons, I guess. Since my father, her first husband, did a midnight flit to Costa Rica after embezzling millions, she had developed a fear of sudden poverty. Especially when the FBI confiscated everything Dad ever touched, including our house. In order to recoup her losses, as well as to put bread on our table, she began marrying up. Given her beauty and breeding, that wasn't difficult. But her continuing marital machinations and all-around bossiness complicated my life. Yes, I stood up to her, but it never made any difference.

"No, I'm not playing detective," I told her. "Merely asking around. For a friend."

"Remember what happened last time you merely 'asked around'? You got shot!"

"Cliff Flaherty was beaten to death, not shot. So I'm safe there." I smirked.

"Think you're funny, do you?" She went quiet for a moment, something rare for her, then started off on another tack. "Oh, well, the talk around town is that they've already caught the killer. But what's this I hear about him being Joe's long-lost son? Surely that can't be right."

"No, it's not. The part about the kid being a killer, anyway. He's a perfectly nice young man."

"Who happens to be *temporarily* out on bail."

"Don't be so judgmental. You spent some time in a jail cell once, remember."

She sniffed. "But I was innocent."

"So is Dylan."

"I also heard that he was staying with that crazy mother-in-law of yours before the police hauled him away. And that his mother's an *actress*." Her stress on the word wasn't one of admiration.

Not trusting myself to talk about Lauren, I picked up the bag full of polar bear feces—the portions Magnus hadn't already batted toward the fence—and took it over to my zebra cart. The dung was headed for the mulch pile at Takamoto's Garden Supplies. After depositing the bag in the back, I called to my mother, "Better move a little farther back. I'm letting Magnus out now."

"I'm not afraid of that little bear."

"Don't say you weren't warned." I unlatched the safety lock on the cub's holding pen.

The little polar bear emerged at a gallop, making straight for Caro, who, besides her fancy duds, was wearing a citrusy perfume. Magnus loved citrus. But I'll give the woman this. As

Magnus skidded to a stop and batted a clump of bear manure toward her; she didn't flinch.

Giving the bear a more accepting look than she'd ever given me, she said, "Frankly, I'm surprised that husband of yours puts up with you."

I grinned. "It's all in the prenup."

Her mascara-enhanced eyes widened. "What prenup? This is the first I ever heard of it." Caro herself was infamous for her lucrative prenups.

"The one that Joe and I wrote ourselves, saying who could do what, and who couldn't." Continuing my work at the zoo had been my first demand; hanging on to the *Merilee* was the second.

"You used an attorney, didn't you?" Her previous tone of disapproval disappeared, replaced by a hopeful expression.

"And have a third party sign off on our marriage? I don't think so."

We'd put it together after imbibing two bottles of champagne. I hadn't listed any "Can'ts" for Joe, because I trusted the man I loved. But there was no point in telling that to Caro.

Tipped off by my grin, she sensed she was losing the argument, so she changed the subject. "Promise me you'll stay far, far away from the Flaherty murder case."

"Hmm."

Alarm tightened my mother's already surgically tightened face. "I expect an answer, Theodora, so what do you mean by '*hmm*'?"

"It means don't worry. I've already got too much on my plate." Which was true, but I've always been good at multitasking. Before leaving for the zoo, for instance, I'd looked up the address of Whispering Willows, the golf resort where an article in the *San Sebastian Journal* said Martin Donaldson, the sole surviving producer of *Tippy-Toe & Tinker,* owned a luxury condo.

"What are you thinking about, Theodora? You have a strange look on your face." She sounded waspish.

"How well do you know Martin Donaldson?"

"Not well; why? I did put together that public protest a couple of years ago when *Tippy-Toe & Tinker* was in danger of being pulled from the KGNN lineup, and to thank me for it, he came to some of my recent fund-raisers for the Otter Conservancy."

I thought about that for a moment. "Did Donaldson contribute much?"

"Some. But Cliff Flaherty contributed more."

Shocked, I turned my attention away from Magnus to her. "Flaherty donated money? For *otters*?"

"High five figures. We were all quite pleased." A sad look fought its way through her cosmetic surgery. "He liked animals. Despite his little drinking problem, he was a lovely man."

"Cliff Flaherty? A lovely man? You're the first person to ever say something like that about him."

With a smug look, she said, "I've always been a good judge of character."

Deciding not to remind her of the time she tried to fix me up with a "lovely man" who'd turned out to be a serial killer, I changed the subject. "Say, Mother?"

A smile. Lately she'd begun to like it when I called her by the proper honorific. "Yes, dear?"

Tugging up my too-big khakis, I asked, "Can I borrow your belt?"

Since Caro wouldn't let me borrow her Chinese red Stella McCartney belt, I pants-drooped my way through the rest of the afternoon, pausing work only for a late lunch—it was already past two—which I ate at one of the tables near the Wolf Run.

Years ago, when Mexican gray wolves were nearing extinction, several American zoos had been chosen to start a breeding program for the animals that would culminate with the release of the species back into the wild. The Gunn Zoo had been one of them, partially because of the unusual "run" designed by the environmental architects Aster Edwina hired. Wolves love to run. Thus their three-mile-long trail circuited the entire two-thousand-and-fifty-acre Gunn Estate, then crossed back on itself and looped around and through the three-hundred-acre zoo, ending at the wolves' cozy den.

Mexican gray wolves also love to hide, so the Wolf Run had been thickly planted with native bushes and trees that allowed the nine-member pack to evade zoo patrons' prying eyes. The only place on the run not heavily forested was near the pedestrian bridge that crossed over it, linking California Trail with Americas Trail. Over the years, it had become one of the zoo's most popular gathering places, not only because lucky patrons might catch a glimpse of the shy animals on the other sides of the bridge's four-foot-high stone-and-Plexiglas balustrade, but because of the Snack Shack adjoining the Wolf Run.

Today the wolf pack was very much in evidence. There's nothing like eating a sloppy chili dog while watching four frisky wolf cubs capering around Durango and Serena, their alpha parents. Granted, my bunched-up, too-large outfit amused more than one zoo patron, but hey, I've never been known for my elegance. The wolves sure didn't care. The entire nine-wolf pack cared more about the noise made by the children on the pedestrian bridge than they did my appearance.

Chili dog finished, I hitched up my baggy pants, climbed into my zebra cart, and headed for Down Under.

The hour being late, most of the wallabies were napping under the large eucalyptus in the center of their enclosure, so they didn't pester me as I swept up. Working quickly, I managed to get my chores done in half the time it usually took, which left me a few minutes for phone calls.

The first call was to producer Martin Donaldson. His voice mail informed me to leave a message, so I did. As a general rule,

I don't like to use my family connections to gain access, but given the trouble Dylan was in, I made an exception.

"Hi, Mr. Donaldson, it's Teddy Bentley. You know, Caro Grissom's daughter? She's the woman who put together that public protest a couple of years ago when *Tippy-Toe & Tinker* was in danger of being pulled from the KGNN lineup? Well, something important has come up, so please call me back. Considerable money may be involved."

If there's anything that excites producers, it's money. Although I didn't yet know how I would work money into the conversation I planned, something would probably occur to me. Or not.

The second call was to Beverly Beaumont, the actress who played Tinker. She wasn't answering her phone, either. While I was leaving my message, Abim, my current favorite of the wallaby mob, woke up and hopped over to see me. As he sniffed around my feet, I scratched the scruff of his neck. Abim liked that enough to flop down on his back, allowing me to scratch his belly. He liked that even better, and chirped his pleasure. Unfortunately, the chirp was loud enough to waken Rambo, one of the more rambunctious of the mob. Irritated, Rambo clambered to his feet, hopped over to the nearest sleeping wallaby, and kicked it. That wallaby—I think it was Delpha—kicked back.

Abim, who was friends-with-benefits with Delpha, decided to help her out, and rushed over to kick Rambo in the head. Kick duly delivered, Abim started back toward me, jostling Geraldo, a dense but scrappy juvenile. Too short to reach Abim, Geraldo's kick landed on Bubbles. By then, the rest of the mob had awakened to a wallaby-wide rumble, and they began taking sides, with each of them hurrying to the defense of their own friends. Before I could do anything, moms kicked dads, sisters kicked brothers, and former friends kicked old friends in defense of new friends. Fur flew.

There were too many brawlers to separate, so I did the only

thing possible. "Dinner!" I yelled, rattling the bag of kangaroo pellets I'd brought with me. It wasn't feeding time, but an over-fed wallaby was preferable to a beat-up wallaby.

My ruse worked. Hisses disappeared and chirps gentled as wallaby after wallaby crowded around the manger.

"Eat up, you little thugs," I told them. Not that they needed any encouragement from me, whose foolish favoritism had started the ruckus to begin with.

Beverly Beaumont, who played Tinker on *Tippy-Toe & Tinker*, returned my call while I was cleaning the emu enclo-sure. Emus are the most dangerous birds alive—last year they killed four people—weighing as much as a hundred and thirty pounds, with razor-sharp talons. I've always been extra cautious around them, and today I made certain their holding pen was securely locked so I could clean without winding up as bird food.

Keeping an eye on the lethal birds, I put down my rake and moved further away to take the call. "Thanks for calling me back," I said.

Having only spoken to me once, at the opening day of the red panda exhibit, she sounded confused as to why I needed to talk to her, but I had my lie ready.

"Before Mr. Flaherty was, um...*died*, we'd discussed an idea I had about the Poonya character."

Silence for a moment, then, "Oh, right. You're the zookeeper who used to live at the harbor. You must have known Cliff from there." I let the following silence ride, and like people usually do, she rushed to fill it. "You should bring up anything having to do with the program to Martin Donaldson, the producer. I'm just one of the cast, and speak whatever lines I'm given."

I was able to talk my way around that by stressing how much I'd like to hear a woman's reaction to my idea, so in the end, mainly to get me off the phone, she agreed to meet me at a mid-town pizzeria on Monday. My second call to Martin Donaldson,

Tippy-Toe & Tinker's one surviving producer, still wasn't successful. Maybe he wasn't as interested in money as I'd believed. I'd have to think of something else.

By the time the emu enclosure was clean, the shadows of the big eucalyptus trees surrounding Down Under had lengthened, foretelling the zoo's imminent closing. With all my animals cared for and happy—except maybe the wallabies, since they were notorious for holding grudges—I began my trek to Admin to clock out. I had just passed the javelinas—they were harassing a raven that had flown into their enclosure—when I heard a woman's scream, then a man's shout.

"Oh, God, no!"

It came from up the hill, in the direction of the Americas Trail. Think cougars. Jaguars. Wolves. Following the screams, I began to run, barely able to avoid tripping over my khaki pants' long legs. Americas Trail being just below the fork that led to the sloths, I cleared the thick tree line within seconds, emerging to see a thin woman climbing the pedestrian bridge's stone-and-Plexiglas balustrade in an attempt to drop into the Wolf Run. A second woman was attempting to drag her back, while a man in a wheelchair called out, "Rita, don't! They'll kill you, too!"

Too?

Near Rita's feet lay an empty stroller, fallen on its side.

Still running, I grabbed my radio and stuttered out an emergency call for help from DART—the zoo's Dangerous Animal Response Team. *"Child in Wolf Run! Get here stat!"*

When I made it to the balustrade and looked over, I saw a horrific scenario.

Ten feet below us, a toddler, no more than three years old, was struggling to her feet while Durango, the zoo's alpha male, approached her, hackles raised, legs stiff. Close behind him came Selena, his mate, saliva dripping from an open-mouthed snarl. Bringing up the rear were Lopez, Fermi, and Camilla, protecting the alphas' four as-yet-unnamed pups.

The toddler misinterpreted the wolves approach.

"Doggies!" she said, proving the fall miraculously hadn't injured her. "Lisa pet doggies!"

Doggies, my ass. The alphas were killing machines when their pups were threatened, and they looked ready to rip that child's throat out with no more thought than if she'd been a marauding badger. There was no time to wait for the DART team with their tranquilizer darts and rifles; immediate action was required.

Not caring about the danger to myself, I ran across the bridge, climbed the balustrade that was supposed to prevent such mishaps, and dropped into the enclosure next to the little girl. Unlike her, I landed badly. As a sharp pain shot up from my right ankle all the way up my leg, I hobbled in front of the child and raised my radio as if it were a yard-long club.

"Go!" I yelled at Durango. If I could turn him, the other wolves would follow.

But Durango didn't care about my "club," and neither did Selena. All the two alphas could see was a threat to their babies. Meanwhile, the screaming and wailing of the human adults on the top of the bridge that spanned the Wolf Run was making the wolves even testier. I didn't dare turn my back on them, and I didn't dare grab the child and run. Either action could initiate an attack. Using the old trick of averting my eyes and playing submissive wouldn't help, either. The wolves were already in attack mode. Acting passive now was a no-starter, unless I wanted a wolf necklace dangling from my jugular.

Think, Teddy. Think.

I needed to treat the situation like I would any problem— one step at a time. My first obligation was to the child, who could not help herself. Only after securing her escape would I have the luxury of worrying about my own welfare.

As Durango approached, his fangs looking sharp as daggers, I saw movement at the corner of my eye. The big woman who had pulled the screaming Rita away, was leaning far over the bridge's sturdy balustrade.

"Here!" Big Gal yelled. "Hand her up to me!"

"Get back or you'll fall, too!" I yelled back.

"Not until you give me that kid!" When she leaned over further and stretched her arms down as far as they could go, I knew what I had to do.

I scooped up little Lisa. Then, holding the struggling child tight—she still wanted to pet a doggie—I walked slowly backward until I entered the shadow under the bridge, with Durango and Selena matching me step for step. Once the shadow crossed my face, I did the scary thing; took one step *toward* the alphas, back into the sunlight. Now I was as close to Big Gal as I could get.

"I'm handing her up now," I shouted to her over the mother's nerve-shattering shrieks. "Get ready!"

Sweat ran down my forehead, down my cheeks, and into my open eyes. It stung, but with my hands full of wriggling toddler, I couldn't wipe it away. All I could do was let it sting.

Another movement overhead. Out of the corner of my smarting eye I saw the man in the wheelchair had rolled forward to grasp Big Gal's lower legs as her upper body dangled over the balustrade. If she came down, there was a good chance he'd come with her.

"Hand her to me now!" Big Gal called. "I can't hang like this forever!"

"Stop wiggling," I told the toddler, trying to blink the stinging sweat away. "You're going back to your Mommy."

"Wanna play wit' doggies!" she whined.

"These doggies bite," I said. "Now put your arms over your head!"

Without turning my back on the wolves, I hefted the little girl as high as I could, moving backward once again until I was almost in the bridge's shadow again. At first I felt nothing but wriggling toddler. Then slowly, as she kicked and kicked, her weight began to lighten.

"No, Bad Lady!" the child howled at me. "Want doggies!" To accentuate her point, she kicked me in one sweat-stung eye.

Although it hurt like blazes, I ignored the pain and held her tighter.

"I've got her now!" Big Gal cried. "You can let go!"

"You sure?"

"Sure's as my name's Lashinda!" A hard jerk upward.

I let go.

With a final, wrenching jolt, Lashinda—her legs apparently well-secured by the hero in the wheelchair—tore the toddler out of my hands and hauled her upward.

The crowd erupted into cheers, which for some strange reason hurt my eye even further, not that I could afford the luxury of worrying about that now. Durango was less than twenty feet from me, closing in, his lips pulled back from those glistening teeth. The rest of the pack was right behind him.

Time to save myself.

Entering into hand-to-hand combat with a wolf pack would be suicidal. But so would turning around and hightailing it down the Wolf Run, because the wolves would bring me down before I cleared the bridge.

I had a better idea.

Zookeeper lore held that if you were ever penned in with a dangerous animal and couldn't run away, you needed to make yourself look as big and dangerous as possible. So I began unbuttoning my khaki shirt, not that easy a task since my fingers were trembling.

One button.

Two.

Three.

How many damned buttons did this thing have, anyway?

Six, as it turned out.

By the time the knee-length shirttail came free, Durango was less than eight feet away. The shirt's sleeves were loose enough that my arms didn't get hung up, so I was able to whip it off in what felt like one smooth motion.

"*Hyawwww!!!*" I roared at the wolves, flapping the humongous shirt above my head, and jumping up and down. "*Hyawwww!!!*"

Durango's eyes widened for a split second, then he turned tail and fled, his pack following close behind.

When the zoo's six-person DART team arrived five minutes later with their fire extinguishers, tranquilizer darts, and fully loaded rifles, I was still pacing back and forth from one side of the Wolf Run to the other, still shaking my shirt, still roaring "*Hyawwww!*"

Just in case Durango changed his mind and came back.

Chapter Ten

Lex Yarnell, one of the DART members who'd hauled me out of the Wolf Run, and then fetched my borrowed shirt with a long stick, chauffeured me around for what remained of my working day. First stop was the Nurse's Station, where Wendy Stafford, R.N., didn't like the way my eye looked. "For all we know, that kid could have stepped in wolf piss," she muttered to Lex, after ordering him to take me to San Sebastian General Hospital's Emergency Room. "If I was a doc, I'd shoot her up with antibiotics."

To me, she said, "There's a full moon tonight, so have Sheriff Joe keep you locked up, just in case." She winked.

I didn't wink back, my usual winking eye being covered with gauze.

When Lex and I arrived at the ER, the doc—Rosalind Widdows, internal medicine, an old friend of mine—did shoot me up with antibiotics, but guffawed at any possibility of my turning into a werewolf. "The last known werewolf died in Romania in 1890. He was replaced by Cthulhu." Shots and smart-assery duly delivered, she gave me a couple of prescriptions and a sterile eye patch. "They have silk pirate patches at the pharmacy. Dressier, if you care for that sort of thing."

From the ER, Lex drove me to CVS, where the pharmacist issued me more antibiotics and a two-yards-long receipt. On the way back to my truck, I called Walt MacAdams at the harbor, and told him what I needed to do.

When Lex deposited me back at my truck, I headed for Gunn Landing Harbor, where the unlikeable Cliff Flaherty had met his untimely end. Sore eye or not, I still had an investigation to conduct.

Walt stood waiting for me on the deck of his *Running Wild*. "Do what you need to do," he told me, "and I'll keep an eye out. Like I said on the phone, none of the cops have gone near *Scribbler* since the day after Cliff bit the big one, but who knows when one of them might drop by for another look-see? If you get caught, leave my name out of it. I don't want your husband more pissed at me than he already is. Hey, what's wrong with your eye?"

"Just got something in it, no biggie," I answered.

As we walked past the *Running Wild* toward Cliff's Gulf 32 Pilothouse, Walt added, "If you wanted to look through his Mercedes Gullwing too, you're out of luck. The cops towed it away yesterday, probably afraid some car enthusiast would steal it. Gave this end of the harbor some class."

Scribbler's cabin was locked, of course; the detectives had made certain of that by replacing Cliff's ancient Yale with a new Schlage. This was disappointing. Once in the not-too-distant past I'd heard Cliff swear at the old Yale—his boat wasn't far from mine—then take a wrench and whack at the thing long enough that the two brawny boaters now living in Hawaii on their *Wipe Out* yelled for him to be quiet or they'd come over and do the same thing to his kneecap. I'd then watched in amazement as Cliff bypassed the cabin door and its recalcitrant lock by sliding into the cabin through a loose window in *Scribbler*'s pilothouse.

After making certain no one was looking, I did the same, the dried-out facing only slightly skinning my hip as I slid through.

Compared to what I'd already experienced today, it was nothing. But as my rump landed on the cabin floor, I realized that Walt's last words had stirred up something I'd been puzzling about.

Why had a man who wrote my mother's charity a large check last week, and owned a '57 Mercedes 300SL Gullwing worth well into a million bucks, been living on a boat as sad as this?

In its heyday, *Scribbler* must have been beautiful, but not anymore. The spacious pilothouse had once been light and airy, but now the salt-encrusted windows dulled the sunny day to a swamp-like gloom. The varnish had been rubbed away from the teak fittings, and the cover on the full-length settee on the port side was ripped and stained. From crime techs looking for drugs? Or from a man who neither cared about people *nor* boats? Probably the latter, since flies buzzed around the dirty dishes in the sink, and unless I was wrong, a family of mice had made their home in one of the galley's open drawers.

The only item that appeared halfway clean in this hellhole was an eight-by-ten framed photograph screwed to the galley wall. The glass had been Windexed to a fare-thee-well, so that even after six days of being abandoned, I could still make out the images of a beaming Cliff Flaherty, a luminous Lauren, and a grinning Dylan, who appeared to be around eight years old.

For some reason that photograph hurt my heart, so I turned away and began looking for...for I didn't know what. I gave the cabinets and drawers—those without mice in them, anyway—a good going-over, then rummaged through the tiny closet. The dead man hadn't been exactly dapper; most of what I found were ancient slacks and shirts that wouldn't have looked out of place at the Midnight Mission. The single exception was a startlingly expensive-looking indigo silk suit that resembled an Ermenegildo Zegna, a brand my elegant stepfather was fond of. It looked brand new.

"Yep," I muttered to myself, checking the label. "Zegna."

After frisking the Zegna's pockets and finding nothing, I

started going through the pockets of everything else, including the crumpled clothes that lay moldering on the floor. The jeans were the worst. Dirt- and oil-encrusted, they could have stood up on their own, but in my first pass-through of their pockets, I found nothing. When I tossed them back down, though, I thought I heard a papery rustle, so I went through them again.

This time I steeled myself to stick my entire hand into the front right pocket, and was rewarded with the scratch of paper. Whatever it was had slipped through a hole in the lining, and now rested stuck between denim and the lining fabric. Maybe that was why the CSIs had missed it. I pulled the paper out to find it crumpled on one end, flat on the other, as if it had been hurriedly shoved into the pocket. It was an invoice for a rebuilt Suzuki outboard motor. Not only that, but it was a third notice, threatening repossession of the *Scribbler*—which had been used for collateral—if payment wasn't rendered in ten days. The warning was dated the day before he'd died.

I frowned. Here was Cliff Flaherty, living in a hellhole, writing large checks to charity while dressed in a three-thousand-dollar suit and driving around in a million-dollar car—all the while his floating home was under threat of repossession.

It made no sense.

With Joe still at work, Lauren back in her hotel room (or wherever goddesses go to kill time), and Colleen and Dylan and the kids in the granny cottage, the house was unusually silent when I made it home from Gunn Landing Harbor. This suited me fine. My eye still throbbed, and all I wanted was to take a shower, and a Tylenol and go to bed. However, this was the perfect time to clear up a few things that had been bothering me about Dylan's story, so after paying DJ Bonz, Fluffalooza, and Miss Priss the attention they were overdue for, I changed out of my baggy but lifesaving uniform and into jeans and a tee. Then I headed for the granny cottage to grill my stepson.

Dylan was sitting on the floral sofa with the kids, the leg of his jeans hiked up far enough that I could see his electronic ankle bracelet. Colleen sat across from him in the matching chair, finishing up that old Irish joke about a broke priest attempting to cadge a loan from a leprechaun. "So that's why you can't borrow money from a leprechaun, because they're always a little short."

Dylan groaned. So did I.

Tonio pretended to laugh. Bridey just looked puzzled.

After catching sight of my eye patch, Colleen cried, "Teddy! What's wrong with your eye?"

"Kid at the zoo kicked me. No problem, since it's been treated, but I need to talk with Dylan. Privately."

Concern replaced by suspicion, she frowned. "Anything you say to Dylan you can say in front of me."

"I'd rather not. Especially not with the kids around."

"Then you're not talking to him." Colleen folded her arms across her ample chest.

"It's important."

"I *said* you're not…"

Dylan entered the fray. "Hey, you two! Don't I have any say in this?"

"Your attorney said you've already talked too much to too many people," Colleen snapped.

Her intransigence irritated me, possibly because my eye had started throbbing again. "Do you want me to help him or not?"

She took a moment to ponder that, then her body slowly relaxed, and Fierce Granny became Plaintive Granny. "Now? But we were all having such a nice time. And by the way, aren't you home early?"

"I take it you weren't watching TV today."

Resuming her Fierce Granny persona, she sniffed, "I've had better things to do."

"For your elucidation, some zoo-goer filmed my striptease in the Wolf Run—more about that later—and she also got a great shot of me getting kicked in the eye," I explained. "Being a self-styled reporter, which everyone is these days, she sent it to KGNN. They've been running it on and off all day."

Colleen shot me a baffled look. "Wolf Run? But what does that have...?"

I grinned, even though it hurt. "At the end of the story they reported that Aster Edwina Gunn wanted me out of the public eye for a while, so she made me take a week's vacation, starting today. I'm going to use it to find out who killed Cliff Flaherty. Like you, I'm convinced it wasn't Dylan."

"Thank you for that vote of confidence, Stepmom," Dylan said. The first part of his sentence sounded like the usual teenage snark, but by the time he made it to the end, his voice was shaky.

Turning to Tonio and Bridey, who had been closely following our squabble, Colleen ordered, "Kids, go into the bedroom and watch *Sesame Street.*"

"I'm not watching that kiddie stuff," Tonio sniffed.

"Then *Tippy-Toe & Tinker*. I think the episode airing today is the one where they introduced Poonya, the red panda. You know, the character played by Jocelyn Ravel."

Upon hearing his lady love's name, Tonio perked up and took Bridey by the hand. "C'mon, Squirt, let's go watch your kiddie show," he said, leading her out of the living room.

Once they were gone, I asked, "Dylan, what do the police have on you? You're not wearing that ankle bracelet simply because of some old grudge against Flaherty. There has to be some hard evidence linking you to his death, and I need to know everything if I'm going to help."

Dylan suddenly found something interesting on Colleen's sage green carpet. I looked down and didn't see anything, other than the fact that the carpet was the exact same shade as the leaves on Colleen's matching sofa-and-chairs suite. Rose and green, green and rose, the color theme carried throughout the small cottage. When it came to décor, Colleen was nothing if not traditional.

Dylan didn't answer my question, so I nudged, "C'mon, kid. What do the authorities have on you?"

"Dunno. And stop calling me *kid*. I'm eighteen." Still looking at the carpet.

"Did it have anything to do with those scraped knuckles of yours?"

"I was working on my car."

"There's no grease under your nails."

"Why do you keep nagging me? You're worse than my mother."

"You got into a fight with Flaherty, didn't you?"

He finally met my eyes. "He started it."

Bingo. "Where'd this fight happen?"

His knee jerked up and down for a few seconds, and just as I was about to repeat my question, he took a deep breath and said, "When I first arrived in town, I stopped by the Circle K to get a Polar Pop, and he bumped into me as I was leaving. Hard. Almost like he'd meant to do it. He made me spill the whole drink, and didn't even apologize."

"And?"

"So I called him on it. 'Hey, man, you owe me another Polar Pop,' I said. Then he shoved me again, even harder, and called me a little fu… Uh, a nasty world. That's when I just kinda hit him. Well, it was really sorta accidental, because I was, um, trying to get around him to my car." Knee still jerking, and he returned to looking at the carpet. Talk about a lousy liar.

"Did you know who he was?"

"Not right then." He met my eyes again, which convinced me he was telling the truth.

Now we were getting somewhere. "Before your arrest, did you tell the police about the incident?"

"Why would I do something stupid like that? I mean, it

wasn't really much of a fight. Once he was down, I tossed my empty cup at him and got into my car."

"You actually knocked him *down*?"

"Like I told you, I didn't mean to hit him that hard, but sometimes I don't know my own strength. It's not like I gave the guy a concussion or anything. He was back on his feet and cursing at me by the time I left the lot, so I just drove to a 7–11 down the road and bought me another drink. So it was all good."

Colleen, who had been sitting quietly during this, exploded. "*All good*? You're recorded knocking a man down, a man who's found murdered hours later, and you say 'It's all good'? What the..."

She quieted down when I put a finger to my lips. But she was right. Dylan might not think there was much to the fight, but the detectives would have checked for a transfer of DNA—Dylan's to Cliff, and Cliff's to Dylan. The kid might even have left a hair or two. Still, the authorities must have had even a stronger reason to arrest him than that one incident, so I persevered. "When you met with your attorney, what did he say?"

He gave me a sour look. "He told me not to tell anyone what I just told you."

"Oh, I'm sure he didn't mean to include me. We're family." I gave him what I hoped was a reassuring smile, but as I was learning, when your eye is bandaged, it's hard to smile without hurting yourself. Who knew the eye was connected to the mouth? "What else might the police have on you, Dylan? There must be more."

A sigh. "As far as I know, just the surveillance camera thing. And, uh, the DNA. But like I said, it was no big deal. It would have shown him getting up. I mean, he wasn't dead or anything."

"You told the police this?"

"I didn't tell them *anything*!"

There was a bit of a disconnect here. "When they asked you about the fight, what did you say?"

"Nothing. I'm not crazy. And... And when this other cop

told me I got caught on a different camera down at the harbor, I didn't say anything about that, either."

I tried not to react to what he'd just said, but Colleen stood up and yelped, "A camera at the *harbor*!? The same harbor where Cliff Flaherty was found dead?"

Sounding more like ten than eighteen, Dylan said in a small voice, "Well, yeah, I guess. If you want to put it that way. How many surveillance cameras do they have around here, anyway? Isn't that against our civil liberties or something?"

"What were you doing at the harbor, Dylan?" I asked.

"Uh, I just wanted to, um, see the boats."

Frowning, I said, "Try again."

"No, really! I like boats!"

"Tell me the truth or I'm walking away from this. What were you doing at the harbor?"

He sighed again. "Oh, all right. When I was driving away from the Circle K, in my rearview mirror I saw the guy I'd been in the fight with getting into a Mercedes Gullwing. I hadn't ever seen one of those other than in a car museum, so I followed him. When I saw him getting into that ratty old boat, I was really surprised, but what the heck, it gave me the chance to get up close and personal with that Gullwing. Geez, what a beauty! Teddy, it's got…"

I waved away his enthusiasm. "That's how you wound up on the harbor cameras."

Colleen groaned. So did I.

Our twin groans worked where my words hadn't. Dylan finally got it. With a face suddenly morose, he said, "I'm screwed, aren't I?"

I was trying to figure out a way to reassure him, when Tonio returned to the living room.

"No Tippy-Toe today," Tonio said. "Just some old *Sesame Street* rerun."

Dylan took advantage of the reprieve. "Oh, that's too bad," he said to his half brother. Then, milking the moment for all it was worth, he shifted around on the sofa so his back was to me, and said, "Say, Tonio, what's your favorite subject in school? At your age, mine was social studies."

When Tonio started yammering about the immense wheat fields in Georgia—the one in the former USSR, not the U.S.— Dylan pretended rapt interest, and I knew our interview was over, at least for now. But that was okay. The lull made me realize how exhausted I really was, so I returned to the empty house, gave the dogs and cat some more attention, then fell asleep on the sofa, with DJ Bonz, Fluffalooza, and Miss Priss snuggled around me.

I didn't wake up until Joe came home and I had to convince him all over again that, no, regardless of the wolf "incident"— which he had seen on the five o'clock news—I was not going to quit my job at the zoo. When he made a disgruntled comment about my striptease, I also told him that if taking off my clothes would keep me alive anywhere, especially in the Wolf Run, then bring on the stripper pole. And, by the way, I was keeping the *Merilee*, too. I didn't care how many corpses floated by.

So there.

Chapter Eleven

Saturday morning all hell broke loose in San Sebastian County. Robbers hit the Snip & Curl, taking off with several dozen cartons of nail polish; there was a twelve-car pileup on Highway One; a commercial fishing boat sank a mile west of Gunn Landing Harbor and dumped twenty-seven people into the Pacific, all rescued via a flotilla of pleasure-boaters.

Around 9:00, Lauren, Dylan's too-gorgeous mother, dropped by to hold his hand, and out of delicacy for my feelings about her onetime relationship with my husband, did the hand-holding in the granny cottage. Not wanting to spend one moment away from their new brother, Tonio and Bridey were back there, too.

This, plus Joe having fled early for the relative calm of the San Sebastian County Sheriff's Office, left me alone in a too-quiet house, so I spent the morning doing laundry, vacuuming, and shining whatever object would hold still long enough to let me shine it. I even bathed both dogs and the cat—separately, of course—then washed their bedding. DJ Bonz and Fluffalooza enjoyed the experience, but Miss Priss squeezed her pristine self under the sofa, where she gave me the Stare of Death. Contrary to popular opinion, not all cats hate water. The Fishing Cats of Southeast Asia has webbing between their elongated toes, which helps them catch fish. To those cats, large bodies of water are no more threatening than the produce aisle at the supermarket.

Miss Priss is not related to them.

It was odd, not being at the zoo on one of its busiest days, and I didn't like it, so during all this frenetic activity, I kept an eye on the clock. Finally, at 1:30 on the dot, I headed out for the San Sebastian Public Library to see puppeteers Gordon "Gordo" Walken and Karla Dollar discuss their work and perform a skit from *Tippy-Toe & Tinker*. Disguising myself as a kiddie show fan would give me the perfect excuse to question them about their relationship with Cliff Flaherty.

In order not to annoy library patrons seeking silence, all the puppetry action took place in the Sierra Room, generally used for teaching ESL classes. But today the room was packed with excited children and their parents. On the dais at the end of the room stood a portable stage similar to the one used on the television show. Its curtain had been raised all the way so everyone could view the puppeteers as they controlled their marionettes. As we quickly learned, when the puppeteers were working their marionettes, they wore plain black tees and slacks, reserving their cumbersome, puppet-matching costumes for other occasions.

Gordon "Gordo" Walken and Karla Dollar introduced themselves by both their own names and their character's names—Tippy-Toe the Tyrannosaurus Rex, and Rosie the Triceratops—then spent a few minutes discussing the history of their art. We learned how the puppets' hand controls had evolved over the centuries from a single line of only a few strings, to the more complicated control bars used in modern times. Since this was the first time the children in attendance had seen their beloved characters' strings being controlled by actual human beings, they paid close attention. So did their parents. And, I have to admit, so did I.

"Archaeologists have found marionettes dating back to

ancient Greece in the fifth century BC, in which simple wooden figures were shown performing religious rituals," explained Gordon "Gordo" Walken. In a departure from his Tippy-Toe voice, he now sounded like a grade school teacher, albeit one built like the Hulk. "Those puppets must have been quite common, because even Aristotle, the philosopher, mentioned them."

With a nimble flip of his huge hand, he made his dinosaur fall on its knees in a prayerful position.

On cue, petite Karla Dollar, said, "Although the form of hand puppetry known as 'Muppets' is more popular today, marionettes remain a popular form of entertainment throughout the world, especially in Austria, France, Sicily, the Czech Republic, Indonesia..." Here she paused, took a breath, and added, "And San Sebastian!"

Holding up her multiple-barred control in both hands, she made her Rosie the fair-minded triceratops give a hippity-hop, then bob its head and clap its claw like hands. The crowd cheered. I cheered right along with them, recognizing how many years of training it must have taken to acquire such skill.

The two then performed a brief skit where Rosie the Triceratops was feeling depressed because of all the turmoil created in Dino Dell after Poonya, the red panda, had moved in.

"My friends are all choosing sides, and I just don't know what to do," Rosie/Karla cried.

"You'll do what you always do, Rosie," Tippy-Toe/Gordo replied. "Which means you'll do the right thing. And don't worry. It'll turn out all right, because in the end, we dinosaurs are good creatures at heart. Even dinos like Zip and Randy will change their minds once they get to know our sweet Poonya, and Dino Dell will be a happy place once again."

With that, the small stage's curtain dropped all the way down, to even louder cheers than before.

When the puppeteers stepped away from the stage, their puppets left behind, children rushed toward them, and for at least a half hour, Karla and Gordo chatted one-on-one with their little fans. I heard several children tell the puppeteers they wanted to be just like them when they grew up. Whenever that happened, big Gordo's unfailing advice was, "Then you must always do the right thing."

"That includes doing the right thing for *everyone*, not just your friends," Karla echoed. She couldn't have been more than five feet tall, and looked even shorter next to six-and-a-half-foot Gordo.

As I waited for the crowd to clear out, I compared the sweet message of *Tippy-Toe & Tinker* to the violent video games currently popular, so despite Tippy-Toe's reassuring words, I didn't feel hopeful. Or maybe I was just tired. I hadn't slept well the past few nights.

When the last child had received personalized life advice from the puppeteers, I approached them. "May I have a minute?"

"You need an autograph for a child who couldn't be here?" Walken asked, with a kindly smile, followed by a wink. "Or perhaps for yourself?"

I fished out a piece of paper from my notebook. "For Bridey, she's five. And if you could sign it as 'Tippy-Toe the T. rex,' she'd be thrilled. And Ms. Dollar, if you could sign yours as 'Rosie the Triceratops'?"

"Call me Karla." Her smile took at least ten years off her age. Forty? Fifty? Age is harder to tell with women because we employ the aid of makeup, and she wore plenty. The tiny woman looked good in it, though, with a blush of pink highlighting her café-au-lait cheeks, and bright red lipstick framing perfect white teeth.

Once they handed me back their autographs (Gordo had drawn a cartoon T. rex on his) I introduced myself, then explained that their producer had been found floating next to my boat.

The smiles disappeared.

"I'm sure that must have been an upsetting situation for you," Gordo said, his heavy brow wrinkling with concern.

Karla's reaction was different. "What's that got to do with us?"

Gordo tapped her on the shoulder with his huge hand. "Remember that weird news story we saw on TV yesterday? The gal in the wolf pen? This is her. She's the sheriff's wife."

Yes, that unfortunate bit of information had made it into the now-infamous "stripper" clip, which is why Joe had been so irritated when he arrived home that night. Few sheriffs enjoy seeing their wives cavorting in the near-nude, even if the cavort saves their lives.

Karla wasn't mollified. Red-faced, she snapped, "He's the sheriff, not you. You have no right to sneak in here and question us."

"I didn't sneak, and I haven't asked you one question yet, except for your autographs."

That didn't fly with her, either. "You think we're stupid or something? I know why you're here. But neither Gordo nor I had anything to do with that jerk's death, and we don't appreciate being followed around and questioned like we're criminals or mur..."

"But, I'm not..."

"Listen, you..."

Gordo, whose calm, Tippy-Toe temperament appeared to carry over to his human life, held up a cautionary hand. "Karla, I'm sure it's all right. Teddy just wants to help."

Karla looked at him like he'd just grown scales, then carefully placed her triceratops marionette into its carrying case and snapped it shut. "I'll be waiting in the van." With that, she stalked out.

"Sorry about that," Gordo said, tucking Tippy-Toe into its own case. "She hasn't been herself since...well, since."

"Since Flaherty was found floating in the harbor?"

He began dismantling the small stage and loading it onto a suitcase-sized wheelie. "I'd like to help you, really I would, but you see how it is. Karla's never trusted the authorities, and if I were her, I'd feel the same way. But go ahead and ask me whatever. Just make it fast." He looked at his watch. "There's an ESL class due to start in here in five minutes."

"Okay, so how well did you know Cliff Flaherty? I mean personally, not professionally."

"Well enough not to like him."

"Any particular reason?"

"Since it's unkind to speak ill of the dead, let's just say I didn't like working with him. We didn't socialize, either."

"Because…?" I let the word hang there.

Gordo promptly forgot his not-speaking-ill-of-the-dead vow, and rushed to answer. "For starters, there was his temper. Cliff was always screaming at someone, at the caterers, the sound people, the director, and even at Marty Donaldson—you know, the show's coproducer. He was especially mean to Karla, although I don't think it was a racist thing; he just didn't like her. He didn't like anyone, for that matter. If you ask me, that bloody temper of his was the main reason he'd gone from being one of Hollywood's more successful screenwriters to the writer of this small-town kiddie show."

I felt compelled to defend my new home. "San Sebastian's not that small. Gunn Landing Harbor, where he was found floating, now *that's* small. Population five hundred."

Gordo gave me a wry smile. "Sorry. San Sebastian is a lovely place. And I'm sure Gunn Landing is, too."

"I take it you're not from here."

"Like most of the cast, I'm LA-born and bred, just moved up here for the show. That was, hmm, let me see, two years…" He halted when the door to the Sierra Room opened and the ESL students began to file in. "Sorry, gotta go. Karla's waiting for me in the van."

"One final question, then I'll let you go. Did you know Flaherty before you started work on *Tippy-Toe & Tinker*?"

"Not really. And that was a long time ago." With that, the big man headed for the door, rolling the wheeled case that carried the make-believe land of Dino Dell. Before exiting, he turned around and said, "Please don't make anything out of Karla's outburst. Ninety-nine percent of the time she's a truly sweet person, but Cliff..." He paused, then added, "Well, he could get anyone's back up. Including mine."

Then he left.

Driving away from the library, several points about the conversation occurred to me. One: Karla Dollar's odd hostility. Two: Gordo Walken's quick leap to her defense. Three: Gordo's following comment about Karla's distrust of the authorities: *If I were her, I'd feel the same way*. Then there was Gordo himself. He'd come across as a big, gentle soul and yet he had—unconsciously, perhaps?—managed to subtly direct my suspicions toward Karla.

When I reached the house, I found it empty except for the cat and dogs, but noticed Colleen's red Mustang and Lauren's opalescent-white Lexus parked in the driveway next to Dylan's silver-blue hatchback, which meant they were still with Dylan in the granny cottage. I would talk to him later, but right now I wanted to see what I could find out about Karla Dollar, aka Rosie the Triceratops.

A half hour with Google found little other than gossipy items about Cliff Flaherty's murder, and polished bios of the show's cast and crew. I was about to give up when I remembered that Colleen, in her guise as mystery writer, subscribed to several private sites, including several that specialized in the Hollywood scene. I'd stood over her one day when she'd logged on to one, and thought I might be able to duplicate her password. So I closed my laptop and went into the kitchen office nook where she still kept her old PC in case inspiration hit her while cooking dinner.

It took several tries, but I was soon cruising around on ZnoopZister, a startlingly intrusive site where it appeared that just about everyone—especially everyone within shouting distance of Hollywood—had run into trouble with the law at some point. It took mere minutes for me to learn the reason for Karla's bristly personality. Twenty years earlier, while she was a single mom living in one of East LA's rougher neighborhoods, her eight-year-old son, Jamal, was being harassed by a twelve-year-old nicknamed Ozee High. Jamal's first encounter with Ozee High left him with a sprained wrist. Like any good mother, Karla had complained to the school's authorities, only to be told that "since the attack hadn't taken place on school grounds and since there had been no witnesses..."

Jamal's next encounter with Ozee High left him with a dislocated shoulder. Leaving Jamal writhing on the ground, Ozee walked away, promising Jamal's pretty face would be rearranged next.

Again, off school grounds, and no witnesses.

At that point, Karla created her own solution. Using her sister Ruella's Wilshire Center address as her own, she enrolled Jamal in the highly respected Caesar Chavez Young People's Academy. Granted, the commute from East LA would take an hour and a half each way, and Karla, who refused to let Jamal ride the city buses alone, was already stressed. Besides taking weekly puppetry classes at Mondrian Ruzicka's School of Puppetry and Marionettes near the old Capitol Building at Hollywood and Vine, she worked back-to-back jobs at Burger King and Popeye's. She considered the extra work worth it because she and Jamal were moving on up.

And they were, until the overcrowded grade school began running checks of students' addresses, which revealed Karla had lied on the school's enrollment form. A felony. As an example, she was sentenced to three years at Chino.

The only good to come out of this was that while Karla was in prison, her sister took care of Jamal, giving the boy a legal home address in the Caesar Chavez Young People's Academy district. The school welcomed him back with open arms.

I grunted in disgust, remembering the miniscule sentences imposed on certain Hollywood television celebrities who had committed similar felonies.

After failing to calm myself down with a cup of chamomile tea, I gave up and used ZnoopZister to run a check on puppeteer Gordon "Gordo" Walken. The results brought up one appearance on a police report involving a stunt man nicknamed William "Moose" Argent. While at a Beverly Hills party, Moose had accused Gordo of stealing his drink, and when Gordo denied doing so, Moose decked him. Gordo, twice the size of the stunt man, didn't bother defending himself, but the host called the police to have Moose assisted out the door. A further search for Moose found several more similar incidents, none involving Gordo, before Moose's death in a rollover on the 405. The autopsy revealed that his blood alcohol content had been .25, extreme by any state's DUI laws.

Other than Gordo's onetime victimization by a stunt man, the puppeteer's history was clean. Not only that, ZnoopZister informed me that while he was living in LA, he performed regularly at various children's charities, volunteered his time at the West Hollywood No Kill Animal Shelter, and had once been photographed helping a little old lady cross the street. The picture was printed in *Variety*, over a caption that read, *"Don't say Hollywood doesn't care."*

Gordo was, however, unlucky in love. The picture taken of him with the elderly woman showed him as young, fit, with plenty of hair. In fact, he was almost, but not quite, handsome, which is possibly why he had once been good-looking enough to lure two women into marriage, and the beautiful Lauren into several dates. But for whatever reason, his relationships didn't last long. After his first wife, Sarah, left him for Cliff Flaherty, Gordo married actress Alicia Blossom, who in turn left him for

Esteban Geraldo, the dashing telenovela star. Astonishingly, Gordo had served as best man at their wedding. The puppeteer was also—this, according to the *Hollywood Reporter*—on such friendly terms with his first ex-wife, he'd agreed to serve as god-father for her new baby. All this goodness made me suspicious, which, in turn, made me wonder where this near-saint had been the night Flaherty was murdered. Talk about a man too good to be true! If he had been a character in a mystery novel, he'd for sure be the killer. But this was real life, and good people didn't run around bashing people's heads in.

Only killers did that.

As I was wondering how hard it would be to whitewash one's digital background—there had been mention of such things on ZnoopZister—the back door opened and Dylan, Lauren, Colleen, and the children trooped in. I hurriedly pushed away from the PC, but not before Colleen noticed what I'd been doing.

She didn't seem to mind.

"That's a fun search site," she said, as Bonz and Fluffalooza yipped and barked their joy at the children's return. "It's great for the Hollywood gang because their scandals tend to be of the sexual kind, but if you want to get down and dirty with a person's past, you need to use the Deep Web."

She leaned over and typed in PlatoSchmato, then a long series of caps and numbers, which brought up a new search engine. "Among other things, this is where old court records go to die or to be looked up by people like us. Now just run your names. Once you're in, it's as easy as ZnoopZister. Not as much fun, though."

Colleen was right about that. As I looked up Gordo and his roommate Ansel "Bird" Yates, the first two names on my list, I was overwhelmed with information, most trivial. Did I really need to know the minutiae of everyone's life, from birth, elemen-tary and high school, college, roommate trouble, small-claims court fusses, divorces, run-ins with the law, etc.? PlatoSchmato thought I did. And PlatoSchmato was right.

While Gordo Walken's background on ZnoopZister had been near-unbelievable in its Nice-Guy-ness (I made a mental note to recheck him on PlatoSchmato), Ansel "Bird" Yates's life was as filled with sex, violence, and adventure as a comic book character's.

Born in Malibu forty-six years ago, and a student at Malibu Montessori, from which his parents were forced to remove him because of his constant mini-assaults on other toddlers, Ansel Yates was first hauled into court at the age of thirteen... My fingers froze on the scroll bar. Weren't minors' records supposed to be sealed? Yes, they were, but apparently no one had told PlatoSchmato, so I continued scrolling. Bird's juvenile record showed that he'd gone after a classmate with a ballpoint pen, almost blinding him. Two years later, at fifteen, he'd committed a similar assault, although the weapon in the case had been a rock. At seventeen, the weapon had been a tire iron.

A tire iron. News reports have identified one as the probable murder weapon.

Colleen, still standing behind me, grunted. We read on.

Several short stays at various juvenile detention installations followed Bird's second and third attacks, the first one apparently having been a freebie.

At the age of eighteen, Bird received his first DUI. Several more DUIs followed, culminating in a short stretch in Malibu Adult Conservation Camp #13. Almost immediately after his release, he was hauled into court again, this time accused of fathering Inger May Prescott's bouncing baby boy. That matter was financially disposed of to Ms. Prescott's satisfaction, eating away at the small inheritance left Bird by his maternal grandmother.

All this was fascinating enough, but what I found surprising was that Bird had once been a championship surfer, winning meets in Australia, South Africa, and Hawaii. That's when he picked up his nickname, after "Surfin' Bird," a song popular in the sixties.

But Bird's prize-winning days ended when he lost a leg during a shark attack.

The tragedy happened when Bird was twenty-two, and warming up for a meet at Oahu's North Shore. By the time the other surfers reached him, he had almost drowned, then upon making it to shore, nearly bled out. But through a combination of innate toughness and spectacular luck—EMTs were already nearby, treating a heart attack victim—he had survived. So had his passion for surfing, which he now did recreationally with a custom-made prosthetic leg designed by an Icelandic orthopedics developer.

After he'd recovered and learned how to deal with the leg, Bird enrolled at Mondrian Ruzicka's School of Puppetry and Marionettes. Upon completion of the two-year course, he worked his way through the children's show circuit, becoming known for his skill in handling two marionettes at the same time. Two years ago, he snagged his first televised job on *Tippy-Toe & Tinker*, taking on the roles of dinos Zip and Randy.

Again, fascinating. But not fascinating enough to make me forget about the information I had read earlier.

Ballpoint pen. Rock. *Tire iron.*

"You thinking what I'm thinking?" Collen said, staring at the screen.

"Yep, tire iron. Wonder if the detectives have talked to Bird yet."

"That would be my guess."

In the living room, I could hear Lauren and the kids laughing at something Dylan had just said, Bonz yipping along in concert. Part of me wanted to join in their merriment, but the other part of me wanted to continue my searches on PlatoSchmato. After all, Dylan's own freedom was the issue here, not my entertainment.

As I continued scrolling down, PlatoSchmato informed me of a property transfer several years' back, from Mrs. Enid Baker Yates to Ansel "Bird" Yates. The legal papers concerned a trailer and the lot on which it rested, located in Surfer's Cove, Santa Cruz, California.

So Bird was that rarest of breeds: a property-owning puppeteer.

"Wonder how Bird and Flaherty got along," I mused.

"Probably not well," Colleen said. "*Tire iron*, remember. But I'm curious about that Martin Donaldson, the show's coproducer. I've never trusted Hollywood money men. Didn't you tell me you were trying to get in touch with him?"

"San Sebastian isn't Hollywood, but I get your drift. Yeah, Donaldson did start out down there, and from what I've already found out, he knew Flaherty back in the day, so if nothing else, he should be a wellspring of information. But he hasn't returned my calls."

Colleen's eyes met mine. "So quit calling."

Chapter Twelve

It was almost five when I set off for Whispering Willows, a relatively new condo complex on the more expensive side of San Sebastian, where Martin Donaldson lived with his fourth wife, Gloria, a corporate attorney for one of Silicon Valley's tech firms. Gloria Marquand-Donaldson spent most of her time in San Jose, and returned to San Sebastian only on weekends. From what I'd heard, her bonuses had helped bankroll the early days of *Tippy-Toe & Tinker*.

I was only halfway there when I noticed the red-and-blue flashers in my truck's rearview mirror. Since I hadn't been speeding or made any illegal turns, I was puzzled, but like any good citizen, I pulled over to the side of the road. Any anxiety I might have had disappeared when I saw my old friend Emilio Gutierrez, Joe's chief deputy, exit his cruiser and amble toward me. Maybe one of my pickup's brake lights was out and he merely wanted to alert me.

"I stopped by your house a few minutes ago," he said, without his usual smile. "Mrs. Rejas told me where you were headed. You need to go back home, Teddy. You're in enough trouble as it is, and I can't keep covering up for you."

You know how in some books the writers say something

like "Her heart fell," as if such behavior by a major organ was physically possible? Well, suspecting what was to come, my heart attempted to fall, but only managed a bump or two. Still, I smiled brightly. "Gosh, Emilio, I'm afraid I don't know what you mean. Did someone accuse me of holding up First San Sebastian Savings and Loan?"

For once, Emilio's face was humorless. "The harbor laundro-mat installed a surveillance camera several months ago, and you were taped having a physical altercation with Cliff Flaherty the day before he was murdered."

I tried again. "*Tape*, did you say? They pick it up at Goodwill or something? Everyone's gone digital."

He frowned. "Lou Caroll likes to save money. Now stop being a smart-ass and tell me what happened."

"It wasn't really physical, just kind of a messy argument, with wet clothes flying all over the place."

All I'd needed was one washer, but when I carried the dirty sheets and towels over from the Merilee, *I found every one of the ten washers in use. Actually, "in use" is the wrong phrase, because not only were the washers stopped, when I opened their lids, I found that each of them contained no more than three or four articles of clothing. They were cold and only slightly damp, which meant they had been sitting there for some time. Where was their owner? Scarfing down Boston cremes at JimBob's Donuts? Irritated, I removed three pairs of ragged skivvies from one washer and placed them on the sorting table. Then I refilled the washer with the* Merilee's *things. Just as I added eco-friendly liquid detergent, Cliff Flaherty entered the laundromat, screaming, "What the frack do you think you're doing!" Only he didn't say "frack."*

"My washing," I'd replied, politely as possible. "Your skivvies are on the sorting table, and I doubt you'll need a dryer."

Next thing I knew, Flaherty was grabbing me by the shoulder, and hauling me away from the washer. Before I could react, he also dragged my sheets and towels out of the washer and dumped them on the floor.

Furious, I picked everything up and told him what I thought of his behavior.

He slapped me.

I slapped him back with a soapy towel.

"Among other things, you struck him," Emilio said, breaking into the memory.

"He hit me first. After that, the floor was all soapy and we were both slipping and sliding around, and yeah, we were grabbing at each other to keep from falling, so I guess from the camera's angle it could have looked more physical than it really was. Once it was over, we both apologized and went our separate ways." A bit of a fib, there, about the apologies.

"You're forgetting we have the services of a lip-reader."

"You showed him the tape?!"

"Her. And not yet. For now, I've heard that the tape's been, ah, misfiled, but if your name keeps popping up in this investigation—which your husband placed me in charge of, remember—I'm sure it'll eventually be found. Probably by that new guy, Orville Thompson. He's as OCD as they come."

Thompson was the deputy who'd given me such a hard time at the harbor the day Cliff Flaherty's body had been found floating next to the *Merilee*.

"Emilio, Flaherty was a rude, crude bully, but I did *not* kill him!"

His face softened. "I believe you, Teddy, but Thompson doesn't, and neither do several people who've never been happy about your interference in police matters. So, as much as you want to help Dylan out, him being your stepson, you can't, because it could blow back on you in a big way. Now go home, and leave the detecting to me and my team. By the way, what's wrong with your eye? It's almost as red as your hair."

Hating the patch, I'd removed it this morning. "Workplace injury. No big deal."

He thought about that for a moment, then said, "Well, the

Flaherty investigation *is* a big deal, so remember what I said. Back off."

With that, he spun on his heel and returned to his cruiser.

I made a lazy U-turn and headed for the house, Emilio's cruiser following close behind. When I pulled into the drive, he gave me a curt wave, then drove on.

I didn't back out of the driveway until he was well out of sight.

Built out of a supposedly fire-retardant faux-wood material and designed to look like a series of Colorado ski lodges, the gated condo complex of Whispering Willows looked woefully out of place amid California's scrubland hills. Within the complex's gated confines were a private golf course and country club, two Olympic-sized pools, a large gym with all the latest fight-the-flab equipment, and a boutique strip mall featuring, among other goodies, a French-ish bistro, an organic smoothie shop, and the Mountain Bean, a coffee café that made Starbucks' prices look cute.

I had no trouble getting through the gate, the attendant being a longtime volunteer at the Gunn Zoo, and made my way to the visitors' parking lot. My informant, the Donaldsons' cleaning lady (also a zoo volunteer), had told me that when his wife was away, he seldom cooked for himself, usually dining early at the bistro before heading over to the golf club for a round of drinks with friends. The bistro was where I found him, hunched over a steaming bowl of pot-au-feu, crunching his way through a baguette almost as long as his arm.

"Well, if it isn't Marty Donaldson!" I called, approaching his table. It being so early, there were only two other customers, and they were on the other side of the room.

He looked up, a crumb of baguette attached to his lip. "Teddy? What are you doing here? I would have thought you'd still be at the zoo."

Sliding uninvited into the chair across from him, I explained it was my day off, then spun a little white lie about dropping by to visit an old friend who'd turned out not to be home, so as long as I was here, I decided to have some of the bistro's lauded onion soup. I added weight to my tall tale by ordering a bowl from the waitress. "And when I'm finished, a decaf latte and one of those delicious-looking raspberry macarons, please." Then, to Marty, I said, "It's been a heck of a week, hasn't it?"

He blinked at me a couple of times, then pursed his lips. "You're interviewing me, aren't you? I was under the impression your husband was no longer involved in the Flaherty investigation."

Busted, but what the hell. "Can't put anything past you, can I? But since you already know about Joe handing off the case to his chief deputy, you must also know that my stepson's been accused of the crime, right?"

"Right."

"Well, what self-respecting stepmother wouldn't do what she could to help get her stepson out of trouble?"

"I could name a few. Want some examples?"

I'd momentarily forgotten about his multiple marriages, but refused to allow myself to be led down that messy rabbit hole. "No, thanks. But I do believe you're in a position to help Dylan, so if you could just answer a few questions..."

"I didn't kill Cliff, Teddy." A thin smile.

"I'm sure you didn't. But who do you think did?"

He brushed the baguette crumb from his lip. "You're kidding, right? An easier question to answer would be, 'These days, who *didn't* want to kill Cliff?' The answer to that would be 'No one.' Probably everyone who ever met him during these past few years harbored fantasies of him dead." The smile turned mean. "Including you. He told me all about that little set-to in the laundromat."

There being no point in defending myself, I said, "Touché. But given his, ah, difficult temperament, how did you manage to work with him?"

"Because at one time I knew a different Cliff Flaherty."

I cocked my head. "What do you mean, *different*?"

He pushed away his half-finished bowl of pot-au-feu and sat back in his chair. "Let me tell you a story. Forty-something years ago, Cliff and I went to the same Beverly Hills middle school. It was a nice neighborhood, but the school had a serious problem. Bullies. Not the kind of bullies you usually see, the semi-illiterate thugs who beat up little kids, but well-dressed bullies with rich, famous parents. They picked on kids who didn't wear the right clothes or who looked different. Not in a racial sort of way, God forbid, in that bastion of Hollywood liberalism, but they were vicious to kids who looked different in any *other* kind of way, especially a physical deformity. Now look deep into my eyes, Teddy."

Frowning, I asked, "Are you trying to hypnotize me?"

His mouth twisted. "No. I meant that literally. Look at my eyes. Carefully. Both of them."

Confused, I did as he'd commanded. At first, I didn't see anything remarkable—his eyes were blue with tiny yellowish strips. In some lights they'd probably appear gray, other times green, but as I continued to study them, I noticed something interesting.

"Your right eye is a bit smaller than the left."

"Correct. That's because I was born with microphthalmia, a small right eye that didn't match the left. It was also bright red, and I was blind in it. When I was thirteen, and in middle school, that tiny red eye called all kinds of hell down on me."

I shook my head. "What are you talking about, red? Both eyes are blue-ish. As for the size, I can barely tell the difference! It took me a while."

"That's because the right eye is an artificial eye, painted by a master craftsman to match the other."

"But..."

"It was put in when I was fourteen. You see, although my mother and I lived in a ritzy Beverly Hills neighborhood, she was a maid for one of the area's wealthier families, and our 'house' was an apartment above the family's garage. We shared one side of the apartment with whatever chauffeur happened to be in hire at the moment. Mom couldn't afford the operation, and the insurance company provided by her employers considered the operation a 'cosmetic' procedure and wouldn't pay for it. So I went all the way through grade school, then part of middle school getting the crap beat out of me."

"Then how...?"

"When I was thirteen, Mom left her old job—something about the guy being 'handsy'—and signed on with a new family. They were the Flahertys."

Excited, I broke in. "And they..."

He held up a restraining hand. "It was the same old snobby school district, and the same old insurance problem, but at least the man of the house wasn't 'handsy.' Then one day, when I was getting beat up behind the basketball court, Cliff, their son, happened to see what was going on and rushed in to help. He wound up getting beat up worse than me, and when his parents saw the damage, they went screaming to the school authorities. The bullies were expelled, and wonder of wonders, some of the parents took up a collection—the Flahertys were the biggest contributors—and I got a new eye."

"All because Cliff Flaherty tried to break up a fight."

"It was more than that. For the rest of our time in middle school, he shepherded me to school and back, making sure nothing bad happened to me again." Then Donaldson leaned forward, made a fist, and pounded it on the table so hard the foam slopped over from my just-delivered latte. "*That's* the Cliff Flaherty I knew."

While driving away from Whispering Willows, I did some heavy thinking. Marty Donaldson had seen Cliff Flaherty behave heroically and compassionately, yet others, including myself, only experienced Flaherty's physical aggression. Was Donaldson seeing his former rescuer through rose-tinted memories? Or given his own spotty background—all those marriages—had he merely been making excuses for another alpha male's bad behavior?

Which led me to an article I'd read recently in *Psychology Today*, where a current scientific study theorized that no one was born "bad." The research suggested that what were formerly labeled as "bad acts" were usually the results of severe childhood abuse, escalated by further traumatic incidents in young adulthood, eventually reaching the tipping point either by a physical blow to the head, or overindulgence in those grand old catchalls, alcohol and/or drugs.

Having personally known several murderers, I wasn't certain I agreed. None of them had fit the experts' criteria. Then again…

Since I was already on the road, I decided to try my luck at a certain trailer park.

Surfer's Cove Mobile Home Park, home of Ansel "Bird" Yates, was located a mere half mile from Steamer Lane, the legendary surfing mecca near Santa Cruz. Unit 73 was a cramped single-wide located in the row farthest from the swimming pool and closest to the busy strip mall behind it. Hardly the classiest of addresses, but, hey, Bird owned his abode free and clear, and in this zip code, that was a big deal.

When the door opened to my knock, I came face-to-face with the realization that even PlatoSchmato didn't know everything. Standing in front of me was Gordo, also known as Tippy-Toe. He appeared perfectly at home in another man's trailer.

"Why, Teddy, what a nice surprise!" he exclaimed, genial as always. "Come in, come in."

Bemused, I accepted the big man's invitation. "Just dropped by to see Bird. Do you, ah…"

"Live here? Sure do!"

Gay? Just roomies? Relevant or not?

"Yo, girl!" boomed a deeper male voice. Bird, standing in the trailer's narrow hallway.

"Uh, yo back."

Gordo waved toward the tiny galley kitchen, "Want something to drink? We've got organic orange juice, herbal tea—I just brewed some—and bottled water, of course, nothing added, just pure H2O."

Having guzzled a bottle of Evian on my way over I wasn't thirsty, but it takes a while to drink a cup of tea, which could lead to a longer visit, so I said, "Tea would be lovely, thanks."

Seconds later I was sipping something horrific; it tasted like a combination of kale and ginger.

"Too gnarly?" Bird asked.

"It's..." I thought of a word that wouldn't be too harsh. "Interesting."

My attempt at politeness didn't fool Gordo. "Maybe some honey?"

"Yes, please." *Or the bitterness will make my tongue curl and I won't be able to talk.*

The forthcoming spoonful of honey didn't work miracles with the nasty brew, but at least made it palatable. As I sipped, I looked around.

Little attempt had been made to turn the single-wide, two-bedroom trailer into a home, other than the surfboards leaning against the wall, and the surfing trophies in an otherwise empty bookcase. No rugs, just a stretch of pink-speckled pea-green linoleum that clashed hideously with the orange-and-brown tweed sofa and the two occasional chairs in front of it. The rest of the "decor" consisted of a row of photographs over the sofa, cataloging the development of a blond, blue-eyed child into a heartthrob teenager. *Bird?*

At second glance, Bird had a star-shaped birthmark on his

neck. The young man in the photographs had none. Bird's son, then, the cause of that long-ago paternity case. Other than the birthmark and the leg thing, he was a younger version of his father. Shoulder-length blond hair, deep tan, heartbreakingly handsome—as his father still was, although streaks of silver now mingled with Bird's gold, shoulder-length locks.

From my vantage point I could see the galley kitchen counter, cluttered by various bottles and vials of herbal remedies, as well as a giant-sized container of Excedrin. Maybe Bird still suffered from phantom limb pain. How long after amputation did that last? When I was done here, I'd place a call to Dr. Leonard "Lenny" Huffgraf, my onetime stepbrother, who had been helpful on earlier occasions.

What I didn't see in the trailer was any evidence of their marionettes, which made me think they probably kept them in their bedrooms. Too bad, because I would have enjoyed examining them close up. Those small dinosaurs were works of art.

Since Bird had been wearing his Dino Zip costume when we'd met at the zoo, I hadn't realized how big the man actually was. Not as big all around as potbellied Gordo, but a tall and solidly built athlete. The surfboards—several well-used foamies, and a couple of antique woodies—testified to their regular use. Bird's claw-footed surfer's prosthesis rested on a shelf underneath the boards, while now he wore a standard, blade-footed one. He hadn't bothered to hide it with Dockers or whatever—just a pair of blue baggies. No shirt covered his tanned and chiseled abs. He smelled like sun and seawater.

Gordo was more demurely dressed in Costco-level jeans and a pale green tee-shirt emblazoned with the cartoonish *Tippy-Toe & Tinker* logo. The shirt did his potbelly no favors. Compared to his gorgeous roommate, he wasn't aging well.

"So to what do we owe the pleasure of your company?" Gordo asked, after we'd settled ourselves onto the ugly furniture.

Gordo picked a green-and-yellow plaid chair; me, its match. Bird flopped down on the orange-and-brown tweed sofa.

I used the old lie that I'd come up with a great idea for the *Tippy-Toe & Tinker* show, which involved walk-on parts by marionettes resembling various Gunn Zoo animals. Gordo listened politely. Bird didn't.

"That's the dumbest thing I ever heard," Bird scoffed. "Expensive—you got no idea how much marionettes cost—and besides, it'd mega-totally destroy our story arc."

Gordo made soothing sounds. "Well, maybe not dumb, since we already have the Poonya character, and she represents a real animal."

"Only because that old bitch at the zoo offered our *producers...*" Bird pronounced the word like it was a particularly nasty Anglo-Saxonism, finishing with, "...a gob of money. That Poonya character's nothing more than a commercial for her zoo, and if you ask me, that squeaky-voice Jocelyn's nothing but a quimby."

In surfer jargon, a quimby was a know-nothing beginner, and its usage made Bird sound less adult himself. He was a middle-aged man, for Pete's sake, not some kid hanging ten. Had he suffered residual brain damage during that long-ago shark attack? After all, PlatoSchmato had revealed that during Bird's rescue, he'd flatlined twice. My doctor stepbrother might help explain that, too. But whatever the cause, Bird's immaturity had just handed me the perfect opening. "Sounds like you had issues with the show's producers."

"Well, *duh.*"

I smiled. "Which of the two was worse?"

"Duh again."

"Now, now, Bird," Gordo placated.

The surfer folded his muscular arms across his bronzed chest.

Despite being forty-four—thank you again, PlatoSchmato—and minus one leg, he was still gorgeous. "Dude, just because you sucked up to him all the time don't mean I have to," he said.

I snuck a look at Gordo to see how he'd handle this but found him seemingly untroubled. Was it really possible that he had *sucked up*—to use Bird's delicate phraseology—to a man who'd broken up his marriage? Eager to follow this thread, I turned to Bird with an expression of admiration. "Sounds like you didn't let Cliff get away with much."

He responded by puffing out his manly chest. "I didn't let Dirtbag get away with nothing. You ask me, it was a miracle nobody'd killed him before, 'cause that dude, he didn't get the concept of boun…boundaries? Is that the word, Gordo?"

Gordo nodded gravely. "Personal boundaries."

Bird continued. "Yeah, personal boundaries. You know that greenroom down at KGNN? Where we tape the show on Mondays? Well, Dirtbag kept popping in every time we was getting ready to tape, telling us make sure we do this, do that, say a line *this* way, say it *that* way, and when Ethan would…"

"Ethan Ganey?" I interrupted. "The show's director?"

"The show sure as hell doesn't direct itself," Bird said, with a self-pleased snort. "When Ethan would tell him to back off, that directing was *his* job, not Dirtbag's, the shit always hit the fan, with Dirtbag saying Ethan didn't know what he was doing, which he sure as hell did. I mean, directing's Ethan's *job*, right?" Not waiting for an answer, he plowed ahead, switching to the present tense, as if it were still happening. "But Dirtbag never shuts up, does he, just keeps yammering on and on, getting Ethan more and more upset, which means he's gonna take it out on us like he always does, so one day last week I…"

Gordo cleared his throat.

Bird took the hint. "Okay, okay, so the past's the past, and all that Zen shit. But I'm telling you for the millionth time there was something wrong in the head with that Cliff dude. Speaking of heads, I think a bad one's coming around." He cast an anguished look at his roommate.

"Close your eyes," Gordo said, his tone gentle. "Take slow, deep breaths. Belly-breathing, remember. One, two, three..."

To my surprise, the bellicose Bird did as he was told, and as the count continued, I could see the surfer's taut body relax.

When Gordo reached twenty, he said, "Now take a cleansing breath."

Bird did.

"Now open your eyes."

Bird opened his eyes, then beamed. "Epic!" To me, he said, "He's something, ain't he?"

It was an impressive performance, to be sure, but I couldn't forget that giant-size container of Excedrin on the kitchen counter. Apparently, Gordo's quick fix didn't always work.

From the view through the trailer's tiny window, I could see the light fading, which made me glance at my watch. 6:05. If I missed dinner, Joe would demand to know why. Still, I was learning too much from this visit to stop now.

"Tell you what, Teddy," Gordo said, still in soothing mode, "while I make us some more tea, why don't you ask Bird to tell you how he got into puppetry? It's an amazing story."

After choking down one cup of the bitter, pungent brew I didn't really want more, but if that was what I had to do to understand the relationship between these two, then I'd drink up. As it turned out, the story that followed was, indeed, amazing.

At twenty-two, Bird had survived a shark attack only to fall into a deep depression, believing he'd never surf again. His physical therapist, alarmed at his patient's degeneration, suggested he take up a hobby. Grudgingly, Bird set out to find one. First came yoga, which ended when Bird got himself ejected from the studio for decking the yoga teacher. Next came woodworking, but during the first class, Bird threatened bodily harm to *that* teacher, resulting in yet another ejection. A spate of other attempts followed, all ending in threats and failure, until the day Bird was sitting on a bench at the Malibu Community Center, awaiting the beginning of a class titled Recreational Rocketry. While he fumed and huffed, he happened to see a group of people carrying marionettes walking down the hall. Curious, he followed them.

"That's when I saw my first marionette show!" Bird said, taking the cup of fresh tea Gordo had just handed him. "It was an amateur deal, but still rad, and, I'm tellin' you that's when I knew it was for me."

The next week he enrolled himself at Mondrian Ruzicka's School of Puppetry and Marionettes, where he neither decked nor threatened anyone. Instead, he excelled, and although he was finally able to begin recreational surfing again, he knew he'd found his true vocation. Sure, he was minus a leg, and that sucked, but his hands and fingers remained intact. Perfect for operating a marionette's control bar. Even better, he'd always been ambidextrous, which made it easy to control two control bars at once—a rare skill in puppetry.

While I was marveling at this tale of triumph over adversity, something he said struck me. "The Mondrian Ruzicka School? Isn't that the place Karla Dollar attended?"

Bird said, "And Gordo, here. And Ethan Ganey, which is why he knows how to direct, although he's not a puppeteer himself. Anybody who's anybody in puppetry goes to Ruzick."

"You left out Jocelyn Ravel."

Bird sniffed an un-Bird sniff. "Didn't ya hear me? *Anybody who's anybody.* She didn't go there. Like I said, nothing but a quimby."

No love lost between those two, then. I was about to ask him about Beverly Beaumont when the color suddenly drained from Bird's face. He stood up so fast he almost knocked his chair over, and made for the Excedrin jar in the galley kitchen, where he shook out four pills, then gulped them down dry. Another headache, this one obviously massive.

"Jesus!" Bird bellowed. "Will this shit never stop?"

With an anguished look on his face, Gordo said, "Sorry,

Teddy, but when he gets like this, he needs quiet, so…" Getting up to attend to his roommate, he gestured me toward the door.

I can take a hint.

When I arrived home, dinner was already on the table. Fortunately, everyone was too busy eating to ask me where I'd been.

I felt relieved until I caught Joe's eye. He looked furious.

Chapter Thirteen

Still on leave from the zoo, I spent early Monday morning on PlatoSchmato, checking out the rest of *Tippy-Toe & Tinker's* cast and crew. I got a lot done, because the house was quiet, the kids being in school, and Lauren and Dylan playing *Monopoly* in the granny cottage with Colleen. As for Joe, he was dealing with an overturned truck hauling a load of live chickens. The truck driver escaped with only minor injuries, but there were chickens in the road, chickens on top of the truck, chickens in the nearby field, and chickens in the scrub oaks.

The image of Joe rounding up the wreck's feathery survivors made me smile. Yes, Joe had been angry last night after receiving a warning from Deputy Emilio Gutierrez about my "behavior," but an especially vigorous hour in bed had soothed my husband's own ruffled feathers.

I had a luncheon appointment to meet Beverly Beaumont at Matteo's Magnifico Mangia, but I was still haunted by yesterday's visit to Bird's trailer. Remembering the unusual interplay between Gordo and his roommate reminded me that I'd checked Gordo's background on ZnoopZister before Colleen had enlightened me about a more rigorous search engine. Time for a recheck.

PlatoSchmato wasted no time in delivering what ZnoopZister had not. Unlike Bird, Gordo had never engaged the attention of the police or law courts. Although his two marriages had been flops—one of the divorces being thanks to the adulterous intervention of Cliff Flaherty—Gordo had a perfectly lawful life. He didn't sue anyone for anything, neither did anyone sue him. Not that it would have mattered, since he'd never owned anything worth suing for. As actors went, he'd been neither a star nor a failure, appearing as a character actor in several low-budget films. His most talked-about role was in *Zombie Lust*, where he'd played the role of a man struggling to keep his family alive during a zombie attack. His acting had been good enough that he'd been nominated for a Best-Supporting-Role Oscar, but eventually lost to Cuba Gooding, Jr. From there, Gordo's roles became smaller and smaller, until he'd been reduced to walk-ons in car-chase movies. His voice was good enough, though, that he'd done voice-overs for several commercials, which eventually spurred him into taking classes at Mondrian Ruzicka's School of Puppetry and Marionettes. Rather than speaking for a tiger on a cereal box, he now spoke for a dinosaur.

But that wasn't all. At the age of twenty-two, Gordo had graduated from Santa Monica's Center for Spiritual and Physical Awareness, where, besides learning how to deal with an actor's hard-knock life, he had obtained the skills necessary to become a "life coach" for the physically and/or mentally disabled. Upon leaving the center, he was also awarded the title "Reverend," which allowed him to perform marriages in the state of California.

Then I realized something else. Since Bird owned the Surfer's Cove trailer and the sliver of land it sat on, that made him Gordo's landlord, whether by formal agreement or not. Did Gordo's semi medical assistance earn him a break on the rent, or was it simply a case of a friend helping a friend? And in the long run, did it really matter?

Deciding I was getting nowhere, I turned my attention to Beverly Beaumont, who played the role of zookeeper Tinker, where PlatoSchmato informed me that Bev's curriculum vitae was all too common. For Hollywood, anyway.

When she'd ridden a Greyhound to California from Milltown, Indiana, thirty years earlier, her name had been Gertrude Scholmaster, and Gertrude's path to Hollywood not-quite-fame and little fortune was an old, old story. Meeting her at the bus stop had been one Cecil Van Allen, her first "agent." Their business agreement ended a year later with Cecil sentenced to thirteen months in jail for pandering, and the parentless Gertrude's stay in an overcrowded facility for delinquent teens. Upon her release at eighteen, young Gertrude legally changed her name to Beverly Beaumont and started making the rounds of various casting couches.

As it turned out, the newly dubbed "Beverly Beaumont" could actually act, and she eventually made her way to a supporting role on *Love Bleeds*, a hospital-based soap opera where she played a nurse. From there, she rabbit-hopped over to *This Shining Day*, another soap, this one set in a small coastal town where she played a Girl Scout leader. That role lasted for two years before an unsigned letter to one of the show's sponsors outed her as a former Hollywood Boulevard hooker.

Her time on *This Shining Day* was over.

A series of small walk-ons followed, a few voice-overs, and several stints teaching acting classes at various acting schools. This appeared to be the best she could hope for until one day, Cliff Flaherty ran into her on the set of *Motorcycle Hussies*, and recognized her as the Girl Scout leader on *This Shining Day*. Remembering that she looked good in khaki, he asked her to audition for the part of a zookeeper in a new kiddie program he and his business partner were putting together. She nailed the audition.

Not that playing a zookeeper on *Tippy-Toe & Tinker* had

brought her fame or fortune or even family. PlatoSchmato found no instances of marriages, children, or property. Along with the rest of the cast, she appeared to be just getting by.

After taking my own cleansing breath, I sat back from the computer and thought for a while about life. Some of us were born under a lucky star; others weren't. Those unlucky folks sometimes had to resort to odd behaviors in order to survive, so who was I to judge?

I was born into money, although thanks to my criminal father, it hadn't lasted long. Then my mother had stepped up to the plate and married rich man after rich man, so in the end, our poverty had been little more than a temporary bump in the road. The point was, I had never been sixteen, parentless, and desperate. The worst thing that ever happened to me paled in the light of what had probably happened to Gertrude Scholmaster/ Beverly Beaumont. If anything, the woman deserved a merit badge for her survival skills.

Feeling magnanimous, I picked up my cell and called Ariel Gonzales at KGNN-TV. She professed herself surprised at hearing from me.

"I would have thought you'd still be home recuperating, Teddy."

"From what? Embarrassment? Besides, you know me, places to go, people to see."

I could almost hear her smile. "Next you'll tell me I'm one of the people you need to see."

"Not you, necessarily, just your greenroom."

I could almost see her eyebrows lift, too. "May I ask why?"

An ex-Marine, Ariel had always been tough to lie to, but I did my best. "As I'm sure you've figured out, there's a good chance— probably a definite—that I won't be doing the *Anteaters to Zebras* show tomorrow, but there's something I might have left in the greenroom the last time I was there. And I need it. So I thought I might swing by today and check."

"Really? Well, we here at KGNN pride ourselves on our hygiene, and our greenroom is cleaned daily. Anytime one of our guests forgets something in there, our janitorial service finds it and delivers it to Lost & Found. What did you lose?"

"Mmm, something. I just thought I could take a look. Who knows? If I find what I think I might find, there might even be a story in it for you. An exclusive, say."

She *mmm*'ed back. "Seeing as how KGNN has enjoyed a long and fruitful relationship with the Gunn Zoo, I don't see what harm there could be by allowing you access, as long as you are properly chaperoned."

"And you would act as the chaperone?"

"Of course."

We made an appointment for me to search the greenroom right after her 10:00 a.m. wrap-up of the morning's news. She'd give me ten minutes, but after that, a group of gymnasts from San Sebastian Middle School would be arriving for their on-air demonstration, and I would have to leave.

"Whether you've found said 'lost' item or not."

She rang off.

I looked at my watch. Only 8:30. Pouring myself another cup of coffee—by now it was super strong, just the way I liked it—I moseyed back to Colleen's desktop to kill some time. I went straight to PlatoSchmato and looked up the next person I was interested in.

Ethan Ganey, director of *Tippy-Toe & Tinker*, had started his Hollywood career making rock videos, but his first full-length feature, *Zombie Lust*, which besides earning an Oscar nom for Gordo Walken, had received Special Mention laurels at the Cannes Film Festival. Ganey's next few films won no awards but performed well at the box office. Then came a few de rigueur Hollywood sex scandals, nothing career-ending, and eventually, a switch to directing television rom-coms. Even worse, commercials.

Most of what followed was the standard Hollywood stuff—no, he hadn't been a Hollywood Boulevard hooker, nor lost a leg to a shark—just a mediocre director who'd once gotten lucky. But several scroll-downs later, I came across a piece written by a blogger who called himself TruthAtAllCosts. Mr. Truth had plenty of snarky things to say about Ganey's various works, among which was this:

"Given Ganey's continued BAD BEHAVIOR, his current job— directing a Central California town kiddie show titled Tipped Toe and Tiffany—*PROVES that there is such a thing as KARMA, and she is INDEED a BITCH!!!"*

Despite Mr. Truth's lack of accuracy, the capitalized snark attack kept me reading. My patience was rewarded with a mega-stack of legal filings that alleged one Ethan Linzio Ganey had illegally transferred funds from a group of film investors' accounts to a numbered offshore account, which had not yet been pinned down. The only way the complainants knew the money existed was because the forensic accountant they'd hired had managed to break into Ganey's Hotmail account and found several references to it. Despite the judge's ruling that the lawsuit could not proceed due to lack of evidence, Ganey was finished in Hollywood.

This led me to read down the list of plaintiffs—there were twenty-six, in all—until I found a familiar name: Cliff Flaherty. As Mr. Truth might say, !!!HOLY SHIT!!!

Traffic being light, and a classic California sun shining bright as all get-out, it took only ten minutes to drive to the KGNN studios. The guards had been alerted to my oncoming visit, so less than another three minutes later I was in the KGNN greenroom. It was overdue for redecorating, and smelled like decades-old cigarette smoke overlaid by Aspen Spring air freshener. The formerly white walls had yellowed to the color of smog, and the black one-piece faux-leather sofa and matching chairs were scratched and ripped. Over the sofa hung a sepia-toned photograph of Walter Cronkite, and next to him, a color photo of the *Tippy-Toe & Tinker's* marionettes.

"Think you'll be back on the air next week?" Ariel asked. Fresh from giving her on-camera news update, she still wore her heavy, on-camera makeup, but the shrapnel scar across on her cheek glimmered through. She was proud of it, and she should be. Her heroism as a helicopter pilot in Afghanistan, rescuing Marines under fire, had won her several medals, including a Silver Star.

I never messed with her.

"Next week? Well, only Aster Edwina knows for sure. She's the one who makes up my schedule, and you know how she is." With Ariel watching me closely, I looked behind and under the sofa, then between the cushions.

"You do know she's now part-owner of the station, don't you?" she asked as I searched.

"Yep." The old bat's holdings just kept growing and growing.

"How is Ms. Gunn, anyway? I've been thinking about her."

For some reason Ariel had always liked Aster Edwina. I guess it takes a hard case to understand another hard case, but as for me, I was just another cream puff who quaked every time the old woman approached.

"She'll outlive us all," I said.

Her face assumed a thoughtful expression. "Look, I know tomorrow's out, but would you *like* to do your program next Tuesday?"

That gave me pause, since it wasn't like Ariel to repeat herself. "As I said, what I want doesn't count."

"Then I'll have a word with her." One corner of her coral lipsticked mouth tilted upward.

"Yes!" I pumped my fist, but not because Ariel believed she could sway my boss.

"Find what you 'lost'?"

On my second sofa go-round I found something that may, or may not, have been what I was looking for. Wedged between the sofa's arm and seat cushion, and crumped into a ball was an invoice for two special-order headlamps from Klaus AutoWerks. The cost of the headlamps, no doubt for Flaherty's Mercedes Gullwing could have paid the *Merliee's* slip fee for the next two years. While that was interesting enough, on the flip side of the invoice was a barely readable note that scratched out "HERBER 10."

HERBER? Okay, so Spellcheck wasn't available for hand-written notes. Or maybe Herber wasn't a badly misspelled *Harbor*; maybe it was someone's surname. Turning to Ariel, I asked, "You know anyone named Herber?"

She shook her head.

If not a person, and by *Herber,* Flaherty had meant *Harbor,* did the one-oh mean a date or a time? Flaherty's body was found last Saturday morning, and the current thinking was that he had died the night before, so one interpretation of the note could easily be "Harbor—10 p.m." Which would mean that Flaherty was making a date to meet his murderer.

Of course, he hadn't known that.

Then something else struck me. "Ariel, about what time does everyone from *Tippy-Toe & Tinker* arrive for their Friday recording?"

"They usually drift in anywhere from 9:00 to 9:30. Why?"

"Was Cliff Flaherty always here for it?"

"Him and Donaldson both. Total control freaks, but it was their money, so…" She shrugged.

Which meant that the "10" could have meant a.m., not nec-essarily p.m.

I stuffed the note in my cargo pants pocket before Ariel could take it away from me.

She didn't miss the motion. "Shouldn't that be handed over to the authorities?"

I gave her what I hoped was a blinding smile. "Sure should. And that's what I'll do as soon as I get home."

"Ah, you're going to give it to Sheriff Joe."

I nodded, but noticing the twinkle in her eye, I don't think she bought it.

Just before noon, I put on gray linen slacks and a matching white-and-gray linen blouse, and shoes instead of boots and headed off to Matteo's Magnifico Mangia for my interview with Beverly Beaumont. But when I arrived at the restaurant, Sal Matteo told me Bev had called and asked him to relay the message that something had come up, and she couldn't make it.

Sal, a handsome, sixtyish Sicilian I'd known forever, added in a soft voice, "The lady sounded like she'd been crying."

I thought back over the few things I'd already learned about Bev Beaumont that morning. Women like her didn't cry a lot, so something big must have happened. Well, then, if the mountain won't come to Teddy, Teddy would go to the mountain.

Thanking PlatoSchmato again, I left the restaurant and drove to 3865 East Mountain Laurel Way, a nice apartment building on the more expensive side of San Sebastian.

When Bev Beaumont answered my knock, her eyes were red. She gave me a startled look. "I can't talk to you now."

Movement behind her.

"Don't you let that nosy bitch in here." Karla Dollar, whose eyes were also red.

"I'm just trying to help."

"Oh, I've seen your kind of help, hunting people down, accusing them of murder. You're worse than the cops." Karla again, daubing her dark eyes with a tissue.

Bev shook her head at Karla. "That's unfair, and you know it. Don't take our problems out on Teddy. She's good people."

Then, turning back to me, she said, "You might as well come on in. Just don't mind the mess."

Although Karla looked like she wanted to kill me, I went ahead and stepped into the small apartment, which turned out to be downright adorable. Smelling of furniture wax and flowers, the small living area was decorated like a fairyland cottage, with the walls painted a pale pink, and the darker-pink sofa and matching chair covered with bright, fairy-tale-themed toss pillows. A large oil painting—not a print—of a unicorn playing with a dragon, hung above the sofa. On the oak end table, next to a pottery vase filled with asters, stood a gilt-framed photograph of a handsome young man whom I took to be Jamal, Karla's son. The only objects out of place in the room were the balled-up tissues littering the otherwise spotless white tile floor.

Beverly gestured toward the small chair. "Plop yourself down and prepare to hear a tale about doom, gloom, and damnation."

Karla responded with a dark chuckle that ended with a sob.

"What's going on?" I sat as directed while the other two took to the sofa.

After a quick daub at her eyes, Beverly said, in a clipped voice, "At 8:00 this morning the entire cast and crew of *Tippy-Toe & Tinker* was called to a meeting at Donaldson & Flaherty Productions, whereupon we were given our pink slips."

"Huh?" That made no sense.

"You deaf or something?" Karla snapped around her sobs. "We got our asses fired! Everybody did, except that asshole writer and the Jocelyn dingbat!"

I shook my head. "There must be some kind of mistake. Your show's the most popular kids' show around."

Beverly, who had probably seen a lot of good things turn bad, nodded wearily. "No mistake. The show's being nationally syndicated."

"But that's good news. The larger audience…"

"The new suits think that with the exception of that Jocelyn bitch, the rest of us are too old to go national."

Confused, I said, "But that's age discrimination."

"Oh, it's legal, all right," Karla snorted. "Bastards made sure it was. Bought us out of our contracts, and we couldn't do a thing about it. Said they were taking the show in a 'different' direction. See? Legal as sin."

"Yet they're keeping the ding…" I caught myself. "Uh, Jocelyn. The young lady who plays Poonya?"

"Little bitch can't be more than twenty."

"And the new writer? They're keeping him?"

"He's twenty-five, tops," Beverly interjected grimly. "Perfect for their 'different direction.' Hell, the new scripts will probably be rap."

Rap hadn't hurt *Hamilton*, but the thought of rapping dinosaurs didn't sound pleasant to me, either, so I let it slide. "What about Martin Donaldson? He's at least fifty."

Karla snorted. "Marty? Nobody cares how old producers are, just their money and their ability to attract more. That jerk's already got a new cereal company lined up, and some organic juice company, maybe a couple more new sponsors. The syndication guys held out for the on-screen talent going younger, so that's what's happening."

A small part of me could understand the finances; the larger and fairer part felt outraged. "The *Tippy-Toe* fans won't buy it. They love you guys!"

Beverly shrugged. "Do the numbers, Teddy. So the show loses loyal viewers in San Sebastian County, the suits don't care. What are a few thousand local viewers compared to tens of millions? Middle-aged actors like me and Karla are just about extinct, like the real dinosaurs. It's happening all over the place, and not just among actors, either. Ever try to get a new job doing anything when you're in your late fifties?"

I thought back to my interview yesterday with Marty

Donaldson. He hadn't said a word about any of this, all the while knowing the show's entire cast—with one exception—was about to be fired. My outrage had neared the boiling point when there was a knock at the door.

The two women looked at each other. "Bet you that's Gordo," Beverly said, jumping to her feet and going to the door.

It was. Gordo Walken, the mild, but soon-to-be-written-out Tippy-Toe, entered the fairyland apartment looking as outraged as I felt. He was carrying a bouquet of roses. As far as I was concerned, a funeral wreath would have been more appropriate.

"Flowers for the fairest," he gulped, handing the bouquet to Karla, who started sobbing again.

"Oh, girl!" he cried. Laying the bouquet on the end table, he sat down next to her, hugging her against his broad chest. "We'll get through this; we will."

Feeling odd man out, I left them to grieve their sudden unemployment together.

From Karla and Bev's apartment, I drove straight to Whispering Willows, but Marty Donaldson either wasn't in or wasn't answering the door. Adrenaline still high, I turned around and headed home.

Matters at the granny cottage were escalating, too, with Dylan blaming himself for everything. Lauren was also playing the blame game, but with herself as blamee. She'd thought she'd done everything right as a parent, yet here was her precious son accused of murder. His constant assurances didn't seem to help. Colleen anxiously eyed them both from the corner desk, where she was pecking away at her laptop, probably killing another victim in her new book.

"Everything would have been fine if I hadn't been so foolish as to allow Cliff into our lives," Lauren moaned, her platinum hair mussed by her son's hugs.

"Stop talking like that, Mom," he said, for what had to be the tenth time. "How were you to know? He seemed all right at first—for a long time, really—and you couldn't see into the future. Besides, you were lonely."

I knew all about lonely women making bad decisions. On the rebound from Joe, I'd married Michael, and all it got me was a divorce. Yet I couldn't help but wonder how a woman as beautiful as Lauren could wind up in the situation she had. Granted, beautiful women abounded in Hollywood, but Lauren possessed more than looks: she had brains, class, and, more importantly, true grit. She could have had any man she wanted, yet she'd settled for Flaherty, a man who turned out to be a brute. Hadn't she seen warning signs before the night he almost killed her? Maybe she had, but mistakenly ascribed them to...what? Overwork? A temporary and meaningless blip in an otherwise healthy relationship? I wanted to understand what had caused such blindness.

"Lauren?"

That incredible face turned from her son to me. "Yes?"

"Can we talk? In private?"

Colleen looked up from her laptop, her expression suspicious. The woman knew me well.

"Sure," Lauren, who didn't, said.

"Hey!" Dylan's voice was as suspicious as Colleen's face. "There's nothing you need to say to my mom you can't say in front of me."

"Guys don't need to be present for Girl Talk," I said to him.

He flushed, and muttered, "Well, then, uh, I'm sorry. I didn't mean to intrude. Really, um, it's just... It's just... Say, think I'll put the breakfast dishes away." He jumped up from the sofa, hurried to the kitchenette, and began hauling dishes out of the dishwasher.

God, I loved that kid.

To Lauren, I said, "How about a walk in the garden? Maybe while we're talking, we can pick some herbs and vegetables for dinner tonight. I hear it's going to be chicken."

Colleen nodded. "Rosemary would be good. And some thyme."

I waited until we were well away from the granny cottage before asking the question that had hounded me since I'd first met her. "Why Cliff, Lauren?"

The answer, which didn't come until we'd reached the garden, was, "You know, over the past few days—ever since I heard about...about all this—I've been going over the past, what I should have seen, what I could have done. But I couldn't see the signs, because there *were* no signs! When I met Cliff, I thought he was the kindest, most loving man I'd ever met. And he was, I swear. That's why he had such early success writing rom-com scripts, all sweet and funny, with happy endings, and not a false or saccharine note in them. So I just couldn't see it. Not once." She swallowed. "We'd been dating for almost a year, he and Dylan had grown close, and I was beginning to think... Well, never mind. I've got Jon now so my lonely days are gone. But back to Cliff. He was fine, *more* than fine, really a great guy, until that awful night when he came over to my apartment, looking like..."

She halted. Stared at the rows of herbs before her. Reached down and plucked a stalk of thyme. "Like he'd totally lost his mind," she finished.

"Nothing before that? A push? A slap?"

"Nothing. If there had been, I would never have let him anywhere near Dylan. Or me. I'd gone through too much and worked too hard to let some violent asshole screw up our lives. And yet that's exactly what happened."

"Did he attempt to contact you afterward?"

For a moment that beautiful face looked sorrowful. "He apologized in phone calls and letters that would break the average woman's heart, but I wasn't buying any of it. In fact, I filed formal charges—I wanted everyone in Hollywood to know what he'd done—and took out an order of protection, and that was that, no more Cliff." She reached up and touched the scar on her face. "And no more scars."

"The article I read about that night said you hit him back."

The sorrow on her face vanished, replaced by an expression of fierce satisfaction. "Damn right, I did. And I'm not sorry. Jesus, he looked crazy enough, *weird* enough, that I really believed he was going to kill me, so when that chair broke..." She clenched her teeth for a brief moment, then added, "He's lucky I whacked him in the knee, not his head."

I thought so, too. "Do you know what set him off?"

"I'm not sure. We'd been talking about the film *Some Like It Hot* comparing Tony Curtis's performance to Jack Lemmon's. Cliff preferred Curtis to Lemmon. I felt the opposite. Then I added that, in my opinion, Marilyn Monroe's performance had been underrated, and that she'd been brilliant in the film. Suddenly, he got this strange look on his face, and called me a dumb blonde. I thought he was joking, but when I laughed, he hit me. Out of the clear blue."

"Could he have been mad about something else, just picked that moment to explode?"

"Cliff didn't work that way. When something annoyed him, he let you know right then. That's why people liked to work with him; he didn't carry grudges."

"Did you ever hear about him getting violent with anyone else?"

She shrugged. "I have no idea. Whenever his name came up, I closed my ears. Who knows? Maybe he'd learned his lesson."

I doubted it, considering my own run-in with Flaherty, and the accounts of other harbor denizens about his behavior, but I asked the next question anyway. "Was he drunk? Or maybe on drugs the night he attacked you?"

She shook her head. "Cliff never used drugs, didn't even drink. Total teetotaler. His joke was that too many Hollywood types were role models for how *not* to behave."

"And yet..."

A nod. "Exactly. And yet."

Carrying stalks of thyme and rosemary we walked back to the granny cottage, where Colleen was still typing on her laptop and Dylan was huddled up on the sofa reading her first mystery, *Murder at the Zoo.*

"Okay if I use PlatoSchmato again?" I asked Colleen.

"Be my guest." She waved me away.

Leaving the three to their various pursuits, I went back to the house and logged on to the site, where I typed in FIND for the name CLIFF FLAHERTY. My conversation with Lauren had left me feeling uneasy, as if too many questions remained unanswered. To hear her tell it, the "kindest, most loving man in the world" had turned into a monster overnight, but that's not the way batterers work. There are always signs, even if you recognize them only in retrospect.

I stayed on PlatoSchmato for almost an hour, but at first all I could find were two problematical civil situations. In the first, Flaherty had gone to the authorities when the mountain cabin he'd rented turned out to be already occupied by a family visiting from Arizona; the real estate company he'd dealt with—and turned his money over to—was fraudulent. Flaherty never got his money back. In the second, a man named Harvey Z. Rexall, had attempted to sell Flaherty a Fender guitar signed by a teenage Johnny Cash, and when Flaherty questioned its provenance, the seller sped away from the scene. But not before his intended victim took down his license number. Flaherty duly reported the aborted transaction to the authorities, and they followed up. The guitar turned out to be genuine enough, but it had been stolen from the Fender Museum five years earlier.

As far as Flaherty's own possible breaches of the law—violent or non—nada, zilch. Not until the night ten years earlier, when he exploded at Lauren, permanently scarring her perfect face. From there on, charges had been filed against him in one violent incident after another.

I shut down the PC and sat there, remembering ten washing

machines, none of them carrying more than four items. I remembered Flaherty's rage-filled face, the hard slap. I remembered him running away, wailing, leaving his precious laundry behind.

Suddenly I had a theory. I placed a call to Dr. Leonard "Lenny" Huffgraf, my onetime stepbrother from my mother's second marriage. We'd remained friends even after our parents' eventual divorce. Lenny was now chief of neurosurgery at San Sebastian County Hospital. Actually, there were three Lennys: Neurosurgeon Lenny, Safety First Lenny, and Bro Lenny.

Safety First Lenny returned my call an hour later when I was on my way to Pinball Wizardess, the game arcade where puppeteer Jocelyn Ravel seemed to be spending so much time these days. As I took the call, I pulled to the side of the road.

"You're not talking while you're driving, are you, Teddy?" Safety First Lenny asked, even before saying hello.

"Just sitting on the shoulder of the road, watching Canada geese fly by."

"Good, because as I continually warn everyone..."

When he was through telling me what he continually told everyone about brain damage from biking without a helmet or texting while driving, or falling into wolf pens, he segued into Bro Lenny. "Terrif to hear your voice, Step Sis. Whazzup?"

I told him what I needed to know, not necessarily expecting an answer because of HIPAA laws, but he surprised me. "That autopsy surprised the hell out of old Jeffers. Here Jeffers was, sawing away, expecting a simple case of murder—which it was, in the end—but what else did he encounter? Only one of the most advanced cases of frontotemporal dementia he'd ever seen in a person of that age. In my opinion—but if you tell anyone I said it I'll say you're a liar—whoever killed Flaherty did him a favor. Otherwise, someday soon, probably within months, the poor shit would have been drooling in a wheelchair for whatever little time he had left."

At my request Lenny spelled out "frontotemporal dementia," then continued, "It's a wonder the guy was still walking around out there. Hey, come to think, they fished him out of the harbor right near the *Merilee*, didn't they? How's the old rust bucket doing these days? Still afloat?"

Lenny had a new Jeanneau Sun Odyssey 64 berthed at the posh north end of the harbor. It had cost him close to a million dollars, and was named *Earned It*.

"The *Merilee*'s still afloat. Why, just last week the kids and I…"

"Oops! Just got beeped! Well, Step Sis, we gotta get together sometime, go over old memories and share terrible stories about our scandalous parents. In the meantime, remember…" Here came another segue. "No talking while driving!" Safety First Lenny demanded, "Or God forbid, posting or Facebooking! And if you take up biking, wear a helmet. And stay away from wolves and bears and anything else with big teeth!"

By the time I got through promising to hardly move, he'd already hung up. I didn't put my phone down right away. Instead, I stayed pulled over while I looked up frontotemporal dementia on my smart phone.

The Mayo Clinic's website was quick to explain everything I needed. Frontotemporal dementia was a fatal form of dementia similar to Alzheimer's, but which struck earlier in a person's life, usually in the mid forties. Symptoms included increasingly odd behavior (like filling up ten washing machines with loads of four items each), loss of empathy toward others, muscle spasms, and poor physical coordination. Violence on the part of the sufferer was not uncommon. Another symptom, which in screenwriter Flaherty's case would have been particularly tragic, was something termed semantic dementia, an increased difficulty in using and understanding written and spoken language.

Life expectancy after the first symptoms appeared was seven to thirteen years.

As I watched the last of the Canada geese fly by, I decided to skip my trip to Pinball Wizardess and track down Nestor Vanderman, instead. Finding *Tippy-Toe & Tinker*'s new co-writer turned out to be easy. I simply called Gordo, who told me something I should have already known. Like so many other underpaid and overworked people in San Sebastian County, Vanderman lived on a boat. In fact, his *Starvin' Marvin*, a 1986 Hunter 28.5, was berthed at Dock 8, only four docks down from the *Merilee*.

Traffic being light, I made a quick U-turn and drove back to the house, where I made another quick search on PlatoSchmato. Then armed with some rather eye-popping info, I headed to Gunn Landing Harbor. For his age, little Nestor Vanderman—actually, Nestor Vanderman, *Junior,* had been a busy boy.

According to PlatoSchmato, as a late teen he'd been arrested three times, convicted once, of possession with intent to sell, before his widower father's money (large real estate holdings in the San Diego area) managed to get that conviction overturned. Before that, there had been minor issues of vandalism, and several bouts of fisticuffs with bar bouncers. But with the drug conviction, he'd finally reached the end of his father's patience. Nestor Vanderman, Sr. gave his son five thousand dollars, a disused sailboat named *Blue Skies*—which his son promptly renamed *Starvin' Marvin*—and told him to sail away and not come back until he'd done something productive with his life. Two weeks later Nestor Vanderman, Sr. was dead, but not soon enough for Junior, because by then Daddy had already changed his will, disinheriting his precious baby boy.

What PlatoSchmato failed to explain was how his history of delinquency led to a writing gig on a children's TV program.

Starvin' Marvin needed a fresh coat of paint, but so did several other boats at Dock 8, the harbor's low rent district, where boats that had been all but abandoned lay tied up in various states of disrepair. Some of their owners were elderly and no longer able to sail, but loved their boats too much to sell them. Still others were working several low-paying jobs to clothe and feed themselves, and had neither time nor money for upkeep. As I approached Slip No. 186, I decided *Starvin' Marvin* had once been blue, but had been bleached by the sun to a weird off-white. On her deck, a young man sat in a cheap lawn chair, tapping away at a laptop.

"Permission to come aboard?" I shouted down to him.

He stopped typing and looked up. "You look familiar, but I can't quite place it. We have a thing one night?"

Nestor Vanderman, Jr. was handsome in the scruffy way that appealed to so many young women. Black hair, untrimmed black beard, and eyes the color of a calm sea on a cloudless day. His white tee shirt, ripped in all the right places, revealed a naturally fit torso.

Despite his tactless question, I gave him my best smile. "No, we didn't have a 'thing.' My name's Theodora Bentley, but everybody calls me Teddy. I live on the *Merilee*, Dock 4." I pointed in the direction of my boat. "Just stopped by for a chat."

"I'm not real chatty."

"Then let's call it a conversation. Did you ever have any trouble working with Cliff Flaherty?" Sometimes directness is the best policy.

He squinted those amazing eyes against the sun. "Wait a minute. I remember now. Aren't you that crazy zookeeper who can't keep her clothes on?"

"Yeah, and I'll tell you all about it if you let me come aboard."

"To converse about Cliff."

"Yep."

To my surprise, Nestor invited me aboard.

After I'd clambered onto the boat and taken a seat on the gunwale, Nestor said, "I can spot a liar several waves away, so I appreciate the truth whenever and wherever I find it. Especially when it's spoken by a natural redhead."

"Thank you so much," I said, my face burning.

He laughed. "Now, *that* was a lie. You weren't grateful in the least to hear that remark. So what do you want to know about Cliff that you haven't already found out? Was he impossible? Yes. Was he likeable? No. Did I hate him? Only sometimes."

"Only sometimes?"

"He was a sick man, so I made allowances. After all, I'm no prince myself." All traces of humor had left his handsome face. "If it hadn't been for Cliff, I'd probably be dead, too."

"Meaning?"

"I'm not going to go into that, other than to say it takes a no-good shit to recognize another no-good shit." Then he changed the subject, or at least, that's what I thought he was doing. "Good old Cliff, a man of many parts. Did you know he used to volunteer at the Seaside Mission in Long Beach?"

Overhead, three gulls wheeled and screeched as they tried to steal a fish away from a passing cormorant. The tip of a gray cloud appeared on the horizon. A promise of weather, or merely a warning?

"Flaherty volunteered at a mission?" I asked. "I'm surprised to hear that. I hadn't pegged Flaherty as the type."

"Neither would anyone else who'd ever been the object of his bile. Like you. Oh, don't widen your eyes at me. Cliff told me all about the crap that went down with you in the laundromat. Quite the little scrapper, aren't you?" He looked down at his laptop and pecked out a few words. From where I was sitting, I couldn't read them.

Looking back up, he said, "Now, I'm not going to say Cliff had a heart of gold, 'cause it was more like tarnished brass, but it was there. That's where we met, the Seaside Mission, when he was ladling mystery meat casserole onto my plate. He didn't turn up his nose at the homeless, not even those of us who smelled like dirty harbor water."

"Ladling out mystery meat casserole's a long way from giving you a job as a co-writer."

"I guess whatever search engine you used on me didn't mention the summers I spent at writers' retreats at Idyllwild, or all those classes I took in screenwriting at So Cal."

"No, it didn't," I admitted.

"*Tsk tsk*. That's search engines for you. They're only interested in the bad stuff."

"Point taken, but back to Flaherty. What happened between you two that you wound up helping him write scripts on a kiddie show?"

Nestor raised his eyebrows. "Helping? *Tsk tsk* again, Red, 'cause for the last two years, every single word that has come out of the mouths of those dinosaurs came straight from these ten fingers." He waggled them at me. They were long and slender, like a piano player's.

"You're telling me Flaherty didn't write *anything* for the show?"

"That's what I'm telling you. Sure, he turned up at all the staff meetings, took notes, did the suit-type shit, but as for the writing itself, he was long past that, all the way back to our Seaside Mission days when he was helping me out with my own little problem."

"Which was?

"None of your business, Red." A wicked grin. "Suffice it to say, Cliff and I were birds of a feather, and that got both of us into trouble multitudinous times. But whereas my bad behavior was very much voluntary—I *liked* being a jerk, still do, as a matter of fact—his behavior wasn't, and all the twelve-step programs in the world weren't going to put Cliff Flaherty back together again. But I could at least help with the writing part, albeit for a price."

"You're telling me he asked you to write scripts for him, using his name?"

"Natural red hair and smart, too! So yeah, that's exactly right. First, I had to unlearn a lot of the stuff I'd been taught in those screenwriting classes, 'cause it was all bullshit. Once I'd done that, he bitched and yelled and bullied me through what amounted to his own class in *The Arc of Action in Six-Minute Segments*. When he thought I was ready, he hand-carried one of my rom-com scripts over to one of his old pals at CBS."

"And they bought it?" I was having trouble believing this.

"Of course they didn't." Here Nestor bared his perfectly white teeth. "But his buddy did advise him to try writing for kids, that the tone in my—uh, *Cliff*'s dialogue—sounded perfect for this cute dinosaur puppet show he'd heard about up in San Sebastian. Due to family issues, its original writer was moving back to Indiana or Kansas or some other godawful place, and he thought Cliff's work would fit right in.

"Well, Cliff worried about that because he couldn't tell a stegosaurus from an iguana, but I could. After I did a little brush-up research and churned out a twenty-two-minute script, we drove it up to San Sebastian. Cliff's the one who took the original meeting, not me, and since he'd worked with Marty Donaldson before, he got the job, plus an opportunity to buy in. Despite his crappy health, he still had some money left, so that's what he did. Anyway, I've been writing the *Tippy-Toe* scripts ever since."

The story was unlikely enough to be believable. Hollywood was weird, and so were the people in it. "What's going to happen now?"

"You mean now that the show's been syndicated? Early this year Cliff took Donaldson aside and fessed up, explained he was sick and couldn't write anymore, that the programs had always been written by me. So, yeah, Donaldson and the other suits are keeping me on. Giving me a nice raise, too. Maybe I'll paint the boat, move it on down to LA Harbor. Or, even better, buy myself some new chick bait. I'm thinking that 41 Morgan Out Island Ketch that's up for sale up at the nicer end of the harbor. Sail it down to La La Land and set up shop."

"What'll you do with *Starvin' Marvin*?"

"Sell it to anyone stupid enough to buy it. You interested?"

I didn't bother giving the question the dignity of an answer. "Are you aware that the whole cast of *Tippy-Toe & Tinker* was just fired?"

"Not my problem. Besides, the new version of *Tippy-Toe* will be animated. Toons are the thing these days."

"Toons? But...but what's the point in buying syndication rights to a TV show, if you want to change everything about it?"

"Mine is not to question why. But you're wrong about one thing you said. I heard that the suits were keeping Jocelyn, too. Not as that stupid red panda character, though. Instead, she'll voice a cute little critter named Eve O. Hippus. Eve, for short."

I shook my head in confusion. "If they're canning everyone else, why keep Jocelyn?"

"Because that helium voice of hers is anime gold."

I finally got it. High voice. Almost childish. "And she's in the right age bracket."

"Brave new world, Red." Nestor's eyes gleamed with dark joy.

A loud squawk overhead drew my attention. One of the gulls had wrenched the fish away from the cormorant and was flying off with it. The cormorant didn't look happy. Neither did the fish.

Chapter Fourteen

"Why didn't you tell me you had an altercation with Cliff Flaherty the day before he was murdered?" Joe snapped at me the minute I came through the door.

He had changed into civvies, but still looked disheveled. His black hair stood out in clumps, like he'd been running his hands through it. The lines in his face had deepened to the point where he appeared to have aged several years since this morning.

I looked around for rescue, but Colleen, Dylan, and the kids must have been in the granny cottage, so I was on my own. At first, I tried to downplay the event. "Well, I knew the Cliff thing would be a problem for you, it happening so close to the time of his murder, so I didn't mention it. After all, it wasn't really a big deal, just a difference of opinion about how many articles of clothing should go into a washer."

"You assaulted him."

So much for downplaying. "With a towel. And he hit me first. If you saw the tape, you'd know that. Speaking of, how'd you find out about it?" I knew darned well that Chief Deputy Emilio Gutierrez wouldn't have told him of the tape's existence.

"Deputy Orville Thompson found it misfiled in the evidence room, and brought the tape straight to me, as well he should. I played it, and there you were, in the starring role. This kind of thing has got to stop, Teddy."

"*This kind of thing*? Like defending myself when someone assaults me? Surely you don't expect me to just stand there and take it, Joe. You didn't marry a wimp."

We were well into our first real marital fight—both of us yelling at each other and scaring the hell out of the dogs and cat—when I finally realized something. Joe was overreacting to a tape that showed me getting hit, yet he was mad at *me*. His reaction was so odd, so *wrong*, and so unlike him that something else had to be going on. This was deflected anger I was seeing.

So I stepped forward, put my arms around him, and found his body trembling. "Tell me what's really wrong, Joe," I whispered.

He looked down at me, his eyes red and raw. After a couple of false starts, he managed, "Laur…Laur…Lauren's admitted to killing Cliff Flaherty."

When I led him to the sofa and sat down beside him, it all came pouring out.

He'd been sitting at his desk, running statistics on extreme DUI as related to head-on collisions when Emilio entered his office to tell him Lauren had come in and demanded to see the officer in charge of the Cliff Flaherty investigation.

"That would be me," Emilio had answered.

During the following interview, she had told him the following story.

Three days before the murder, Lauren had found the note Dylan had left for her, describing what he'd discovered on his DNA test, and that he was driving to San Sebastian to meet his paternal grandmother, with whom he'd been exchanging emails. She stewed about the situation for a while, and after hearing nothing more from Dylan—he wasn't answering his cell—jumped in her car and drove all the way from Burbank to San Sebastian. Upon her arrival, she had the bad fortune to pull in for gas at the Circle K at the same time Dylan was being manhandled by a man she recognized as Cliff Flaherty, her violent ex-boyfriend. She was about to get out of the car to lend Dylan assistance when Cliff fell to the pavement.

Witnessing the altercation made her think. Through the Hollywood grapevine, Lauren had heard that Flaherty had left LA and was working somewhere near Monterey. She'd given him no more thought at the time, but now she'd seen him abusing her precious son.

Worrying that Cliff might continue being a danger to her precious baby boy, she waited until Cliff staggered back to his car, then followed him to the harbor, where she watched him weave his way along Dock 4 to *Scribbler*. It being midweek, most of the boat owners were away at their jobs, rendering the dock nearly deserted. But being cautious, Lauren waited until dark, then took the tire iron from the trunk of her car, and made her way to *Scribbler*.

When Flaherty answered her knock—he'd always suffered from insomnia, she'd explained to Emilio and the detectives—she hit him over the head with the tire iron, then dumped his body into the greasy harbor water.

Deed done, she drove straight through the night, all the way back to Burbank.

"Oh, c'mon, Joe, does that sound credible to you?" I asked. If a murder hadn't been involved, such a tall tale would have been amusing.

During Joe's recounting of Lauren's story, he had calmed considerably, as if for the first time realizing how ridiculous Lauren's story sounded. He even managed a half smile when answering, "Emilio and the detectives are following up on her movements. They're checking the appropriate surveillance cameras again to see if she appears on any of them during the right time frame, and…"

"And have them look at the odometer on her Lexus. Then check with her Lexus service reps in Burbank to see what the mileage was last time it was in, and find out if it was up at least another twelve hundred miles since then. It should still be under warranty, and you know how fussy car companies are about regular checkups to keep it that way. They're worse than dentists."

He gave me a puzzled look. "Twelve hundred?"

"Eight hundred miles for the first round trip, then another four hundred for her trip back up here. You'd also have to factor in the average amount she drives per week, and…"

"Teddy, sometimes you scare me."

Sometimes I scared myself. But I didn't want him to know that, so I asked, "With that 'confession' being a steaming pile of you-know-what, where's Lauren now? Back in her room at the San Sebastian Hyatt?"

"Still being questioned at the station." The half smile was gone. "Someone walks in and confesses to murder, cops have to take them seriously, no matter how crazy they sound. It's my guess she'll be there overnight."

Which meant so would Emilio and the detectives, even though they all had wives and children waiting for them at home. Families disappointed, time wasted—those were the main reasons authorities took filing a false report so seriously.

"Has Dylan heard about this?"

He shook his head. "I haven't told him yet."

"Colleen?"

"I called her as soon as I found out."

"Maybe she's told him already."

"I ordered her not to."

Joe should have known by now that ordering Colleen not to do something was an exercise in pointlessness, but he clung to his idea of old-fashioned mothers baking apple pies and agreeing with everything they were told. While Colleen is a terrific baker, she'd never been great at following orders.

Arms around each other, we trooped over to the granny cottage to see how Dylan was holding up upon hearing that his mother had confessed to murder. But, miracle of miracles, it turned out that Colleen hadn't said a word. Leaving Joe in the flowery living room to deliver the bad news to Dylan, she pulled me into the bedroom where she'd stashed the little kids, and explained she had remained silent because she'd been afraid he would charge over to the sheriff's office to tender his own murder confession.

"He's a strong boy, Teddy. I wouldn't have been able to hold him back."

From the noises in the other room, it was clear Joe wasn't finding it easy, either. Grunts, thumps, bumps, a high-pitched clatter of something that sounded like china.

"Hope that wasn't one of my Wedgewood bowls," Colleen mourned.

"Maybe we'd better go back in there."

My mother-in-law could only sigh.

Forcing the children to stay behind—Tonio was desperate to see the tussle—we closed the door behind us as we left the bedroom. Yes, that crash had been the prized Wedgewood bowl Colleen had been using as a serving dish for butterscotch candy. In the struggle to keep Dylan from charging out the door, Joe had knocked over the coffee table, sending the bowl onto the floor. The carpeting hadn't been thick enough to save the dish, and now blue pieces of china and golden, cellophane-wrapped candy were scattered all over the place. As a color scheme, it didn't quite work.

Joe had forced Dylan into a sitting position on the sofa, and stood over him, his hands pinning the boy's wrists against the sofa's back. He was talking to his son in the same soothing way I talked to my charges at the zoo.

"Going down there will only make the situation worse," Joe said. "Deputy Gutierrez is no idiot. He knows what your mother's trying to do, and I can promise you she won't be charged."

"Unlike me, you mean?" Dylan hissed up at him. His face was red with anger, but there were tears in his eyes.

Seeing her chance, Colleen sat down on the sofa next to Dylan, slipping an arm around his waist. "You can't think only of yourself now, Dylan. Think of your mother."

"But I am!" he howled.

"No you're not," she said. "If you went down there, you'd immediately be arrested for breaking bond. Remember the conditions? That you stay on your father's property? How do you think your mother would feel then, seeing her boy in a jail cell? Staying here, obeying the law, *that's* the way to help her."

He flicked his eyes toward her. "You believe that?"

"Not believe. *Know.*"

After a few moments, Dylan slumped, the fire fading from his face. Joe released his wrists and stepped back. "You okay now, kid?"

"No, I'm not okay, and that's a really dumb question." But he tried for a smile.

Crisis averted.

We spent what was left of the evening chowing down on pizza from Matteo's Magnifico Mangia and discussing what we'd do when Lauren was released from police custody. Tonio wanted a blow-by-blow description of the tussle between Joe and Dylan, which Dylan happily gave him, hyping up the action to a full-on brawl.

"How come nobody's bleeding?" Bridey asked.

"Because we cleaned it all up; didn't want to scare you." Dylan said, winking.

"There was no blood," Joe corrected. "Just a calm exchange of opposing ideas."

"Awwww!" Tonio, sounding crushed.

Eager to do something that would make our waiting time easier, Colleen suggested we bake a batch of her cranberry-apricot scones for dessert. We eagerly agreed, and spent the next hour or two chopping, sifting, and blending. Even little Bridey helped by shaping the dough into rough triangles. Fifteen minutes later, we were sitting at the table, butter and honey dripping from our fingers.

While we were eating, our faith in the San Sebastian Sheriff's Office was rewarded as Lauren walked through the cottage door. "It's over!" she announced, after Dylan finally let her go. "Charges will be dropped against Dylan sometime tomorrow."

Joe was aghast. "Gutierrez actually *believed* you? That you killed Flaherty?"

She turned to him, her beautiful face glowing. "Turns out Deputy Gutierrez didn't believe a word I said. There's a good chance I'll be charged with filing a false police report, but I don't give a damn about that. I'll pay the fine and sign whatever they want. The only thing that matters is that tomorrow Dylan will get that stupid bracelet cut off his ankle and will finally be able to come and go as he pleases." She shot him a look. "Which means going straight back to Burbank. Now, can I have one of those scones? I'm starved."

Joe reached out and snagged her arm before she reached the table.

"Wait a minute. What makes you think charges are going to be dropped against Dylan?"

She stopped and looked up at him in a way that made me distinctly uncomfortable. "Because of that other dead guy."

"*What other dead guy?!*"

"You haven't been watching the news?"

"No, we've not been watching the news," Joe said in irritation. "We've been too worried about you and your crackpot confession."

I cast a glance toward the master bedroom, where Joe had left his pager after changing out of his uniform. What had we missed?

"Lauren!" he snapped. "*What* other dead guy?"

With an almost joyful look on her beautiful face, Lauren replied, "Martin Donaldson, Cliff's coproducer. Somebody just bashed his head in."

Chapter Fifteen

The next morning, KGNN-TV News reported that Martin Donaldson had still been alive when the garage attendant found him at 8:15 p.m., bleeding out next to his new white 740i BMW. The two-level garage was located in a small business complex at the far eastern end of San Sebastian, where the production offices of Donaldson & Flaherty were housed.

The garage attendant told the on-site reporter that Donaldson's last words were, "Why? I... I don't..."

Sad.

Not so sad for us was the fact that the electronic tracker on Dylan's ankle proved that at 8:15, he was twelve miles away from the parking garage, helping his grandmother bake. While doing so, the San Sebastian County Sheriff, a zookeeper, two minors, two dogs, and a cat looked on. Even better was the fact that at 8:15 on the same evening, Dylan's mother was lying her head off to Chief Deputy Emilio Gutierrez and two disgruntled detectives in Interview Room #2 at the San Sebastian Sheriff's Office.

Breathlessly, the reporter rushed on: "Our source tells us that the murder weapon left beside him was a tire iron, quite possibly the same weapon used on Cliff Flaherty last week. Speculation is high that both crimes were committed by the same person!"

"Well, no shit, Sherlock," Dylan muttered, slathering butter onto another scone.

"Language!" Lauren hissed.

"Sorry," he mumbled.

Dylan's defense attorney, my stepfather Albert Grissom, had already petitioned the court for an emergency hearing on his behalf, and Joe, before leaving for his office, speculated that Dylan's much-hated ankle bracelet would be off by the end of the day. In the meantime, emotions in the house ricocheted back and forth from elation to guilt over that very elation. A man was dead. An inoffensive man who, with his coproducer Cliff Flaherty, had created *Tippy-Toe & Tinker*, thus bringing joy to children everywhere.

Well, maybe not everywhere, but certainly in and around San Sebastian.

Later, while we were clearing away the breakfast dishes I asked Lauren, who had spent the night on our convertible sofa, why she had believed her "confession" would be taken seriously.

"Well, I'll admit I didn't think it through, but so what? After speaking with Dylan's attorney, I realized my kid was in serious trouble. That fight at the Circle K, where he'd knocked Cliff down? On video? I had to come up with some story that would take the heat off him and transfer it to me, so I said I'd been gassing up my car and saw the altercation. And then, out of anger at what Cliff had done to Dylan, after…" Here, she touched the scar on her cheek, "After what he'd done to me, I just snapped. So I said I followed him down to the harbor and killed him with my tire iron."

That woman had never picked up a tire iron in her life. "I'm sure the detectives noticed that your car was nowhere on the store's surveillance camera."

"I told them there was probably a kink in the system."

"And your supposed drive of eight hundred miles in one day? Four hundred up here from Burbank to kill him and another four hundred back? What kind of lunatic would do something like that?"

She gave me a smug look. "The mother kind of lunatic."

In a way, Lauren scared me. There was nothing she wouldn't do for Dylan, absolutely nothing, and that kind of single-minded commitment could be dangerous. To ease back the conversation, I asked, "Are you planning to see your own family while you're here? Bury the hatchet, as it were?"

"No." She rubbed the platter she was holding so fiercely that I thought it might break.

"Eighteen years is a long time. I'm sure your family, especially your mother, would love to see you again. And meet Dylan."

"She tried to take my baby away from me." Her beautiful lips compressed to a thin line.

"I'm sure they were all doing what they thought was best for both you and Dylan."

She put the platter down. "Did you know that my mother came into my hospital room and literally tore Dylan from my arms and started toward the door? As sore as I was, as weak as I was, I threw myself out of bed and ran after her. I grabbed him back and began screaming so loudly the nurses came, then Security. After that, she was banned from the hospital premises."

Her face had turned red with rage and love: Mama Bear protecting Baby Bear.

After taking a few deep breaths, she added, "Then my aunt came and collected us, and that was that. No more kidnapping attempts from dear old mom."

While I thought her mother's behavior was reprehensible, I was also confused by it. "What do you think she was going to do with him? Surely she wouldn't hurt her own grandchild!"

"She was going to take him to the adoption agency, like she'd promised. *Against* my wishes!"

"You'd just turned eighteen. They wouldn't have accepted him without your signature."

"Maybe not. But healthy, white, blue-eyed babies were at a premium. She could probably have gotten a small fortune for him in the underground adoption sector, and I wasn't about to take the chance. Dylan was *my* baby, not some toy to do with as she pleased!"

"Where was your father when all this was going on?"

"Letting her do whatever she wanted, just like always."

Families. It's a wonder so many of us emerge from them alive. But like children, some families grow up. Mine did. Well, more or less. "Maybe your mother has changed, Lauren."

"Maybe Hell's frozen over, too."

Conversation ended, she exited the kitchen, leaving me to finish the dishes. Not that I minded, because it gave me time to think. What was Lauren's family really like? Granted, they had behaved badly during the pregnancy crisis, and from the little information I'd been able to wrest from her, they hadn't even attempted to contact Lauren or their grandchild during the last eighteen years.

What kind of family was that?

What kind of *mother* was that?

I thought about my own family, my many-times-married mother, my felonious father on the run from the FBI after embezzling several million dollars. How would they have handled the same situation?

Try as I might, I just couldn't imagine either of them attempting to steal a baby away from its mother. If I'd been unfortunate enough—or *fortunate* enough—to have gotten pregnant during that brief time Joe and I had together when we were teens—I knew my parents would have supported me all the way. There would have been no forced march to a faraway aunt, no attempts at baby-stealing.

Adoption wouldn't even have been on the table.

Then I remembered my mother's intervention into Joe's and my relationship. From her point of view, and it hadn't changed much, he was nothing more than a Hispanic migrant-worker's grandson, whereas I was a *Bentley*, the descendant of one of San Sebastian's founding families. Before I could protest, Caro had shipped me off to a girl's school in Virginia, and there I stayed until Joe, on the rebound, married another girl.

If Caro had deemed that dating Joe was unacceptable, what would she have done if I'd gotten pregnant by him?

Out of curiosity, I called and asked her.

She was home, but on her way out. "Make it fast, Teddy. I promised to help set up at the Women's Club luncheon and I'm already late."

"Fast it is, then. What would you have done if, when I was in high school, Joe had gotten me pregnant?"

She snorted. "I'd have killed him, of course. That's if your father hadn't already killed him by the time I got there. Now is that all? I'm really in a rush."

"But what about the baby?"

Her tone changed. "Teddy, are you trying to tell me something, that…?"

"No, no. I never got pregnant. I'm just saying, *what if*?"

"What if what?"

"What if I'd gotten pregnant with a mixed-race baby? What would you have done about that?"

In an irritated voice, she said, "Well, we'd have had to add another room to the house, of course, probably where Albert's study is now. No, make that two rooms, one for you, and one for the baby. They're loud, you know. You were a holy shrieking terror for eight months before you settled down, so we'd have wanted you two located as far away from our bedroom as possible so we could get some sleep. And we probably would have decorated the nursery in bright colors, which pediatricians believe provides more stimuli for the baby than those wimpy pastels everyone else was using. As for furniture, definitely Italian decor. That store in the mall, Bambino, has the most cunning…"

"That's okay, Mom. You've answered my question."

Feeling relieved, I hung up. Mother would have driven me crazy with her nursery-decorating schemes, but she'd have let me keep the baby.

After killing poor Joe.

I'd been making a list of all the people Cliff Flaherty had had run-ins with when I received a surprising phone call from my boss.

"It's Tuesday," Aster Edwina said, seemingly apropos of nothing.

"Yes, I've noticed," I answered, adding the old bat's name to the list of suspects. Flaherty must have insulted her at some point.

"Tuesday's the day of your TV program, so why haven't you picked up the animals?"

"You're kidding, right? You told me to stay away from the zoo, so that's what I'm doing. Staying away from the zoo."

"I never said don't do *Anteaters to Zebras*, so put your uniform on and get down here. They're waiting for you in Animal Care."

Ah ha. She'd finally remembered how much free publicity the program gave the zoo. Well, fine. If she wanted me to do it, I would. The zoo—and the animals who called it home—was more important than my hurt feelings.

I put my suspect list away.

For the trip to the TV station, I was accompanied by Lex Yarnell, the armed Gunn Zoo park ranger. Following direct orders from Aster Edwina, the star of today's show was a member of an endangered species, and apparently our boss wanted to take no chances. The other two animals were Basuri, a tiny muntjac, otherwise known as a "barking" deer, and Billie Jean, a leash-trained warthog. While Billie Jean had issues, she never failed to entertain.

"I can't believe Aster Edwina told us to bring Farzeen instead of Poonya," I said, as we wrestled the cages from the van into the station.

"Every now and then the old bat thinks of something other than her own interests," Lex replied. "Thanks to the puppet show, Poonya's been getting plenty of publicity, but these little guys…" He motioned to the back of the van, where Farzeen lay quietly in her carrier, "well, the news out of Asia isn't good, and Aster Edwina wants everyone to know it."

Ariel Gonzales was just finishing her newscast when we entered the greenroom. Via the monitor, we learned that the morning's coastal fog would clear by noon, and that the San Sebastian Women's Club had raised more than ten thousand dollars to donate to San Sebastian's No Kill Animal Shelter.

Just as Ariel's assistant was about to usher me and my charges onto the set, Ariel held her hand to her earpiece and said in a serious voice, "Viewers, I have just been informed that there have been important developments in the Cliff Flaherty murder case. According to the police, certain materials left at the scene of TV producer Martin Donaldson's murder—which we at KGNN reported on this morning—have had a major impact on that aforementioned investigation. According to a press release from the sheriff's office, Dylan Ellis, the young man once considered a suspect in the Cliff Flaherty murder case, has been cleared of all charges. We will have a follow-up on what is now the Flaherty/Donaldson case during our noon news hour, so stay tuned to KGNN-TV, your Friends in the Know."

Ariel's face blanked for a moment, then resumed its former cheeriness. She lowered her hand, smiled, and said, "In a moment we'll greet Teddy Bentley, who will present her regular Tuesday morning feature, *Anteaters to Zebras*. But first, a word from our sponsor, Captain Queeg's Bait Shop, where the worms are guaranteed to be juicy or your money back!"

My cue. I picked up Basuri's cage and took my place on the set.

We chatted for sixty seconds while the viewers at home watched a tape of worms squirming around on a pile of manure, then when the camera's red light came back on, Ariel plastered on a phony smile—she'd never liked worms—and introduced me.

"Here she is, KGNN's very own Teddy Bentley!!! Why, what's that cute little thing you've got on the leash, Teddy? And am I wrong, but are those fangs?"

I plastered on my own phony smile. "Well, Ariel, Basuri here is a muntjac, otherwise known as a 'barking deer.' He only stands seventeen inches at his shoulder…" When I leaned forward to illustrate, Basuri took that opportunity to bark, although it sounded more like a cross between a throat-clearing and a yelp. I let him bark himself out, then resumed my spiel. "…and weighs only twenty-six pounds. Those 'fangs,' as you call them are actually tusks, and they use them to fight over territory. And females, of course. An interesting thing about muntjacs is that they have no actual breeding season…" I winked. "And therefore, do the wild thing whenever they feel like it."

Ariel tried to look disapproving but didn't quite manage it.

"Their round-the-year amorous activities have led to an interesting situation in England. In 1925, several muntjacs escaped from the Duke of Bedford's estate in southern England, and now these Sri Lankan natives can be found throughout England, Wales, and even Scotland and Northern Ireland."

"Oh, my!"

Then I added another feature of the cute little things that I knew would delight child viewers while not-delighting their parents. "Those Dracula-like tusks are useful for something else, too. They eat the dead!"

For once the Silver Star-winning Ariel looked horrified. "What!?"

"Yes, it's all too hideously true. Muntjacs have a taste for corpses, and the deader the better."

When Basuri barked again, Ariel leaned back away from him as far as she could.

Taking mercy on her, I said, "And our next guest is…"

At my cue, Lex hurried onstage with a small animal carrier, carefully set it down on the floor, then grabbed Basuri by the leash and led him away while the little deer was still barking. He was probably hoping to scare up a nice, juicy corpse.

I opened the carrier door and scooped out the real star of the show, and held up what appeared to be a gray-green soccer ball. "Ladies and gentlemen, I give you Farzeen the pangolin! Her name means 'Gift of God,' and that's how we treat her at the Gunn Zoo, because she truly is a precious gift."

Then I set her down on my lap, gave her a brief loving look, and began to stroke her smooth scales. "But these days pangolins are an increasingly rare precious gift," I continued, looking back up at the camera, "because pangolins are the most poached animals in the world. If the trafficking doesn't stop, Farzeen and her brothers and sisters will become extinct within the next decade."

Then I told the viewers that at first glance, pangolins appeared to be reptiles, but they weren't. Like armadillos in Texas, pangolins were mammals. Also like armadillos, pangolins would roll up into a ball when they were frightened, as Farzeen was doing now.

Still stroking her, I said, "These wonderful little animals believe their keratin scales will protect them," I told the camera, "but sadly, those very scales are the reason pangolins are so often poached. The same kind of ignorance that leads some men to believe that a rhinoceros's ground-up horn will cure their impotence also makes them believe that a pangolin's scales cure cancer."

I sniffed. "It doesn't."

For the next few minutes I discussed the various threats to the declining pangolin population—deforestation, poachers, etc.—until Ariel made a slashing movement in front of her neck. *Wind it up, commercial's coming.*

The set's monitor let us know that Barnacle Bill's was running a special on surf and turf on Wednesday night, but to ensure there would be a lobster with your name on it, you needed to call ahead for reservations. While the commercial was playing, Lex returned to the set, put Farzeen in her carrier, then disappeared. Seconds later he was back again, leading Billie Jean, a yearling African warthog, on her leash while some wit in the studio played the Ramones's hit single, "Warthog" as background music.

If anything was going to go wrong, it would be now, because experience had taught me you couldn't trust Billie Jean as far as you could throw her.

But Billie Jean's appearance started off nicely. Mild-mannered, for a warthog, she let Ariel scratch her broad back while I started the standard monologue.

"Remember Disney's feature film *The Lion King*? A cousin of Billie Jean's here was the break-out star. Natives of sub-Saharan Africa, warthogs are as varied and interesting as their continent. Female warthogs, for instance, live in family grounds called 'sounders,' where they sometimes share parenting duties. See Billie Jean's adorable little tusks? When she matures, those tusks can grow to be ten inches long!"

Ariel, who had been silent up to this point, said, "I hear that decorative carvings on warthogs' tusks—similar to the old scrimshaw art on whalebone or elephant tusks—are being sold on the black market. Is that true?"

"Unfortunately, yes. And not even the black market. No one has thought to pass laws protecting warthogs yet."

In sympathy, I reached down and scratched Billie Jean behind the ears, eliciting a grateful grunt. She loved to be petted.

Smiling at the red light again, I continued. "Although a warthog's tusks are quite lovely, they're mainly for protection for themselves, and for their families. Warthogs are tremendously loyal, and will fight to the death to protect their own—especially their piglets. By the way, another admirable trait of female warthogs is their willingness to foster piglets who have lost their own mothers, suckling them until they're able to take care of themselves. And woe be to anyone who tries to harm their fostered babies! Billie Jean here, as an adolescent, weighs only a hundred and thirty pounds, but when she reaches full size, she'll clock in at three hundred, and Heaven help anyone who messes with her or her piglets."

During all this, Billie Jean remained supine, oinking and snorting and flicking her tufted tail, the very picture of porcine tranquility. But that ended when one of the talk show's producers—who up to this time had watched silently out of camera range—picked up a bag from the nearest desk. With the lights blinding me, I couldn't make out what it was, but I heard the rattle. Billie Jean, who like all warthogs had an impressive sense of smell, clambered to her feet, her beady eyes homing in on the bag.

Oh, dear Lord, please don't let it be Cheetos.

"*Hawog?*" Billie Jean asked, wrinkling her snout.

Then the shit-for-brains producer opened the bag, scrambled his hand around, and lifted out something orange.

I tightened my hold on Billie Jean's leash. Despite the big DO NOT FEED THE ANIMALS sign at the Gunn Zoo's entrance, which was repeated in front of every enclosure, not everyone follows orders. People who should have known better had begun tossing Cheetos to her, and she'd developed more than just a taste for them.

She'd developed an addiction.

When her addiction had been discovered, she'd promptly been put in the zoo's version of rehab with other sufferers of her ilk, but you know what they say: it's not the last Cheeto that hooks you, it's the first.

"HAWOOOGG!!!" Billie Jean bellowed from the depths of her porcine being.

With that, she ripped the leash from my hands, along with a layer of skin, and charged the producer.

Showing a nimbleness that surprised me, the producer hopped onto the top of his desk, foolishly hoisting his bag of Cheetos.

"Drop those Cheetos!" I yelled, tearing after the warthog. "Before she climbs up there after you!"

Warthogs can be nimble, too.

The producer, a kid who was probably too immature for his job, dropped his Cheetos, although not without a look of anguish.

By the time I reached Billie Jean, she had demolished the Cheetos, along with a goodly portion of the plastic bag. I grabbed the leash with my sore hands—another workplace injury to report—and dragged her back to the set.

Staring right into the red light, I said, "Next time you're at the Gunn Zoo, please don't feed the animals."

After Lex and I had delivered the animals back to the zoo and I'd picked up my truck, I decided to drive by Lauren's parents' house.

Just out of curiosity.

Lauren's maiden name was Ellis and Colleen's old phone book—she used it to come up with her characters' names—had shown me there was a family named Ellis not too far from the San Sebastian Library. Although I knew I shouldn't be sticking my nose in someone else's business, I drove over to Stardust Creek, a quiet, suburban-style settlement of one-family homes. They weren't fancy, and some people might even have considered them starter homes because they were small, and from what I could tell, had three bedrooms at the most. But each yard was neatly kept up, creating an environment of community harmony. Number 8453 Stardust Circle, a pale-yellow Colonial, was especially tidy, with a small, closely mown lawn bordered in asters and chrysanthemums. A pebble stone path led from the curb to the dark-green front door, where a woman in her fifties stood cleaning a brass door knocker. She and Lauren shared the same straight nose, the same high forehead, the same pale blond hair.

I cruised to a stop on the other side of the street, and watched until she'd burnished that door knocker into a dazzling brightness. Then she started on the doorknob.

Should I?

Smart Teddy knew she shouldn't.

Hopeful Teddy felt she should.

On this one occasion, Smart Teddy won the struggle, and pulled away from the curb and headed toward home. But not before Hopeful Teddy had taken out her cell and snapped a picture of the sad-eyed woman.

Just a little after one, Dylan received a phone call from the San Sebastian Sheriff's Office, inviting him to come down to the station so his electronic monitor could be legally removed. Lauren accompanied him, a triumphant look on her face.

After they left, the house fell silent. Joe was at his office, the kids were in school, Colleen was in the granny cottage working on her latest book, and I'd already finished my list of likely suspects in the Flaherty murder. But no matter how long I stared at it, I couldn't see my way clear to pick a favorite. The man had hurt and offended so many people. As for Donaldson, maybe he'd known something about Flaherty's killer that he hadn't bothered to tell the police.

It was all just too confusing.

Stymied, I turned on the local TV channel and found a few *Tippy-Toe & Tinker* reruns, but they didn't hold my interest.

Then I tried reading the latest issue of *World Wildlife Magazine*, but I was too jumpy to stay focused. So I did what I always do when the world gets to be too much for me.

I went back to the zoo.

Unfortunately, being a mere observer instead of working with my animal friends didn't hold the same kind of magic. For instance, I found myself paying almost as much attention to the zoo's visitors as I did the animals. Could that portly, genial-looking man holding his daughter's hand be a murderer? And how about that elderly woman taking delight in her grand-children's excitement? As unlikely as it seemed, grannies had murdered before, and would murder again.

Don't think about murder, Teddy.

At least certain animals were happy to see me—Abim the wallaby, for instance; Lucy the anteater; and Alejandro the llama—but they did appear confused at seeing my approach on the public trail rather than on the keepers' trail. Truth be told, I felt confused, too. It was wrong to be out here with the public instead of taking care of my friends.

Don't think about murder, Teddy!

So much had happened recently. Dylan's addition to our family. Cliff Flaherty murdered. Dylan arrested. Lauren show-ing up. Martin Donaldson murdered. Lauren's fake confession. The sadness in Lauren's mother's eyes.

No wonder I was a wreck.

I was standing in front of Poonya's enclosure, watching the little red panda scamper up a small tree, when someone bumped into me.

"Sorry!" a male voice boomed. "Tripped!"

I turned around to see the cast of *Tippy-Toe & Tinker*. Gordo, who for some reason had chosen to wear flip-flops for his visit to the zoo, had come up behind me with Bird, Karla Dollar, and Bev Beaumont. The only cast member missing was Jocelyn Ravel, who still had a job.

"I'm surprised to see you all here," I said, before I could stop myself.

Gordo gave me a sympathetic smile. "Considering everything you've been through, we could say the same thing about you."

I flushed, realizing he was probably referring to my near-naked romp (I'd still had on my pants and shoes) through the Wolf Run. "I missed my friends. And you?"

"The same. That's why I rounded everyone up and came out to see the sights. Since we're all animal-lovers, we wound up here."

Although the group didn't look ecstatic, they appeared less glum than previously. Now that the shock had worn off, maybe they'd started thinking about the future. Nope. Cancel that. It was doubtful that the future for the forty-plus-years-old puppeteers included continued employment in their chosen craft. Instead, their probable future included asking, "You want fries with that?" at McDonald's or advising Walmart shoppers to have a nice day, until even those jobs were taken over by robots. The so-called Golden Years were in the process of vanishing, replaced by Grade Z trailer parks and rapidly diminishing unemployment checks.

I forced a smile. "There's nothing like a zoo to cheer people up. That's why I'm here." Then I remembered. "Ah, it's sad about Marty Donaldson, isn't it?"

"Depends on your point of view," grumbled Bird, his still long golden hair gleaming in the sun. "As for me, I call it Karma."

"Bird!" snapped Karla. "That's a terrible thing to say."

"But hardly incorrect," Bev said, taking Bird's side.

"People, people," Gordo admonished. "No point in speaking ill of the dead now. Remember why we're here."

"To see if we can come up with any ideas for a new program," Bev said. "But good luck with that, since the only decent writer around is Nestor Vanderman, and he's sure as hell not going to write anything for us, not now that the new suits are tripling his salary for some damned cartoon."

"More than triple, I'll bet." Bird, scowling. "There's no loyalty in this gnarly business. Just worshippers of the Golden Calf."

"You're wrong about there not being any other writers around," I interjected. "My mother-in-law's a successful writer. And I happen to know there's a writer's workshop that meets at the library every other Saturday, and some of them are writing scripts. Come to think of it, I'll bet one of you could write one, so don't be so quick to give up hope." Then, directing my next comment to Gordo, I said, "From what I hear, you've been in the business longer than anyone in the cast, so why don't you give it a try?"

He looked startled. "Me?! Write a script? About what?"

I thought fast. "About the same kinds of things Flaherty used to write about, but with the stories played out through mario-nettes representing living animals, not extinct ones. You could set it, say, around animals that live in a place like the Gunn Zoo." I waved around me, taking in the entire three hundred acres.

"We'd have to get new marionettes," complained Bird. "Do you know how much professional level custom-mades like ours cost? Over a thousand each."

"Surely the new people had to buy the rights to your original characters, Tippy-Toe and the others, even if they weren't going to use them."

The silence that ensued was so long that I repeated the question, adding, "Or am I wrong?"

Bev finally answered. "At the time, we were all just so thrilled to have a paying gig on TV we didn't pay that much attention to the wording in the contract."

"But still…"

"What it boils down to, Teddy, is that our marionettes don't belong to us."

The others listened shamefacedly as Bev went on to explain that the puppeteers' earlier marionettes, paid for out of their own pockets, were deemed not flashy enough, so the show's producers—Cliff Flaherty and Martin Donaldson—had hired an Italian craftsman to replace theirs with the dinosaur marionettes the viewing public had grown to love. "Therefore, the contract we signed stated that any marionettes used in *Tippy-Toe & Tinker*, belonged to the show itself, not us."

I thought I saw a glimmer of hope. "You guys still have your original marionettes?"

"Sure, but we're not allowed to use them 'for profit,' just for charity shows and children's birthday parties," Gordo said. "But even for low-rent events like that, we have to change their appearance and voices enough that they won't be mistaken for the characters on *Tippy-Toe & Tinker*."

Another embarrassed silence followed as the puppeteers rued their collective naivete.

Chapter Sixteen

Another evening, another pileup on Highway One. While Joe was out there helping mop up, Lauren and the kids were glued to the TV watching another *Tippy-Toe & Tinker* rerun. That gave me a chance to do what I probably should have done earlier.

Use PlatoSchmato to pry into another dead man's past.

Up until Marty Donaldson's death, I'd thought only of the enemies Cliff Flaherty had made, and that included my friends at the harbor. Now, though...

At first glance, Martin Donaldson's background appeared rather dull compared to his battle-prone business partner's. No DUIs, no beat-downs, no abuse of laundromat privileges. I did, however, take note of a lengthy list of lawsuits he had been involved in while doing business with Flaherty and some other guy named Richard Caton Strayle, most of the cases having to do with contract disputes. They'd won most, but lost two notables.

Twenty years earlier, Rhonda Estancia, heiress to an herbal tea company, had filed a lawsuit against Donaldson, Strayle, & Flaherty, Ltd. for contract fraud, alleging she'd signed a contract stating that for a certain amount of funding, she would be given coproducer credit as well as the starring role in *Swamp of the*

Undead. The film would be designed to look like a documentary based on the government cover-up of a zombie outbreak in Giverney, a small Louisiana parish. Rhonda would play the part of a wayward, sexy nun who, with the help of her priest boyfriend, bullied the zombies into returning to their graves. The movie was never made, purportedly because Donaldson, Strayle, & Flaherty couldn't raise enough funding to start filming. The heiress had to eat her losses because the firm claimed everyone involved lost money on the deal.

A year later, *Zombie Lust*, set in a small Texas town, featuring rising stars Marissa Corazon and Nick Hornsby as headliners and coproducers, opened to terrible reviews but terrific box office. Rhonda Estancia, who happened to be in the audience on opening night, discovered that the script was an almost word-for-word retelling of *Swamp of the Undead*, right down to the film's now-infamous final line, "Who needs God when I've got you?" Since Rhonda was still in possession of the original script, the judge awarded her thirty-five million dollars, the large amount based on what she'd already lost, plus the amount she could have conceivably made if she'd produced and starred in *Zombie Lust* and its sequels: *Zombie Lust II, Zombie Lust III,* and *Zombie Lust IV.*

Donaldson, Strayle, & Flaherty, Ltd., appealed, then reappealed the verdict, but the verdict was affirmed by the state's highest court. Giving up, the company declared bankruptcy, but whether Rhonda Estancia ever received her millions wasn't clear.

In the second case, which happened two years after *Zombie Lust* had staggered its way through the court system, Richard Caton Strayle, former partner at Donaldson, Strayle, & Flaherty, sued Martin Donaldson and Cliff Flaherty for misappropriation of funds—more commonly known as embezzlement. Strayle won, but as in the case of Rhonda Estancia, whether he collected or not remained a mystery.

I stared at the screen, finding it amazing that neither Donaldson nor Flaherty had been criminally prosecuted for fraud. I also found it amazing that the two had been so greedy that they had even screwed their own business partner.

Hooray for Hollywood, indeed.

Come to think of it, wasn't that exactly what my own father had done? Stolen millions from his business partners before skedaddling off to Costa Rica with his ill-gotten gains? But Dad was still alive and living the high life with his new wife, whereas Donaldson and Flaherty were both dead. Maybe someone from their past had finally caught up with them.

Where were Rhonda Estancia and Richard Caton Strayle now?

Another PlatoSchmato search gained me a little more information. In January of 2014, Estancia had married an architect named Augustus Kinsella; on Christmas Day in 2015, she had received a speeding ticket on the PCH, just north of Malibu. Nothing since then, other than the fact that two years later, Rhonda Estancia-Kinsella had died from a fall down her mansion's winding staircase, leaving the bulk of her estate to several animal rights organizations, and the proceeds—if any—from her lawsuit against *Zombie Lust*, to her twin grandchildren, Waylon Estancia-Barnes and Honey Bee Estancia-Barnes. Waylon died of a drug overdose a year later, and Honey Bee dropped from sight.

As for Richard Caton Strayle, after his lawsuit against his former partners, PlatoSchmato had nothing on him: no wants, no warrants, no property transfers, no marriages, no divorces.

The Invisible Man.

As soon as Tonio and Bridey were sent to bed, Lauren announced that she was driving back to Burbank the next morning and that Dylan would follow her in his car.

Which was, apparently, news to Dylan. "What? I'm not going back to Burbank yet!"

"If you stay here, the cops may arrest you again," Lauren said.

"No, they won't. Thanks to whoever killed Martin Donaldson, I'm off the hook."

"Whomever."

Dylan shot her a look. "That's what I said."

"No, you said, 'whoever.'"

I could almost see the steam leaking from Dylan's ears. "Whatever. Besides, I want to look up the other side of my family. The Ellises."

"The hell you will!"

Colleen and I stared at her. Did Lauren really believe she could tell an eighteen-year-old boy/man what he could or could not do? Then I answered my own question. Sure she did. In the past, her beauty had probably given her an argumentative power that always squelched her male opponent's mere rationale.

But not Dylan. He had his father's backbone. "I'm through letting you run my life," he said, firmly.

At that point, Colleen interrupted. "All right, you two. It's been a rough day, and my nerves are shot. I don't need any more drama."

That shut down mother and son for a while, but they continued to glare at one another across the kitchen table, where we sat drinking decaf and chomping on cranberry-apricot scones. I'd been feeling as snappish as my mother-in-law, so I was relieved to hear Lauren was returning home. Her beauty was breathtaking, but husbands weren't supposed to notice that kind of thing, yet Joe's sneaking glances had been making me wonder if he'd told me the complete truth about their relationship. Maybe it had been more than a Prom Night drunken one-nighter.

Pretending it was a mere attempt to lighten the mood, I chirped, "So. You and Joe were lab partners!"

Lauren stopped glaring at her son long enough to give me a quizzical look. "Uh, yes. Joe was better at chemistry than I was."

"Chemistry." I didn't like the sound of that.

"Yes. Especially the periodic weight table. I had trouble remembering how many atoms each element had, you know, like did oxygen have three atoms or two?"

"Oxygen has eight atoms."

"See what I mean?"

"Hmm." I was just about to ask her another question when Colleen stood up and announced that she was going to the granny cottage and wanted me to follow her for a private chat. "Dylan, you stay here with your mother for now."

He agreed, but he didn't look happy about it. His mother was a formidable foe, and now the two women on his side were abandoning him.

When we walked into the serenity of the cottage, Colleen turned around and waggled a well-manicured forefinger at me. "Teddy, what in the world is wrong with you?"

"She's just so beautiful," I said glumly, sitting down on the flowery sofa and burying my face in my hands.

"Silly girl," she said, putting her arms around me. "Joe loves you, not Lauren."

"Ever since she arrived, he hasn't been able to take his eyes off her!" I wailed.

"Neither can you. That's the problem with jealousy; it makes you obsess on the very thing you feel threatened by. You keep staring at the woman like she's a snake and you're some poor little mouse she's about to chomp. So stop thinking about Lauren, and for God's sake, stop comparing yourself to her. You're pretty cute yourself."

"Pretty cute isn't the same thing as beautiful," I muttered, wiping my eyes. "And I have this big bump on my nose."

"It's a perfectly fine nose. You're only self-conscious about it because your mother keeps harping on it."

"She's right about my nose."

Colleen vented an exasperated sigh. "All this downtime from the zoo must be making you crazy. There is *nothing* wrong with your nose! So let's drop all this talk about Lauren and noses, and talk about something we can do something about—like what's happening with the investigation into Flaherty's and Donaldson's deaths. The authorities don't seem to have a clue, but I noticed you've been back on PlatoSchmato."

The only reason she'd brought up the murder investigation was because she wanted me to stop obsessing about my husband's fascination with Lauren. But she was right. I was beginning to feel foolish about my foolishness.

"Okay, here's what I found out on PlatoSchmato..." After condensing all the various court cases Flaherty and Donaldson had won, I told her about the two civil cases they'd lost, and ended by telling her I hadn't been able to find out if the company had ever paid up.

"They sound like those two guys in *The Producers*," Colleen said, with an almost-admiring grin. "Scamming other people into investing in a terrible play that was certain to fail."

"Except *Springtime with Hitler* turned out to be a big hit. Just like *Zombie Lust* and its three sequels. And don't forget *Tippy-Toe & Tinker*. Like *Zombie Lust*, that one actually came into fruition. It's like those two guys kept making hits despite themselves."

"Ruining lives in the process," she pointed out.

I nodded. "They also left an entire herd of murder suspects behind them. Just for starters, there's Strayle, and everyone in the *Tippy-Toe* cast. Not to mention most of the liveaboarders at the harbor. I only wish I'd been able to find out whatever happened to Strayle. PlatoSchmato didn't come up with anything after his former partners declared bankruptcy."

Colleen gave me a stern look. "Then you didn't look deeply enough. Remember, I warned you that PlatoSchmato includes records dating back almost to the Ice Age, so it can be cumbersome. You have to have patience." Then she made me promise again to stop obsessing about Lauren and keep my mind on murder. And to never think of the two at the same time.

Thus given my marching orders, I returned to the house, only to see that in my brief absence, Joe had returned home and was sharing a cranberry-apricot scone with Lauren and their son. One happy little family.

Murder. Lauren. Murder Lauren.

Somehow, I managed to get past them without acting on the voice in my head.

The next morning Lauren decided not to go back to Burbank just yet, which surprised no one. She was still having trouble cutting the umbilical cord. Or apron strings. Or cut whatever, not that I cared.

"Teddy, could you pass me the apricot jam?" she asked politely as we shared a communal breakfast in the dining room.

I passed the jam.

"I love you, Dylan," Bridey said, looking at him with adoring eyes.

"And I love my new sister," my stepson answered, smiling. "*And* my new brother." This, to Tonio, who promptly flushed.

Perhaps to break up the saccharine moment, Joe held off taking another bite of his Denver omelet and asked Dylan, "Anything interesting on the schedule for today?"

"Gran and Mom and I thought we'd try our luck at Pinball Wizardess." To me, he said, "You ever been there, Teddy? Maybe you'd like to come along."

With my husband sitting at the table I didn't dare mention my talk with Jocelyn at the arcade, so I merely said, "Sounds too noisy for me." When I glanced at Joe, he'd gone back to eating his omelet, oblivious to the strained note in my voice. I couldn't wait until everyone was gone so I could get back on PlatoSchmato. It was my fifth day away from the zoo, not counting that sneaky visit yesterday, and Colleen had been right; too much downtime was making me crazy. In the bright light of day,

I felt myself returning to normal, and for me, *normal* meant finding out who'd killed Flaherty and Donaldson.

A half hour later, the kids had left for school, Joe for the sheriff's office, and Colleen, Dylan, and Lauren were back in the granny cottage burying themselves in my mother-in-law's old photograph albums while waiting for Pinball Wizardess to open its doors.

As for me, I was trolling through old court records on PlatoSchmato, beginning where I'd left off yesterday. Every now and then, dull court records were enlivened by tidbits about Hollywood's dirty linen. Among them, who had "really" killed JFK (Marilyn Monroe's jealous boyfriend), who had "really" murdered Nicole Brown Simpson and Ron Goldman (the mailman), and what had "really" caused the car wreck that killed James Dean (an alien spaceship landing too close to the highway). Wading through those and other improbables, I couldn't help but wonder how sites such as PlatoSchmato hadn't been shut down or sued, or a combination of both. But here it still was, doing a brisk business in blind articles where names weren't always given, but with hints so obvious you'd need to have been buried under a rock for centuries not to recognize the victims' identities.

After I'd waded through almost three hours of ancient court records and paranoid conspiracies, PlatoSchmato finally came through with an item in a gossip column titled *Hollywood Knows All.*

What Hollywood producer, after winning a giant lawsuit against his two former business partners yet failing to collect, attempted suicide the night before he was to be evicted from his Brentwood mansion? The maid, who had returned to the house to help pack, found Mr. X in the garage, slumped over the steering wheel of his still-running 1965 Shelby Cobra Roadster. Our sources say that Mr. X,

*who is now undergoing treatment at a Los Angeles mental
health facility, is alive only because of the prompt intervention of Maid X, who had at one time been a member of the
Girl Scouts, where she learned CPR. We here at Hollywood
Knows All award a big shout-out to heroic Maid X!*

Another search, this one going back to a happier time,
resulted in a photograph of Richard Caton Strayle, former partner of Donaldson and Flaherty, beaming from the seat of his
newly acquired 1965 Shelby Cobra CSX 8000 Roadster.

To my shock, I recognized him.

Somewhere along the line he had gained at least fifty pounds
and changed his name to Big Rick Stevens. He now ran the
San Sebastian car dealership where I had purchased my Nissan
pickup truck several years earlier.

Small world.

Chapter Seventeen

It being a Wednesday and October not a big car-buying month in the first place, Big Rick Stevens's dealership wasn't busy, so the moment I stepped out of my truck I found myself swarmed by car sales reps.

"You here to trade that in?" asked one, a young guy who didn't look much older than Dylan.

"Sorry, I'm just here to see Big Rick," I said, waving them all away. "It's a personal matter."

I was certain I remembered where Big Rick's glass-walled office was located—down the hall, last office on the left. I was right. The door was open, and Big Rick, appearing only a little older and a little heavier than he'd been when he sold me my pickup, looked up with an expectant smile.

"Theodora Bentley, isn't it?"

"Good memory." I entered, only partially closing the glass door behind me. Like I had years earlier, I felt like I was in a fishbowl. I could hear soft conversation down the hall, so that gave me the courage to start right in. "Why did you change your name?"

"Excuse me?"

"You used to be Richard Caton Strayle. I'm just curious why the change, that's all."

He put down the legal-sized papers he'd been looking at, but the smile was still there. "Oh, I doubt that's all, Ms. Bentley."

"Actually, it's Bentley-Rejas now. I changed *my* name, too."

"When you married the sheriff. Nice guy, I hear."

"I think so." *Except for his attraction to beautiful platinum blondes.*

"You're not here to buy another truck are you? But if you are, I'd be glad to give you a Friend-of the-Boss discount."

"Is that a bribe?"

Over the silence I was able to hear a clatter of footsteps down the hall, and a female salesperson explaining to a female customer the benefits and drawbacks of four-wheel-drive vehicles. The customer was worried about the cost—not of the vehicle itself, but with rising gas prices, and how much it would cost her to run a four-wheeler.

Big Rick finally spoke. "Bribe? Oh, please. I wouldn't be foolish enough to try and bribe the sheriff's wife. I was just offering you a good deal, that's all. Your truck's what, eight years old now? How many miles do you have on her?"

Interesting. The pronoun for boats and ships was usually female; this was the first time I'd ever heard a pickup truck called "her." Big Rick couldn't have known that my truck's name was Brad, after one of my favorite insurance commercials. I appreciated his effort, though. It was a further sign that motor vehicles had always been an important factor in his life. Did he still have the 1965 Shelby Cobra CSX 8000 Roadster from the newspaper photo? Or had that gone the way of his Brentwood mansion?

"Why are you really here, Mrs. Bentley-Rejas?"

"Call me Teddy."

"And you can continue to call me Big Rick. The other name…" He looked down at the stack of legal papers. "Well, it brings back a time I'd rather forget. Besides, Stevens was my mother's maiden name. Although the lady had her faults—Jesus, what a temper—most of my memories of her are pleasant."

"And it's easier to keep the same initials."

"That, too. Now again, at the risk of sounding redundant, why are you here?"

"To find out why you've been hiding out."

One side of his mouth pulled up. "Especially now that the two men who screwed me over have been murdered?"

"Correct." Before entering his office, I'd noticed another salesman right across the hall from us—a big, burly guy. So was his customer. Nice to know, if I had to shout for help.

I doubted that would happen, though. Despite my nosiness, Big Rick's demeanor remained calm, if careful. "You think that, after all my 'hiding out,' I'll finally break down and tell you the truth?" A question, not a statement. The open joy in his eyes when he'd had his photograph taken in his beloved Shelby Cobra was long gone, replaced by an intimidating watchfulness.

"What do you have to lose, Big Rick?"

That made him chuckle. "You're really something, you know that? But yeah, I get it. What do I have to lose? The old life may be gone, but I have this new one, and I like it a lot." He flashed a gold wedding ring I hadn't noticed before. "Noelle— thank God she's not an actress—and the kids. They make up for everything."

"Even the money Donaldson and Flaherty stole from you?"

He rested his hands on the legal documents. "Granted, I no longer have my Hollywood millions, but I'm doing fine. Great cars for a fair price. No one gets cheated at Big Rick's. At night I can go to bed and sleep the sleep of the angels, which wasn't always true in the old days. I was always up half the night worrying about this or that, and who was going to come for me next. You want to know why I changed my name? Legally, by the way. Because I didn't want any vestiges of my old life trailing after me, and that included my former business partners."

I wasn't sure I bought it. "You had to have known they'd moved up here and were producing *Tippy-Toe & Tinker*. Why didn't you go after them for the money the court awarded you? That judgment must still be in effect."

"Oh, it is. Believe me, it is." A cagy smile. "Sure, I knew they'd moved their sleazy selves to San Sebastian, so I did a little snooping around and found out exactly how much money *Tippy-Toe & Tinker* was bringing in. It wasn't as much as you'd think. Donaldson was basically living off his wife—she's some high-powered dot-com attorney in Silicon Valley—and there was Flaherty, living on some sleazy old barge…"

"It's a sailboat. And it's not sleazy, just needs some upkeep." Why I felt I had to defend a boat, I don't know, but I did.

Down the hall, the two women were still discussing the expense of running a four-wheel drive. The customer had begun thinking about a Toyota Land Cruiser, which excited the saleswoman. Or maybe a Land Rover, which thrilled her even more.

After another long silence, Big Rick started talking again. "Okay, so I know nothing about boats, just cars. Sorry to have offended. Back to Flaherty. I ran into him at the mall one day, and realized immediately that something was seriously wrong. Physically, I mean. He looked like hell. When I said hello, it was obvious he didn't even recognize me, yet we'd shared the same office for years. Long story short, neither of those guys was doing as well as me, so what would have been the point of dragging that old lawsuit through the courts again?"

He paused, and his face hardened. "However, once I read the announcement in the paper that their cute little TV show about dinosaurs was being syndicated, I changed my mind. Now they had money worth going after." With that, he picked up the sheaf of legal papers his hands had been resting on and waved them at me. "And that's exactly what I was about to do, until, well, you know. So if you think my grudge against those two embezzling bastards turned me into a killer, think again. Theoretically, they were worth more to me alive than dead."

Stating the obvious, I said, "You can always sue their estates."

"And join the parade in court." For a moment, his face was sour, then it brightened as he leaned over his desk and said, "Say, I've got a beautiful Nissan Titan out there, bright blue, V8 engine, priced to sell, and you'd look great behind the wheel. Why don't you...?"

After the test drive, during which I felt like a flea on an elephant, I returned to my loyal old pickup and went over everything Big Rick had told me. Some of it I bought; some of it I didn't. The alibi he'd finally offered me looked good, though. At the time of Donaldson's death, he had been sitting in his glass-enclosed office closing a deal on a new Chevy Silverado 3500HD. And like during all deals at Big Rick's, the surveillance cameras had been busily recording.

When I reached the house, I found yet another element had been added to the family drama—the arrival of Lauren's husband, Jon Overholdt.

Fresh off the plane from Burbank Bob Hope International Airport, he sat at the dining table, sharing coffee and scones with Joe—who had returned home for lunch—Lauren, Colleen, and Dylan. In between bites, he was comparing San Sebastian weather to the weather back in the LA area.

"We're warmer than usual, ten to fifteen more degrees than you are here, and... Oh, hi, you must be Teddy!" Big, bright grin.

"Sure am," I replied, sitting next to Joe and taking a scone for myself.

You'd think that given the dynamics involved, the *Joe & Jon Show* would be rife with tension, but it wasn't. Instead the two men had bonded over their shared fondness for Dylan, who now enjoyed the new privilege of having two dads. As if by unspoken agreement, their connection to Lauren wasn't discussed. When I snuck a glance at her, she looked relieved. So did Dylan and Colleen.

As we talked, I studied Jon Overholdt. He was a tall man,

sinewy instead of beefy, and no stranger to the gym. Certainly strong enough to wield a tire iron. And unlike Lauren, he obviously had no fear of flying. While the man with the engaging grin didn't look like a killer, killers seldom looked like killers. They usually look like your neighbors, which they sometimes are. As to motive, that was a given. Cliff Flaherty had once hurt Overholdt's beautiful wife, and what loving husband wouldn't relish a chance to take his revenge?

However, the scar on Lauren's face was an old one, barely noticeable. And besides, how would Jon Overholdt know that Flaherty, after his Hollywood career had tanked, was residing on a boat in Gunn Landing Harbor? It seemed so unlikely that I brought my attention back to the scone-fest.

"Not that I believe in global warming or any of that alarmist stuff, but it does make you think," he was saying to Joe.

"I hear ya," Joe said back, nodding sagely.

"If we don't do something about it, we're all going to die. First the plants, then the animals, then us." This, from Dylan.

"Say, I hear you guys have some fruit trees in back," Overholdt continued, after agreeing we were all in trouble. "What kind?"

Now it was Colleen's turn to shine. "Orange and apricot. Joe's father planted them when he built the house. We also have a large kitchen garden. Would you like to see it?"

Overholdt's grin grew. "Would I!"

With that, everyone except for Lauren and me headed for the backyard. Once they were gone, I turned to her and asked, "What's your husband doing here?"

"He thinks he can drag me back to Burbank, not that there's any chance of that happening. Men, you know."

"Yeah, I know. Men."

For the first time, we actually smiled at each other.

After the kitchen garden tour was over, Lauren and her husband left for the San Sebastian Hyatt for a little "alone time," as she phrased it, leaving me to suffer Joe's questions about what

I'd been doing all day. My answers involved a certain amount of fibbing, using the word "library" twice, and "pinball" three times.

"You'd be surprised how much fun pinball is," I finished. "Why don't we go together some evening when you're not mopping up wrecks on the One?"

He shook his head. "Sounds like fun, but you know me. When I have time off, I like to spend time with you and the kids on the *Merilee.*"

Joe didn't have the makings of a sailor, but since our marriage he had learned to enjoy the lazy pace of life at the harbor. It was the opposite of a cop's life, which was three-quarters boredom, one quarter heartbreak.

My fibs about my own life having passed muster, he headed back to his office. As soon as his cruiser was out of the driveway, I made a few calls. The first was to Gordo Walken. After some initial wariness, the puppeteer agreed to meet me tomorrow at JimBob's Donuts, a place that advertised itself as "Where the grub is sweet and the calories cheap." He sounded less morose when I told him the grub would be on me.

My other calls included those to Karla Dollar, Bev Beaumont, and Ansel "Bird" Yates, all *Tippy-Toe & Tinker* alumni. I called a couple of harbor friends who had experienced run-ins with Flaherty, namely Walt McAdam and Linda Cushing. Other liveaboarders had probably undergone similar situations, but at this point, I had no names. Maybe Walt and Linda could help.

Calls completed—and on a few occasions, messages left—I left to do something many people would consider heartless.

Interview a grieving widow.

At the outset, Gloria Marquand-Donaldson, the producer's fifth wife, didn't appear to be particularly upset over her husband's recent demise, and our talk quickly turned from "Who are you and what do you want to talk to me about?" to "Marty was no saint, but neither am I, so let's just get on with this. Understand, though, that I won't give you any information which might have a negative impact on the negotiations he and his partner entered into with CFZ Productions or any impending lawsuits that might arise therewith."

"Sounds fair to me," I agreed.

Gloria was a bone-thin brunette of about fifty, and the severe black dress made her look even thinner. Her unlined face would have better fit a thirty-year-old, whispering discreetly of a top-flight cosmetic surgeon, possibly the same one my mother used.

With a chilly smile, the grieving widow said, "Then let's move it along. I have a casket to pick out."

Unnerved in the face of such briskness, I let her lead me into a gray-on-gray living room that fairly screamed for a spot of color. Even the large painting on the wall across from the gray rock fireplace was a medley of grays. I'd seem homier hotel rooms. Then again, she spent most of the week in San Jose, didn't she? I wondered about the decor of her other home. Same old gray? Or black-on-black?

Taking a seat on an uncomfortable gray chair, I took out the notebook I'd brought with me, only to have her say, "Put that away. Anything I tell you is off the record."

Had she confused me with a journalist?

When I started to clarify the reason for my visit, she interrupted. "Yes, yes, you're the sheriff's wife, I know that. And from what I've read about you, you may be nosy enough to find out who killed my husband. That chief deputy of your husband's certainly hasn't."

"Well, Deputy Gutierrez has to follow proper police procedure."

That wintery smile again. "But you don't."

"Like you said, let's just move it along, okay? So..." I took a deep breath. "Who do you think killed your husband?"

"Someone connected to the show, of course."

"*Tippy-Toe & Tinker?*"

"That's the only show Martin and Cliff were involved in now, unlike in the old days when they'd have a dozen pots boiling on the stove."

"Do you have a favorite suspect?"

She thought for a moment; after all, she was an attorney. Then she said, "I'm not making any accusations, you understand, but Marty once told me he was concerned about Karla Dollar, that puppeteer who plays, ah, *played* Rosie the triceratops. She's a felon, you know."

Yes, I knew. In order to get her son into a good school, Karla had lied, and wound up serving three years in Chino for it. Gloria Marquand-Donaldson saw only the crime, whereas I saw a mother's love. "Do you have any children?" I asked her, although I already knew the answer.

"No, thank God. But I understand what you're getting at. You're trying to minimize the fact that she broke the law. If every woman whose child was bullied resorted to committing a felony, God only knows where we'd be. Karla's a smart woman. She knew what she was in for if she got caught, but she went ahead and falsified those papers anyway. Which was Martin's whole point. Her past behavior proved that when the law didn't suit her, she'd simply break it."

As opposed to finding legal ways to ruin someone's life. I thought back about Donaldson's and Flaherty's history of predatory business dealings. They'd cheated others—legally—for money, never for love.

That thought about love made me ask my next question. "You're Martin's fifth wife, correct?"

She narrowed her eyes. "Fourth. And as for me, I've only been married twice."

Same with me, so no judgment there, but I just had to ask the next question. "Do you inherit his estate?"

To my surprise, she laughed. "Jesus, Teddy, you've really got balls!"

I don't know what I'd expected, but laughter wasn't it. Astonished, I started, "Well, I was just…"

Waving me quiet, she said, "Yeah, yeah, I inherit, but only kinda. Given your own past divorce…" She flashed a grin. "Yes, I looked *you* up, too. I'm sure you understand the weight of California's community property laws re divorce, but here's something you might not know, that community property also affects inheritance when someone dies intestate. A couple of years ago he inherited several hundred thou from some long-lost relative, but thanks to his lack of planning, I won't see a penny. I sure as hell have to pay his bills, though."

"Martin didn't have a will?"

"Sloppy of him, wasn't it? But don't go worrying about me. I'm already well-provided for, and it happened the old-fashioned way—my own family inheritance."

A light went off in my head. *Marquand. Marquand Oranges*! Some sleuth I was, not connecting Gloria's maiden name— Marquand—to the family famed for vast land-holdings in the Inland Empire, southern California's verdant agricultural center.

As I was still adjusting to the shock, she added, "I had no reason to kill poor Marty, not a financial one, anyway, even though I'll eventually reap the benefits of the *Tippy-Toe & Tinker* syndication. Isn't that sweet?" Another bright smile.

"And while we're still on the subject of wills, dear Teddy, let me tell you about the one I myself notarized a couple of months ago. I can tell you this because a reporter from the *San Sebastian Journal* has already asked my opinion on it, which is how I know the news will appear in the paper tomorrow. The cops are aware of that particular will, too, and earlier today they stopped by to question me. I gave them a little more information than I gave the press." Here every trace of her former humor vanished as she

eyed me like a hawk ready to pounce on some unfortunate creature. "Despite, or maybe *because* of his ill-health, Cliff Flaherty
made a will, and guess who's going to get his oh-so-recent ill-
gotten gains?"

Although I feared I could already guess the answer, I asked
anyway. "Who?"

"Dylan Ellis."

Chapter Eighteen

As I sat there trying to keep my shock from showing, Gloria Marquand-Donaldson told me about the sealed letter accompanying Flaherty's last will and testament.

"It was hand-addressed to Dylan Ellis, and I suspect it contains some sort of apology," she said. "Look, Cliff wasn't always the nicest guy in the world, but every now and then he'd surprise you with some act of decency."

"Such as?" I asked, finally finding my voice. Flaherty's problems were physical, not moral, so despite his symptoms' obnoxiousness, I felt pity for the man.

"Such as the day last month when he got out of his car in order to keep some wayward sea lion from getting hit as the dumb thing scooted its ass across Harbor Road. That made the online version of the newspaper. *Cliff Flaherty, Crossing Guard!* Then two hours later on the very same day, he turned Neanderthal again and insulted some poor woman in the supermarket parking lot who wasn't loading her groceries into her car fast enough for him. Why? Because he wanted her parking spot and he was tired of waiting. Without going into details, let's just say it was a racially insensitive insult, followed by a purposeful and repeated ramming of her shopping cart with that stupid Mercedes Gullwing of his."

That sounded like Bad Cliff, all right, but how would Gloria have found out about it? Could she have been nearby, putting groceries into her own car? Since I couldn't picture Gloria Marquand-Donaldson ever doing anything as domestic as food shopping, I asked, "And you know this how?"

"Because she was bringing him to court, and he came by here to get some free legal advice. When I told him to suck it up and pay the woman off, he insulted *me*, too. Or rather, he insulted my cosmetic surgeon, saying he'd done sloppy work and it showed."

With that, one half of her face managed a smile, while the other half struggled to keep up.

Later, as I left her condo, I couldn't stop thinking about Cliff Flaherty's disease. It had been slowly but steadily eating away at his brain on its grim march toward death. Yet every now and then, it had allowed him a brief respite at his former level of awareness—only to confront the ugliness Bad Cliff left in his wake.

Oh, what hell.

My bad day wasn't over, even though the extra misery occurred at an unlikely place. Thinking about Good Cliff had driven me down to Gunn Landing Harbor, where I counted on the *Merilee* to act as an island of calm in the midst of my emotional whirlwind.

The shush-shush of waves. The cry of gulls. The bark of harbor seals.

Blessed peace.

I spent a sorrow-free hour dusting and fussing around my boat, not thinking about anything, just focusing on the glow of teak and the gleam of brass fittings. Once the *Merilee* was shipshape, I poked my head out of the cabin to breathe the fresh salt air.

It being a weekday, most liveaboarders were at work. The only person I spotted was Linda Cushing, struggling across the parking lot toward the laundromat carrying what looked like several loads of laundry and in danger of losing them all.

"Let me help you with that," I said, catching up with her. As she turned around to greet me, several socks slipped off the top of the pile and onto the asphalt.

"Now look what you've done," she groused. "I had everything perfectly balanced until you came along." But she was smiling, and she tilted her load so that half of it wound up in my arms. "Haven't seen much of you lately, Teddy. Been busy solving crimes? Or just stripping for dollars at the San Sebastian Honey Pot?"

At first the comment took me aback. "Meow to you, too, Linda. How'd you know about my dances with wolves? I thought you didn't have a TV."

"Saw it on Walt's big screen. He came over to get me, said they were about to rerun it on that Ariel woman's newscast. But don't worry. They blurred out your Ts and A, although I must say, you are in great shape. Must be all the shit-shoveling at the zoo."

"I've demanded residuals." I was serious, having made the call earlier.

"If you do, they'll stop running it, and..." She looked blank for a moment, then said, "Oh, you clever girl, you. That's exactly what you wanted, isn't it?"

"Great minds think alike."

When we arrived at the laundromat, we found it empty, but I couldn't help remembering the last time I'd been in here.

Loaded washers. Wet towels.

Cliff Flaherty, with only days left to live.

As Linda separated her clothes, I asked, "What's the current buzz about Flaherty's murder?"

"Just gossip and not much sympathy. Oh, wipe that shocked look off your face, Teddy. He was a nasty man who got what he had coming."

"That's cold."

"Not really. He offended so many people around here it's a miracle he didn't end up in Davy Jones's locker much earlier."

Linda finished loading the third washer, then bought several packets of soap from the dispenser on the wall. Dumped the soap on the clothes. Slid her credit card through the slot. Heard the hiss of water filling the washers. Satisfied, she motioned to the bench against the end wall.

We sat, listening to the washers' *ka-rump, ka-rump* as their cycles started and the scent of dissolving detergent filled the humid air...

"You say Flaherty offended 'many' people," I said to Linda. "Who else around here that you know of?"

She vented a sound that was half disgust, half laugh. "Well, there weren't many people he didn't insult at one time or another, so most folks learned to give him a wide berth. But me and Walt, us being such close neighbors, we got the lion's share of his crap. The only good thing I can say about the man is that he liked cats. He seemed especially fond of Toby, who started spending way too much time over on *Scribbler*. At first I worried about that, but one day I saw Flaherty sitting on the deck with Toby in his lap, and I'd swear that the son of a bitch was singing nursery rhymes to that little cat. Toby was loving it, too. He stayed on Flaherty's lap until sundown, then came padding back to the *Tea 4 Two* like it had been no big deal."

Poor Toby. Left orphaned after his original owner had been killed by a lunatic, the little Siamese had now lost another friend to murder.

"Cats are weird, aren't they?" Linda said, rhetorically. "They love the unlovable and treat us nice guys with contempt."

My experience had taught me that all living creatures were weird, from three-toed sloths to boat cats. But unlike sloths, boat cats had an innate sense of danger. Toby had trusted Flaherty enough to sit on his lap, apparently sensing something most humans couldn't—that hiding underneath Flaherty's disease, an untouched section of his brain remained gentle. Thinking about Toby purring on the man's lap reminded me of the photo screwed to the wall of *Scribbler*, and the joy on Flaherty's face.

I blinked away the memory.

"Eye still bothering you, Teddy?" Linda asked. "I heard you got wolf piss in it."

"I'll live. So answer me this. Let's say one of the liveaboarders tired of Flaherty's crap and finally did him in. Who's your guess as to who that would be?"

"Oh, that's easy. You."

My shock must have been apparent because she began to laugh. "You think the whole liveaboard community didn't find out about that fight you two had in here? The cursing? The shrieking? The towel-slapping? C'mon, Teddy, you must have known that once Lou Caroll saw that videotape he'd blab about it to all and sundry."

I made a face. "Okay, okay. After me, who's your favorite suspects?"

She thought for a moment. "Me. Then Walt."

Bypassing the possibility of Linda, who was in her seventies and not the tire iron type, I asked, "Why Walt? He's a firefighter. His job's to save lives, not take them."

She snorted. "My, my. Aren't you the high-minded one? But remember that cute brunette Walt was seeing for a while? The one with the little girl?"

"Annette and Terri? Yeah, that was the first time I ever saw him get serious about anyone."

Like most firemen, Walt was a decent sort of guy, but he had been notoriously free in sharing his virility, and the series of beautiful women spending the night aboard Walt's *Running Wild* had provided Gunn Landing Harbor countless instances of gossip over the years. For a while it looked like his escapades would continue until Walt became the World's Oldest Living Playboy. But then one weekend Annette and her daughter showed up. In contrast to his standard bikini'ed-and-thonged conquests,

Annette dressed demurely in a one-piece that matched her daughter's. The two soon became the only females to spend full weekends on *Running Wild,* and the other liveaboarders began calculating the odds that Annette would wind up with an engagement ring.

As if to make certain she wouldn't be overheard, Linda flicked a glance at the laundromat door. No laundry-laden liveaboarders approached. Satisfied, she continued, "Did you notice how a couple of weeks ago Annette and the kid stopped coming around?"

I sighed. "Not really, since I'm not down here much anymore, myself. But what does Annette have to do with Cliff Flaherty? Wasn't he a bit old for her?" I tried to make a joke out of it.

Linda narrowed her eyes at me. "Last time Annette and the kid were down here, Flaherty shouted something rude. Something about Annette's, ah, bust size. Only that's not what he called them."

Bad Cliff coming out to play again, leaving Good Cliff to suffer the consequences.

Even for a one-piece, the swimsuit I'd seen Annette in was conservative. High neck, a coy ruffle around the hip. However, there had been no disguising the fact that Mother Nature had been generous with her topside, bestowing at least a 38-D onto her slender frame.

"Please tell me she didn't hear that. Or the little girl."

"*Everybody* heard it. Walt, Annette, and the kid just happened to be guests on my *Tea 4 Two* when Flaherty sounded off. You know how sound carries over water. Jesus, Teddy, you should have seen Walt's face."

Imagining his reaction wasn't hard. "What'd he do?"

"Went over and talked to Flaherty. Politely, I think. At least there was no blood. Not that I saw, anyway."

"Politely? Tell me another one, Linda. I know Walt better than that."

"I'm serious! That's all he did—talk. Then, anyway. Probably because the kid was there."

"What was Annette's reaction?"

"She got a bit red in the face, but given her build, I'm sure she'd heard it all before. You know what men are like. Still, we never saw her down here again, did we? Anyway, you asked me who'd be my other choices for the killer, so there you are. You. Me. Walt. In that order. But we both know you're no killer. And neither is Walt."

I couldn't help but notice she hadn't included herself in the No Killer category.

Being back at the harbor had not only relaxed me, but it had given me an idea. No one knows as much about the goings-on at a harbor than its harbor master, so after leaving Linda to babysit her laundry, I headed over to Jean Novello's office.

Halfway across the parking lot, though, I spied Walt pulling in, fresh from his shift at the firehouse. I waited next to his authorized spot while he unloaded some equipment from the bed of his Dodge Ram 3500. From what he hauled out, it looked like he planned to spend the rest of the week working on his *Running Wild*.

"Good to see you at the harbor again," he said, hazel eyes sparkling. "And here we have all been saying you'd turned into a landlubber."

"Never happen," I said. "You know me; things get crazy, I have to come down for a little R&R."

His broad smile dimmed somewhat. "Crazy, yeah. Lots of bad things happening these days. First Flaherty, then his business partner. Now there's a rumor going round that there's been a big shake-up over at KGNN. Some kiddie show or something got canceled."

As I helped carry some brushes and varnish to *Running Wild*, I filled him in.

"Geez, that's even worse than I thought, 'cause I bet puppet jobs aren't easy to come by these days," he said. "Except for kids' birthday parties and all. But try making a living out of that."

"Speaking of kids, how's little Terri, Annette's daughter? For a six-year-old, she seemed especially bright."

What was left of his smile vanished. "She's fine, I guess."

"You *guess*?" I raised my eyebrows. "What, you haven't seen her and Annette lately?"

"No, and I don't want to talk about it."

When Walt says no, he means no, so when he boarded the *Running Wild*, I handed over the varnish, bid him a polite good-bye, and left.

Harbor Master Jean Novello was scratching some notes in what looked like an old-fashioned accounts book when I entered. She'd only been on the job for a few months, but had settled in nicely. A former lieutenant in the Coast Guard, she was in her late forties and her weathered skin was almost as brown as her hair. Her eyes, though, were a startling topaz, almost the same color as a cat's.

She looked up from her messy desk with a warm smile. "Well, hello, Ms. Bentley-Rejas. What can I do for you on this fine California afternoon?"

"For starters, you can call me Teddy."

"Roger that."

"Not Roger, *Teddy*."

Having performed this greeting joke several times in the past few weeks, we both cackled. It took us both a moment to calm down, and when we did, the ghost of our laughter still lurked in the background.

"What can I do for you, Teddy?" A further display of white teeth.

Harbor masters see all and know all. Their duties range all the way from enforcing California navigation laws, to assigning boats to specific moorings, and to helping boaters batten down the hatches in case of typhoons or tsunamis. And, of course, to interface with the authorities in the case of high crimes and misdemeanors committed in the harbor.

They are also known for their abilities in keeping their lips zipped.

But Novello was worth a try. "Are you aware that Cliff Flaherty's business partner was killed yesterday?"

A careful nod. "I heard something to that effect, yes."

"With a tire iron, just like the one that killed Flaherty. This time the killer left it behind."

"I would take that to mean that he—or she, as the case may be—does not plan to kill again. Or maybe just forgot it." She looked lazily out her sparkling-clean office window, where outside, a small boat was being winched out of the water. Its furled sails were stained and the hull looked like it hadn't been debarnacled in ages.

"The *Sea Sprite*," Novello said. "The owner died, and the family just forgot about her. The boat, I mean. Sad, isn't it? Seeing a good boat go bad?"

Talk about an opening. "Did you know Cliff was suffering from frontotemporal dementia?"

Those topaz eyes swung back toward me. "I knew something was wrong, but not being a medical person…" She raised her hands in a helpless gesture. Her nails were broken, and grease stained the cuticles.

"How'd you know?"

"I can't tell you that." She looked back out the window. "Like the *Sea Sprite* out there, *Scribbler* was beautiful once, too. When you really love something, it tends to show, agreed?"

I remembered the pristine photograph in *Scribbler's* filthy galley. "Definitely."

"So you make certain nothing happens to it. Legally, I mean. Let's say you've leased a beautiful apartment, one you've decorated with loving care. You'd make certain you paid your rent on time, wouldn't you?"

"Definitely."

"You wouldn't let the rent slide for so long that you get hit with an eviction notice, would you?"

"Definitely not."

"And you certainly wouldn't run out and make an offer on an even more expensive apartment, would you, not without updating your current contractual obligation, would you?"

"Nope."

She turned away from the window again, an anguished look on her face. "Poor *Sea Sprite*. All that beautiful teak, all those memories, yet she's headed for the wrecker." Then her voice changed, became more businesslike. "Did you know someone finally made a serious offer on *Lotta Luck* last week?"

"Uh, no, I didn't." *Lotta Luck*, moored at the expensive north side of the harbor, was a Gulfstar fifty-foot ketch tacked for a round-the-world voyage. She was a gorgeous vessel, but I felt she was a bit overpriced. Most interested buyers had thought so, too.

"The offer was accepted. Papers just need to be signed and witnessed."

"Who's the lucky buyer?" I asked.

Topaz eyes met mine. "Actually, the sale fell through. Seems the buyer was murdered last week."

Before leaving the harbor, I returned to the *Merilee* to pick up the abalone shells I had found on the sand spit near the harbor and forgotten to take home. Colleen had begun using seashells to separate the herbs from the rest of the vegetable garden, and they would make a nice peace offering after our morning squabble. While I was gathering them, it occurred to me that someone else needed a peace offering.

In the past couple of weeks, my husband had not only discovered that he had an eighteen-year-old son, but he'd needed to step aside from a high-profile murder investigation when it appeared to involve that son. As the cherry on top of this Shock Sundae, he'd also been confronted with his ex-girlfriend and needed to deal with a jealous wife. Although I was alone in the cabin of my boat, I felt myself flush with embarrassment over my lack of understanding.

Well, that would end right now.

I pulled out my phone, sat down on the galley bench, and speed-dialed my husband.

"Love you," he answered. He was sweet that way.

"Love you more." My rote, but heartfelt, answer. "Sweetie, do you happen to be pulling bodies from wrecked cars or anything awful like that?"

A chuckle. "Nope. Just leaving the Mastersons. They're fighting again."

"Any blood?"

"Nah, they're both too old and feeble to hurt each other. It was more of an insult-fest, but the noise was bothering their neighbors, so we had to show a presence. So what's up? It's not like you to call when I'm working. Not having trouble with wolves again, are you?"

"Oh, ha. Just missing you, that's all. And wanting to apologize for my bad behavior this last couple of weeks."

"Teddy, you have nothing to…"

"Joe, don't you dare let me off the hook so easily. I need to apologize, so I am. Furthermore, I've decided how I can make it up to you."

"Hmmm?"

"We need some alone time, just you and me, alone *together*."

"I like the sound of that."

Was it my imagination, or had his breath begun to quicken? "And you know where?"

"Wh…where?" No, it wasn't my imagination.

"On the *Merilee*."

No immediate answer, just more rapid breathing. Then, "Just you and me on that slow-rocking boat?"

"You got it, bud."

"Oh, I *really* like the sound of that." *Pant, pant.*

So we made a date.

Amends in the process of being made, I pulled my attention away from the happy future to the problem of the less-happy now.

Who had killed both producers of *Tippy-Toe & Tinker* and why?

Visiting murder scenes is not one of my favorite things, but since my earlier visit to Flaherty's boat had turned out to be helpful, I had high hopes for the parking garage where Martin Donaldson had left this vale of tears. My visit there turned out to be helpful, too, but in a different way.

When I drove my truck up to the parking garage's entrance on Sycamore Street, I found it blocked by a sign announcing GARAGE FULL—USE ELM ST LOT. But on the next block I spotted a parking spot next to a boarded-up store, so I parked there and hoofed it through the evening's dimming light back to the garage. This side of town wasn't the best—at least half the buildings were marked for demolition—and purse-snatchings weren't unknown. The offices of *Tippy-Toe & Tinker*'s producers had been here since their less successful days, and as they say, beggars couldn't be choosers. But I made it into the parking garage unmolested, only to notice that the camera on the first-floor level was smashed, so I felt no safer in here than on the trash-strewn street. Hopefully, the camera on the basement level, where I was headed, remained intact. Like most women, I don't like underground parking garages, not even those in better neighborhoods. They were too dark and lonely. It was well past quitting time, so no herd of white-collar workers would be rushing to their cars, eager to get home.

The door leading to the office building and presumably to

the lower level stood in the middle of the garage, so I had my choice of entering the stairwell or walking down the corkscrew-shaped car ramp. Not being a fan of stairwells, I chose the ramp. Although most of the garage's ground level was poorly lit, at least the ramp was aglow with luminescence.

Still, when I started down the ramp to the basement level, the hairs on the back of my neck prickled and goose bumps emerged on my arms. If something happened, my only defense was the canister of pepper spray that Joe had given me for Christmas on a sterling silver key ring. It might give me time to run. As it was, the pepper spray turned out not to be needed. Nothing awful lurked in the ramp, but it was so narrow that on its blah-beige walls I could see scrapes of color left by arriving and departing autos. Black. Silver. Several shades of red, and even Rental Car Teal and that bright chartreuse dubbed Alien Green.

Looking more closely at the paint smears, I remembered that Dylan's hatchback was painted silver-blue, Karla Dollar's Chevy Cruz was teal, Jocelyn Ravel's Kia was that weird new color called Alien Green, and unless I was mistaken, Beverly Beaumont's Toyota Camry was the same Lipstick Red as one of the smears on the wall. Most of the other cars of the people I'd spoken with were white, like Gordo Walken's Ford Contour, or silver, like Martin Donaldson's 740i BMW and Cliff's Gullwing. Plenty of those colors on the ramp, too. Paint smudges on a parking garage wall wouldn't prove anything, but I still made a mental note to myself to see if any of my suspects' cars had had any run-ins with blah-beige walls lately.

On down the ramp I went, reaching the basement level just as a white Jeep Explorer was starting up. At its irritated honk, I flattened myself against the wall, and even then, the Jeep passed unnervingly close.

I should have chosen the stairs.

In the end, I made it to the basement level without getting splattered all over the wall. It took a few seconds for my eyes to

adjust to the relative darkness, and to overcome the claustrophobia I felt at the garage's low ceiling. My claustrophobia increased
when I saw another surveillance camera out of commission;
this one not only cracked, but with its lens spray-painted black.
A different set of thieves? Or just vandals?

As I stepped out of the ramp and onto the parking area, two
men and one woman came out of the stairwell door together,
and headed for the spaces marked CARPOOL ONLY. As soon
as they'd driven off in a white Chevy van, two more men came
out of the stairwell. One wore a suit and carried a briefcase,
the other wore gray overalls and carried a heavy-duty mop and
bucket.

Briefcase Man climbed into a silver Audi and drove away,
whereas Janitor Guy stood there for a moment, staring at me.
He was somewhere in his early thirties, and his weathered
face revealed considerable time spent outdoors. Interestingly
enough, although I'd never been in this parking garage before,
he looked familiar.

When I approached, he said, "Ohmigosh! You're Teddy
Bentley, the gal from that TV program, *Anteaters to Zebras*! Can
I have your autograph?"

I now recognized him as Jerome Lukasik, a yearly subscriber
to the zoo. He was an all-around animal-lover who had never
played favorites until Poonya arrived, and then it had been love
at first sight. His love was requited, too. The little red panda
never went into her *Eek!* mode when Jerome was around.

Although I felt strange giving someone my autograph, I
reached for the small notebook he took from one of his overall
pockets and signed my name. At the same time, I couldn't help
but notice the facing page, which was covered with handwrit-
ten notes about red pandas: their size, their weight, their dietary
habits. He'd done considerable research, but why?

When I asked, he flushed. "I'm, uh, writing a kid's book. Not
that it'll ever get published or anything because I don't have

the slightest idea of what I'm doing, but it's fun, y'know? I just wanna make sure I get everything right."

Handing the notebook back, I said, "My mother-in-law's a mystery writer, and next semester she's teaching a class on creative writing at San Sebastian Community College. She might be able to help."

His flush deepened. "I'm already enrolled! Isn't her *Murder at the Zoo* just the greatest thing ever? My book, well, it's a mystery, too, and this red panda named Poonya—guess who for!—is the detective who solves the case of a kidnapped black-and-white panda cub and brings him safely back home."

Every now and then the Fates are kind. After a few minutes of discussing red pandas versus the more popular black-and-whites, I shared a few facts he hadn't already come across in his research. With the conversational ice well and truly broken, it was easy to bring up Martin Donaldson's untimely demise.

"Terrible, wasn't it?" I said, shaking my head. "And right here in this garage!"

"I'm the one who found Mr. Donaldson," he responded, looking like he was about to cry. "I tried to stop the bleeding, and when he stopped breathing, I tried CPR, but it didn't do any good. The EMTs and the cops got here pretty much at the same time. It couldn't have been more than five minutes, but it was too late. Poor guy was gone."

Faced with such compassion, I decided to play it straight. "If you've been watching the news, you probably already know that my stepson was originally charged in the murder of Mr. Donaldson's business partner, but when authorities realized they'd made a mistake, they let him go. Still, I'm worried that they may change their minds, so I'm trying to get to the bottom of this. Maybe you could…" I let my voice trail off.

"Help you?" he finished for me. "Sure, Teddy! What do you need?"

"Show me where it happened."

Grunting an assent, he hefted his bucket and mop and headed toward the back of the garage with me trailing close behind.

Martin Donaldson had died in Space 76. It was still roped off by yellow police tape, but there was nothing to see, anyway. Just a dark spot where his blood must have pooled, and a smaller spatter area four feet away where the murder weapon had been tossed.

"I've been scrubbing like crazy," Jerome explained, nodding toward the bucket he'd set down. "And I've got most of it out, but you can still see what...what it was."

"In time people will forget and think it's an oil spot. Or engine coolant or something. By the way, I've noticed that two of your security cameras are out of commission. How long have they been like that and why haven't they been fixed?"

"The police asked me the same thing. It happened two nights ago, when we had several car burglaries. Windows smashed, glove boxes rifled, you know. Any packages, gone. When I noticed that the cameras had been tampered with—not hard to do, because there was glass and broken plastic all over the place that night—I reported it to Management. Turns out they were an old model and couldn't be fixed. New ones have been put on order, but they haven't arrived yet."

"You couldn't get any from the hardware store?"

He shook his head. "They were all out. After all those purse-snatchings and car burglaries, everybody and his canary wants the things. So here we are. Big, dark garage and no working surveillance. The women in the building are all freaked out about it, and I don't blame them. The cops were able to get something off that one, though," he said, pointing at the damaged camera. "Just before it got spray-painted, it showed some guy dressed up all in black, face covered and everything, just like a ninja. But then he whipped out a spray can and that's all she wrote."

"A well-informed thief is a successful thief," I said. "Before the ninja showed up, were there any other incidents down here?"

"Nothing violent. But we get complaints every now and then when someone scrapes his car up in that narrow ramp, but we can't do anything about that, can we?" He turned his hands over in a helpless gesture.

I thought about the timing. Two nights before Donaldson's murder, two surveillance cameras in this parking garage of his office building had been taken out of commission. While both acts could have been committed by the car burglars, the damage to the camera down here could have been caused by whomever killed Donaldson.

With Jerome's permission, I ducked under the police tape. Even close up, the stain looked innocuous. If you hadn't known what it was, you... Well, you wouldn't know. While Jerome continued his attempt to erase it completely, I searched the surrounding area. I found nothing, not even a chewing gum wrapper or cigarette butt. Whatever detritus had been lying around where Donaldson had been killed had already been scooped up by the CSIs.

Giving up, I bade goodbye to Jerome and headed back through the failing light to my pickup, only to find a piece of paper stuck under the windshield wiper. A ticket? Disgusted, I looked around, wondering if there had been a NO PARKING sign I hadn't noticed, but I didn't see one. A flyer, then. Someone advertising a charity car wash or upcoming yard sale. I slid the paper out and looked at it, then immediately wished I hadn't.

STOP SNOOPING OR YOUR NEXT

Chapter Nineteen

When your husband has ordered you to stop snooping around in a police investigation, you can't exactly show him a threatening note accusing you of that very thing. The note felt like it was burning a hole in my pocket as the family assembled for the superb dinner Colleen served up: thick ham steak with red-eye gravy, homemade dressing, and a ratatouille of vegetables from her garden, followed by warm peach cobbler topped with hand-whipped cream.

The food was so good that Tonio and Bridey stopped their squabbling and chowed down peacefully. Lauren was back from her visit to the Hyatt with her husband, who had given up trying to make her go home and flown back to Burbank alone. She sat across from Dylan, gazing at him with adoration. Joe had made it home for dinner, the elderly Mastersons having promised to not shoot each other.

As genial family chatter rose around me, I tried not to think about the note in my pocket, but it was like telling a child not to put beans up his nose. Once you've given the child the idea, a game of Beans-Up-Nose is certain to follow. My own personal bean was STOP SNOOPING OR YOUR NEXT. That misspelling, for instance. It should have been YOU'RE, contraction for "you are," not YOUR, possessive. An uneducated writer? Or an educated writer attempting to appear otherwise? Or, maybe, just a writer in a hurry. Then again…

"You're looking thoughtful tonight, Teddy," Lauren said, tearing her magnificent eyes away from her son.

Don't talk about murder, Teddy. Don't talk about murder. I forced a grin, even though it felt like a rictus. "Oh, I'm just thinking about everything that's happened. Dylan. You. This wonderful expansion of our family."

"I'm so glad you see it that way, but I was afraid, what with Joe and I…"

"Have you noticed that when children help with the gardening, they tend to enjoy their vegetables more?" This, from non-gardener Joe, who couldn't tell a rutabaga from a radish.

"Why, yes I have." Colleen.

"I've always loved ratatouille." Me, who hated the soggy stuff.

By now, Lauren, who wasn't stupid, realized her near-gaff and changed the subject. "I read in the *San Sebastian Journal* that the entire cast of *Tippy-Toe & Tinker* will be giving a farewell performance Saturday night at the college. Are any of you going?" She looked around the table.

"I wanna go!" Bridey immediately yelled.

"Me, too," Tonio said, no doubt thinking of Jocelyn Ravel, love being blind.

"Why don't we all go?" Dylan suggested. "Considering what's about to happen to them, losing their jobs and everything, it would be a nice gesture of support."

The adoration in Lauren's eyes intensified.

As for me, I was mentally kicking myself for not asking Marty Donaldson's widow when Dylan was going to be advised of his upcoming inheritance.

Maybe he already knew.

If I had known how tough Thursday would turn out to be, I'd never have gotten out of bed.

Instead, I arose feeling happy and refreshed after some late-night lovemaking, followed by a just-as-delightful early-morning co-ed shower with my husband. But in a suddenly crowded household, it's best to keep your joy to yourself; otherwise, once you reach the breakfast table, you'll be letting yourself in for some embarrassing questions. Such as...

"Gee, Teddy, you seem so chipper this morning! Care to share?" This, from Lauren, goddess eyes twinkling.

"It's such a beautiful day, is all." Me.

"You haven't noticed it's raining?" Dylan.

"Rain is good for flowers."

"You're not a flower, Teddy." Tonio.

Colleen, cottoning on to the drift of things, said, "Teddy is so a flower. She's an open-faced sunflower, shedding light wherever she goes."

Gagging sounds from Tonio, immediately mimicked by Bridey, which made them sound cute.

"Stop it!" Joe, mock-angry. "I've got places to go, people to arrest. In the meanwhile, I want you to behave yourselves. Especially you, Teddy."

I beamed my sunflower self at him. "I promise to be good as gold."

As soon as Joe was out the door, Dylan said to me, "Let's go pick some radishes."

"In the rain?"

"I was telling him that radishes picked in the rain taste twice as good as those picked on a sunny day," Colleen said. "Wasn't I, Dylan?"

"You sure were, Grandma Colleen."

Lauren gave the two a puzzled look.

I knew enough about my mother-in-law to feel secure she was planning something, so I said, "You know, I read something like that once. Say, it looks like the rain's slowing down, so why don't we get a move on before it picks up again? I can already taste those radishes."

When Lauren stood up, intending to accompany us, Colleen touched her arm. "Lauren, I need your help clearing the table."

Lauren, having learned a few things since she'd arrived in San Sebastian, obeyed.

"So why are we picking radishes?" I asked Dylan as we splashed our way to the vegetable garden.

"Because my mother won't leave me alone long enough for what I need to say. Here it is. I want to go see her parents today, and I want you with me."

Just when you think someone has no surprises left to spring on you, they pull a wet rabbit out of a hat. This brave young man who'd driven four hundred miles alone from Burbank to a strange town to meet a father and grandmother he'd never seen before, was scared.

"I'd be honored," I told him.

The Ellises weren't the open-hearted Rejases. After Dylan had made his doorstep declaration, I don't think they would have invited him in if I—the recognizable star of *Anteaters to Zebras*—hadn't been along. Lauren had painted her mother Winona as cold and controlling, and she'd been correct. Victor Ellis, Dylan's grandfather, was no warmer.

We were in for a rough ride.

After following orders to leave our umbrellas outside and wipe our feet on the mat, we walked into an icicle-white living room. White walls without pictures, white tile floor, white sofa and white occasional chairs—it was like walking into a snowstorm. It felt like it, too.

"I don't see what you want from us." Winona Ellis crossed

her arms in front of her chest, after taking a seat in one of the chairs. "We don't have any money."

"Correct," her husband agreed. "We owe you nothing. We don't owe our daughter anything, either. When she left our house eighteen years ago, that was the end of it."

Dylan seeming to have trouble speaking, I decided to warm the room up a bit. "Speaking of, Lauren's over at our house right now. The way I heard it, she didn't 'leave' your house—you forced her out."

When Winona turned those once sad, now frosty, eyes on me, I could see where Lauren had got her looks. "None of this is any of your business, Mrs. Rejas."

Since Dylan and I were sitting together on the iceberg sofa, it was easy for me to slip my arm around him. "It's Ms. Bentley-Rejas, and oh yes, it is my business. Dylan and I are family." I wanted to add, *What the hell's wrong with you people?* but I didn't.

I'd known people like this before. Having once made a mistake, they'd rather double-down than apologize, no matter how many hearts it broke, or how many dreams were destroyed. Part of me pitied them. The other part wanted to wring their stubborn necks.

Clearing his throat, Dylan said, "You being my maternal grandparents, I thought I'd just stop by and introduce myself, that being the courteous thing to do." Then he stood up, dragging me with him.

God, that kid was strong.

Still dragging me, he walked over to each grandparent, and much to their dismay, shook their hands. Then, frigid handshakes accomplished, he dragged me to the door.

Once outside, he finally let my hand go. "That went well, didn't it?"

Despite our horror, or maybe because of it, we howled with laughter all the way to my pickup.

Miracles do happen; they just don't always arrive in the guise of burning bushes. Sometimes they show up waving DNA results.

And sometimes, we don't know what to do about it.

Deciding that I didn't want to be around when Dylan told Lauren where we'd gone after dumping all those wet radishes into the kitchen sink, I decided to get the next unpleasant chore out of the way as quickly as possible. Then maybe I'd go back to the *Merilee* and spend a couple of relaxing hours with my cell phone turned off. But for now, I set off for Beverly Beaumont and Karla Dollar's apartment. My previous visit had been cut short by the entrance of Gordo Walken, bearing consolation roses.

I arrived to find their apartment as pristine as before, and the roses still alive.

"You again," Karla grumped, as Beverly invited me in.

"Yep, me again. Still hate me? There's a lot of that going around today."

"Oh, nobody hates you, Teddy," Beverly said.

After what I'd been through at the Ellis house I didn't feel up to playing any more games, so I said, "Look, I meant to talk to you guys about something before, but it was a bad time since you'd just lost your jobs and…"

"And then Gordo came in with the flowers," Beverly finished, her eyes alert. Had she already figured out why I was here?

"Correct. Well, I need to ask you some pretty personal questions, about the past and all, so, ah…"

To my surprise, she laughed. "Like about the time my name was Gertrude Scholmaster, and I screwed my way to the middle rung of the soaps?"

"Uh, something like that, yes."

Her smile didn't go away. "In case you're wondering, I had nothing against Cliff Flaherty."

"Really? That's odd, since by all accounts he was a difficult man. Yelled at you a lot, I hear. Insulted you. Brought up your past." That last was a guess, but I could see it scored.

She didn't weaken, though. "Since when is getting insulted a good reason to kill your employer?"

Karla finally spoke up, as feisty as ever. "Hell, as far as name-calling goes, I had as good a reason to kill Flaherty as Bev here did."

"Such as?"

"Every now and then he'd call me Ms. Felon in front of others. It really ragged on me."

Sympathy has no part in a murder investigation, but I felt it anyway. "That would have ragged on me, too. But..."

"But?" Karla's voice turned downright waspish. "So of course I killed him, then turned around and killed Martin Donaldson, who would never have dreamed of calling anyone names? Sure, why not? Pin the tail on the felon, right?"

Speaking of being ragged on, my sympathy vanished and I decided I'd had enough from Karla Dollar. "Oh, stop playing victim. It's getting tiresome."

Karla opened her mouth, the better to scorch my ears with a comeback, I figured, but the sound that emitted was a chuckle. "Oooh, snap! You've got quite the bitch quotient, girl!"

"That has been called to my attention on occasion." *Twenty minutes ago, for instance.*

Stunning me even further, Karla—aka Ms. Felon—reached over and patted my hand. "I'll go make you some herbal tea. You look like you could use some."

"Nothing with ginger, please."

A snort from Beverly. "You've been drinking Gordo's tea, haven't you? And here we were beginning to believe you were smart."

When Karla's tea arrived it was delicious, and yes, it calmed me down considerably. After that, we had a chat that only veered out of the comfort zone when I had to bring up Flaherty. But it started nicely enough.

Motioning to the photograph of the young black man in cap and gown, I asked Karla, "Your son?"

"Jamal, yes. Graduated from USC last year, master's in computer sciences, already working for Google."

"I'm impressed. But USC's an expensive school. It must have been a financial strain putting him through, and then paying back those student loans…" I waved my hands in a gesture of hopelessness.

Her smile had a touch of gloat in it. "Full-ride scholarship."

I smiled back; sometimes the good guys do win. "Get to see him often?"

"He works at their headquarters in Mountain View, so sure. We have dinner every Saturday. And in case you're wondering, he pays my rent…" Here she gestured at the lovely apartment, "… the food bill, and utilities. I may be jobless right now, but I won't starve. Neither will Bev. Once I told Jamal what had happened to us, he upped my allowance and told me to take my time finding work, to just find a job I enjoy as much as he enjoyed his. He also said that if I wanted to actually retire, it would be all right, too, that I earned the right to a nice life. He's even giving me a clothing and vacation allowance. Enough for two!"

Beverly, who'd been quietly sipping her tea, spoke up. "He's a fine young man. Really loves his mom."

Most boys did love their moms. Joe loved Colleen. Dylan loved Lauren. But it was a fine and rare thing when sons actually stepped up to support their jobless mothers, and in some cases, even their roommates. Which brought me to another question. "You two sure seem pretty close."

"Captain Obvious strikes again," Karla said to Bev, who laughed.

I wondered if I should ask the obvious question, then decided it didn't matter. Love is love. But as it turned out, I didn't have to ask.

While refilling my tea, Karla said, "Of course we're close. Bev was my roommate at Chino Prison. You see how tiny I am, how small-boned? I can't begin to tell you the beatings I didn't get because she always stood in the way. She's my Bestie for life, and Jamal knows it. Even if I was dumb enough to fall in love with another jerk like Flaherty, Jamal would see to it that she'd still be taken care of."

My mouth dropped open. "Wait a minute. Did I hear that right? Did you really say *'fall in love with another jerk like Flaherty'*? Do you mean to tell me that you and Flaherty were A Thing once?"

She shot me a quizzical look. "You didn't know?"

If my jaw had dropped any farther, it would have hit the pretty flower-print area rug. "You fell in love with him even though he kept calling you Ms. Felon?"

She shook her head. "Naw. I'm talking about a time before he got so awful. It was back in my LA years, just after I got out of Chino and no one wanted to hire me to do anything other than ask, 'You want fries with that?' Jamal and I were really struggling—Bev was still in Chino, by the way—when Cliff happened to show up at an audition I went to. It was for some candy bar, I forget which. Anyway, I didn't get the job, but he turned me on to another audition, where I did get the role! Along the way, he asked me out, very polite-like, and yeah, we eventually became A Thing."

Remembering, the look in her eyes softened. "I got enough jobs that I was able to enroll in that puppet school." Here, she blushed. "I had a marionette as a kid, and I always dreamed of being a puppeteer. And living with Cliff, he made me believe that I'd be a success at whatever I wanted to do. For a few months it was all wonderful, me doing what I loved, living with a guy I loved and who seemed to love me back, but then one day…" Here, her eyes turned cold. "I've never been one of those women who goes for creeps—after all, I had Jamal to look out for—so the day he slapped me for overcooking the roast, Jamal and I split."

Already knowing the date Karla was released from prison, I did a little math in my head. She'd probably met Flaherty before he fell for Lauren, when a slap had turned into a fist.

"Were you surprised when you found out he was one of the producers of *Tippy-Toe & Tinker*?"

"Not at all, since he was the person who let me know about the job in the first place."

There went my jaw again, headed for the rug.

"You're serious?"

"Serious as a heart attack. Regardless of how crazy Cliff got in the end, he never stopped helping me. Rosie the Triceratops isn't the only role he got for me over the past few years."

Good Cliff making amends for Bad Cliff.

Something else occurred to me. "Karla, has an attorney reached out to you lately?"

"You mean that fancy-dancy Marquand-Donaldson broad? Yesterday, as a matter of fact. Swanned in here out of the clear blue and handed me an envelope. And guess what? Seems I'm an heiress!"

Karla and Beverly beamed twin smiles.

On my way to Surfer's Cove to clear up a few things, I made a phone call.

Dylan didn't answer.

Karla already knew she'd inherited money from Flaherty, which meant that Dylan had probably already been apprised of his good fortune, too. So why hadn't he told me?

Or maybe, just maybe, the content of Dylan's letter hadn't been so cheery.

I pressed REDIAL.

Still no answer.

My call to Colleen went unanswered, too, so I left a message for her to call me back, then rang off.

On the off chance, I tapped in Gloria Marquand-Donaldson's phone number.

She answered.

I half expected Gordo and Bird to be at the beach—surfers surf, rain or shine—but they were both in. Recreational marijuana being legal in the state of California, they were enjoying a little R&R and were already comfortable enough to offer me a joint. Bird wasn't even wearing his blade-footed prosthesis.

"No thanks," I said, taking the chair next to him, but slightly upwind of the joint he was smoking.

"Tea?" Gordo asked lazily, his bulky body taking up most of the ugly sofa. "There's some already brewed on the stove. All you have to do is heat it up in the microwave."

I shuddered. "I'm good." Then, concerned about the very real possibility of a contact high, I decided to make my visit quick by getting straight to the point.

"The other day when I was here, I forgot to ask a couple of questions, so I thought maybe you'd..."

"Ask away, pretty lady," Bird said, after a deep inhale, followed by a slower exhale. Gordo copied him, then leaned back on the sofa with his eyes closed. I couldn't tell if he was awake or asleep.

"Where were you guys last Friday night?"

"Friday?" Bird turned to Gordo. "Dude, wasn't that the night we was over at Stoke's?"

Without opening his eyes, Gordo answered, "Nope. We were at Stoke's on Thursday. Friday's when we did our grocery shopping."

"But that was in the daytime," Bird protested. "I'm pretty certain we went to Stoke's afterward 'cause Friday nights is Ladies Night and all the babes get drinks half price, so they come streaming in..." Bird waggled his eyebrows in the same manner I'd seen his character Zip waggle his. "The pickins over there are sweeeet." He took another toke. Inhaled. Exhaled. "Hey, bro, I remember that blonde, even if you don't. You know, the one with..." Not too stoned to notice my frown, he didn't finish what he'd been about to say. "Anyways, you know. She was a total classic. Gave me her number, and I'm gonna give her a call one of these days."

"I'm telling you, Bird, that was Thursday." Eyes still shut, Gordo spoke again. "Never learn, do you?"

"Nothin' to learn. With me, it all comes easy. You're the one who struggles."

"I liked the brunette. And I think she liked me."

Considering how Gordo behaved around dark-haired, dark-skinned Karla Dollar, his preference for brunettes didn't surprise me one bit.

"Get her number, bro?"

"Next Thursday I'll give it a try."

"Friday, I'm telling you."

"Oh, for Pete's sake!" I snapped, out of patience. "Forget Friday! Where the hell were you guys on *Monday*?" Not that it mattered, because the two were so stoned, they didn't even bother to ask why I wanted to know.

Or at least they acted that way.

"Monday? Bro, don't we always rehearse on Mondays?" Bird took another toke, waited.

Gordo finally opened his eyes. "Usually. But last Monday was when Ethan was out of town, so they called off rehearsal. And by the next day we found out Donaldson got his ass killed, so no more rehearsals. Ever."

"Righteous." A deep chuckle.

I leaned forward. "Wait a minute. You're telling me that Ethan Ganey, *Tippy-Toe & Tinker*'s director, was out of town the day you guys were supposed to be rehearsing? That doesn't make any sense."

Bird threw me a bleary grin. "*Ex*-director. There's gonna be a new one now, Ethan knowing squat about toons."

Ever compassionate, Gordo said, "Give the poor guy a break. He's as upset as we are."

"Ethan'll land on his feet. Guys like him always do. When we was talking to him about that San…"

"Bird!" Gordo suddenly sounded less stoned.

"Huh?"

"Shut it."

Bird gave him a stunned look, then stoned as he was, or seemed to be, shut up.

What was I missing here?

More questioning availed me nothing. Neither of the two knew for sure where they were when either murder was being committed—or so they pretended. And stoned as Bird was, he certainly found the fortitude to say nothing more about *Tippy-Toe & Tinker's* former director or whatever *that San* thing was.

So I left them to their real or staged cannabis dreams.

It was still raining when I stepped outside of the weed-reeking trailer. Fortunately, I wasn't too stoned to realize that, yes, I most certainly did have a contact high, it having been impossible to avoid in the confined space of the cramped single-wide. The rain-blurred palms surrounding the trailer park appeared to be doing the hula in the light breeze, and the scent of seawater was strong enough to lure surfboards into the water without their human masters. The breakers, as they hit the shore, sounded like a barrage of cannon fire.

Far out, man.

Since it would be foolish to drive in my condition, I decided to walk it off. I didn't get soaked, because I still had my umbrella in the pickup, so I snatched it off the floor of the passenger's side and strolled two soggy blocks to the beach, where I stood for the next ten minutes, sipping Cokes from the refreshments kiosk, and watching the surfers ride the waves.

Rain or shine, surfers didn't care.

Water was water.

Here's the lovely thing about the ocean. You can be half out of your mind with confusion or anxiety, with anger or with grief, but when those big waves come breaking in, you recognize how microscopic you are and how little your personal world actually matters in the great scheme of things.

In a way, it's freeing.

So much so that—how did the old Bible verse go? *Once I saw through a glass darkly, but one day I knew.*

As the stiff ocean breeze blew away the fog of cannabis, my own dark glass began to clear.

Chapter Twenty

Brain working again, I splashed back to my truck and headed for Gunn Landing Harbor, where I found Nestor Vanderman's *Starvin' Marvin* bobbing sedately in her mooring on Dock 8.

Rapping against the window, I called, "Permission to come aboard!"

The writer stuck his nose out of the cabin, "Granted, Red. Now get the hell in here out of the rain."

Vanderman had been packing, and the boat's cabin was filled with cardboard boxes already taped closed. Two cartons were separated from the rest, not packed as neatly. He pushed one of them from the galley bench so I could sit down. As I shook myself dry, I said, "You're moving."

"Yep, due in LA Harbor next week."

"But not with *Starvin' Marvin*, right?"

"How right you are. Yesterday I closed the deal on *Huzzah!*, that 41 Morgan ketch I was telling you about. Wanna come along? We could have some good times."

"You and I probably have different definitions of 'good times,' so I think not."

He pasted a tragic expression on his handsome face. "Aw, Red, you don't know what you're missing."

"I'll live. What's going to happen to *Starvin' Marvin* now? You just going to junk her?" The boat wasn't much, but all boats have souls, and I hated to see another boat cast aside like the *Sea Sprite*.

"Some cop bought it."

How like Vanderman, to refer to his boat as an *it*. "Which cop?"

"Oh, that's right, you know most of them, don't you? Hubby being the sheriff and all. Some deputy named Emilio Gutierrez said it'd make a nice handyman project."

At that, my cranky mood lifted. Joe's chief deputy and his young family would make a nice addition to harbor life, and I did like the idea of *Starvin' Marvin* becoming all she deserved to be.

"Ah, I see that pleases you. But tell me, why are you here? Since you don't really like me much, I know you didn't drop by to chat."

I'll say this for the man, he did understand people, and that was probably what made him such a good writer. "Okay. Who do you think killed Flaherty and Donaldson?"

Despite his put-upon air of nonchalance, Vanderman looked startled.

"Jesus, you don't mess around, do you, Red?"

"As you so correctly surmised, I'm not here for the pleasure of your company."

He scratched at his scruffy beard. "Hmm. Who killed Flaherty and Donaldson? Sounds like a board game, doesn't it? But I'll bite. My guess? Gordo Walken. Anybody that nice has to be hiding something."

"Sounds reasonable to me. What do you think he's hiding?"

"Something that didn't show up on whatever search engine you've been using, probably. Hit-and-run, killed a kid, never got caught—something on that level. Or…" He drummed his fingers on the galley table. "Gordo Walken is a serial killer, slyly working his way through the kiddie show network with the avowed life goal of killing every single kiddie show producer. And they do deserve to be killed, Red. They are slime."

As I had hoped, his answer revealed more about him than he realized. "No thoughts about Bird?"

That made him laugh. "Bird? He couldn't find his own ass without a map, and then he couldn't read the map. You ought to watch him trying to memorize a script. Painful. Ask me, he didn't just lose a leg to that shark, he lost half his brain cells, too."

I stood up. "Thanks for all your help."

"Leaving so soon?" He actually seemed disappointed.

"Oh, you know, places to go, other killers to see."

I left him with his mouth open.

Walt was in, too, but he wasn't alone on the *Running Wild*. Annette was in the cabin with him, along with Terri, her little girl. They were both bundled up in blankets, watching a rerun of *Tippy-Toe & Tinker*, the one where the dinosaurs got into an argument about allowing Poonya, the red panda, to move into their neighborhood. Apparently, Annette had decided that with Flaherty's death, the harbor was now safe to visit again.

Thirty minutes later I arrived home to find a burgundy-and-silver 1956 Rolls-Royce Silver Cloud sitting in my parking spot, its uniformed chauffeur dozing behind the wheel. I almost kept going, but realizing that I'd be tracked down to wherever I ran off, I parked on the street and slumped into the house.

The gang was all there, except for Joe, who was still at work, of course. Colleen looked bemused by our visitor; Lauren, jealous at having to share the limelight; Dylan looked suspicious; and Tonio and Bridey were clearly excited to be in the company of such splendor. As for me, I straightened my spine and told my biggest lie of the day.

"Nice to see you again, Aster Edwina," I said to my boss.

The old harridan threw me a wolfish smile. "And lovely to see you, too, Teddy. I just dropped by for a nice little visit."

Knowing full well that the eighty-something Aster Edwina never "just dropped by" on anyone, I prepared myself for the worst.

Which arrived quickly, disguised in sheep's clothing.

"The zoo is so quiet without you."

"Uh huh."

"Dull, too." Sharp canines gleamed.

"Uh huh."

"So it's time you returned."

"Uh huh."

"Teddy, why don't you sit down?" Colleen said. "You're making us all nervous, hovering like that."

Because I want to be ready to flee if necessary. "I've been sitting all day, and it's nice to be standing for once."

"I was thinking Saturday," Aster Edwina said.

"What!?"

"How's your eye?" Her voice fairly dripped with insincerity.

"My eye's fine, and Saturday's out." There were things I needed to do, such as find a way to convince Joe who had killed Flaherty and Donaldson, and God only knew how long that would take.

"Saturday's *in!*"

"No, it's not." I started for the bedroom to change into dry clothes.

"The governor's going to be at the zoo on Saturday and she wants to meet Poonya."

I turned around, wanting her to see the fury on my face. "Good. Then let whoever's been covering for me do the honors."

Aster Edwina's eyes narrowed, but not before a glimmer of her dark, dark soul leaked out. "Poonya behaves better with you. So if you want a job to come back to, you'll be at the zoo at 6:00 sharp Saturday morning." Having issued her royal decree, the Empress of the Gunn Zoo rose and left the house without saying goodbye to us peasants.

"Shit," I said.

"Language." Colleen, of course.

Because there were children in the room.

After changing into dry clothes, I called Dr. Leonard "Lenny" Huffgraf, and was gratified to reach him at home. This meant he was able to answer my questions more leisurely. Yes, being bitten by a shark could cause brain damage, my step-brother explained, because when the shark pulled you under, there was a good chance you'd breathe in enough seawater to make you flatline. More than one flatline, you'd probably experience recurring headaches. As for phantom limb pain, the syndrome had originally been treated by the liberal use of opioids, but because of attendant addiction problems, 'scripts written for opioids were becoming rare. Tylenol was now the treatment of choice.

"Not Excedrin?" I asked.

"Too much caffeine," Lenny said. "If someone already has behavior problems…" He made a whistling sound.

"Oh, c'mon, Lenny. You live on caffeine."

"I don't have behavior problems."

"Then you've changed a lot since our parents were married."

"That was a long time ago. I now make Eagle Scouts look wicked."

We teased each other some more, just like in the old days, and finally hung up, promising to get together soon.

Now it was time for a less pleasant conversation.

While I'd been changing, everyone had moved over to the granny cottage, which is where I caught up to Dylan.

"Let's go outside and talk."

"In the rain?" he said, surprised.

"It's stopped. You should see the rainbow."

Glumly, he followed me outside. I had a hunch he suspected what I was going to say. Since the radishes had proven helpful for our earlier conversation, I stopped where some stragglers remained.

Looking Dylan straight in the eye, I said, "When did you find out about the money Flaherty left you?"

His face went ashen. "I don't know what you're talking about."

"Don't lie to a liar, kid."

It took him a few seconds to get his courage up, but when he did, he responded, "You knew?"

"You weren't the only person he felt it necessary to make amends to."

He shuffled his feet in the garden patch mud, pretty much ruining his Nikes. "He should have left it to my mother. She's the one he hurt, not me."

"He knew your mom was already well taken care of, but you were just starting out. And he probably felt guilty about you having to witness your mom getting beat up. But you didn't answer the question. When did you find out?"

"Several days ago. I got a manila envelope in the mail, registered letter, but when I saw it had an attorney's return address on it, I threw it in the trash."

"You did *what*?"

By now his face was no longer ashen—it flamed with embarrassment. "Then the next day I got to thinking, what if it was good news instead of bad—which attorney's letters usually are, I've learned—so curiosity got the better of me, and I fished it out of the garbage. Anyway, I opened the thing and read it, and I guess I'm kinda rich because *Tippy-Toe & Tinker* is part of Flaherty's estate now, and it being nationally syndicated and all…" He shrugged his shoulders.

"Well, you're not the Aster Edwina kind of rich, and there's one other heir you'll be splitting the proceeds with, but I don't think you have to worry about starvation, not as long as you manage your money well. I am curious, though. Did the envelope also contain a personal letter?"

"Yeah. It was filled with all kinds of apologies. Made me feel really bad about all the nasty things I'd thought about him all those years, because I hadn't known he was sick."

"I don't think he knew it, either, when he hit your mother."

"Yeah. I mean, no, he probably didn't. Sad, isn't it? What can happen to a person?"

Yes, it was.

After dinner, Dylan came clean about his newfound wealth to everyone, and we all trooped off to McSorley's Ice Cream Parlor to celebrate.

An hour later, sweet teeth sated, we returned home and engaged in several rounds of *Monopoly*.

Colleen won them all.

As for me, while Colleen was bankrupting the rest of the family, I paid a final visit to PlatoSchmato. The search wasn't easy, names and faces changing over the years, but I finally found the link I was looking for.

And yes, I'd been right all along.

At bedtime, Joe and I settled ourselves in front of the master bedroom's television set to watch the late evening news. Sandwiched between the usual updates about purse-snatchings and thefts from parked cars, came the announcement that the cast, crew, and sponsors of *Tippy-Toe & Tinker*, as a parting gift to their loyal watchers, would be presenting a free Farewell Show on Saturday evening. It would take place in the auditorium of San Sebastian Community College, and everyone was invited.

"We need to see that," Joe said. "All of us. Between my hours and yours, we don't spend enough family time together. But afterward, let's do what you suggested. Mom can take the kids home, while you and I head for the *Merilee*. Then it'll be just you and me, on that slow-rocking boat."

"Yes, yes, yes, a thousand times yes!" I cuddled closer. "But first..."

He really liked what I did then.

Chapter Twenty-One

Director Ethan Ganey lived in a less-impressive part of town than I'd expected, but then again, his career had pretty much tanked after the *Zombie Lust* series. I guess that's what happens when directors get typecast.

The building, a four-story faux Spanish hacienda, wasn't too bad. Whoever owned it had patched the cracks left by last month's earthquake, and the narrow strip of lawn in front had been recently mowed. However, no one had bothered to pick up the advertising circulars and plastic Circle K bags that littered the entrance. Muttering "Keep California beautiful," I grabbed one of the bags and stuffed the others into it, along with the advertising circulars. I was about to take my haul over to the dumpster when the apartment door opened and Ganey emerged.

"What the hell are you doing?" he asked. "That's the super's job."

His wet hair testified that he'd just stepped out of the shower, and the neatness of his clothes proved that he either had a live-in girlfriend or knew how to iron.

"Looks like the super didn't come to work today."

He snatched the bag from me, rustled through it, then—apparently not finding what he was looking for—tossed it back onto the ground.

Whereupon I picked it up and delivered it to the dumpster. There. A little less mess in the world.

"Oh, wait. I know you, don't I? You look familiar." Ganey had followed me, and was standing so close I could smell his after-shave. Something expensive, which, given his low-rent domicile, surprised me.

"You've probably seen me on TV," I said, meaning on the *Anteaters to Zebras* show, but judging from where his eyes traveled, that wasn't where he recognized me from. "Yes, yes, I'm the naked zookeeper, but I'm also the sheriff's wife, and I've got some questions I'd like to ask you."

He raised his eyebrows, but his eyes stayed put. "Surely you jest."

"I'm not against a joke here and there, but not about murder." Melodramatic, sure, but at least his eyes moved from my chest to my face.

His mouth twitched. "I've directed enough cop shows to know your qualifications are zilch."

"True, but in this case, irrelevant. Several members of the *Tippy-Toe* cast already told me you missed a rehearsal the day Flaherty was killed. I found that to be quite interesting, since the show was scheduled to run the next day. It didn't, though."

"Of course it didn't. Cliff having just been found dead, running the show would have been in bad taste."

"You're all about taste, are you?" I smiled, to take the edge off my question.

That soothed him somewhat. "Well, there are limits, even in show business. Look, I know what you're after here, and I still say you've got no business poking your nose into an offi-cial police investigation—especially into the murder of a man nobody cared for and nobody misses—but if you're so deter-mined to know where I went that day, what the hell. I was in So Cal. A little bird had told me what was about to happen with *Tippy-Toe*, so I was down there trying to put something together for myself and a couple of the cast members."

"Which ones?"

"Bird and Gonzo. But not their marionettes, for legal reasons. Just voice-overs for some anime piece of shit."

Poor marionettes. Left out in the cold again. "And?"

"The suits haven't made up their minds yet. Zombies are out, werewolves back in, but I did make a werewolf picture back in the nineties, so hey, we've at least got a chance."

"Who was the little bird?"

"I don't kiss and tell."

Interesting answer, especially since I hadn't asked him about his sex life. Nor was I going to, because I had bigger fish to fry. "Then maybe you can answer this. A little bird told me—probably not the same bird you're involved with—that Cliff Flaherty once brought a civil action suit against you. What's your side of the story?"

Instead of denying it, he laughed. "Talk about the pot calling the kettle black. Yeah, Flaherty sued me, but he didn't get zip, because there was nothing to get. For every film that actually gets made in Hollywood, a couple hundred of them die in Legal. Besides, I didn't take anything that wasn't legally mine—salary for time spent. Now, Red, not that this hasn't been fun and all, but I'm expected someplace. So *hasta la vista*, baby."

He raised his hand, and for a moment it looked like he was about to slap me on the butt, but after catching sight of my expression, he lowered his hand and hurried down the street.

Interview Number One down, I took off for Interview Number Two, not that I expected much, but you never can tell, can you? I finally caught up with Jocelyn Ravel at Pinball Wizardess, her home away from home. It being this early in the day, half the machines stood silent, making the din almost bearable. Jocelyn was cozied up to a machine titled *Alien Babes*, and when she caught sight of me, she bumped the machine so hard the *TILT* buzzer sounded.

"Dammit!" she spat. "What the hell are you doing here?"

Since it was only 10:00, and this made the second time I'd already been asked that question, I figured I must be doing something right. Cheered by the insight, I said, "Jocelyn, did you know that Ethan Ganey's been pitching some cartoon about werewolves, and that it involves Bird and Gonzo?"

"So? No way that's gonna happen. Not with those two losers on board." She scowled at the tilted *Alien Babes* as if the machine had personally insulted her.

"When did you find out and who told you?"

The scowl traveled to me. "None of your business."

"Big secret, is it?"

"No. I just don't feel like talking to you."

Three black-clad teens, young enough they should have been in school, took over the machines in the row behind us. The din in Pinball Wizardess increased.

"Was it Bird?" I yelled, above the noise. Given the man's brain damage, he probably had trouble keeping secrets unless his roommate was there to shut him up.

"Bird?" Her laugh had a cruel edge. "That retard doesn't even know what day it is, let alone what's going down in Hollywood with toons."

Somehow, I managed not to slap her. "Gordo, maybe?" I yelled again.

She rolled her eyes. "As if."

No one in the cast, then, which made sense. When I'd run into them at the zoo the other day, they'd all seemed like one big happy family. Several more teens came in, firing up more pinball machines. Where were the hooky police when you needed them?

"Did you ever run into someone connected with the *Zombie Lust* movies?" I yelled louder.

At that, Jocelyn reached behind her and pressed *Alien Babes'* PLAY button. It lit up again, dinging and clanging and screeching out some god-awful tune.

"Go away, Teddy," I lip-read. "Can't you see I'm busy?"

Chapter Twenty-Two

It was a relief to be back at work. Even the razzing I received in the employees' break room as I helped myself to a cup of coffee felt good.

"Durango's been asking about you," Robin Chase, big cats, said. "He wants to take you out to dinner."

"*For* dinner," corrected Jack Spence, bears.

I drank my coffee slowly, letting them tease me all they wanted; in fact, it felt good. I was one of the gang again, back where I belonged. This time, fully clothed.

Some people dislike doing the same old thing day after day, but for me, it's Heaven. Heaven to stop by the cafeteria to get my charges' food. Heaven to see their excited faces when I showed up with their worms, monkey chow, or whatever. Heaven, even, to rake up their feces. A couple of times my llama friend Alejandro almost knocked me down in his desire to nuzzle me, but he eventually settled down enough for me to clean his Friendly Farm enclosure. Then he followed me happily as I raked the enclosure clean, stopping every now and then to pet an animal that needed petting.

The day couldn't have been finer. Last week's storm had cleared away the pollutants in the air, and the sun had driven back the fog that had earlier crept through the eucalyptus trees. Birds sang, wolves howled, lions roared.

I was so happy I felt like singing, but taking pity on the animals' delicate ears, I didn't. I am not Maria Callas.

When I showed up at the red panda's enclosure, Poonya acted just as thrilled to see me as Alejandro had been. But maybe it was because of the armful of fresh bamboo shoots I carried.

"Yummies for my honey," I announced, as the little red panda scampered down from her tree.

Tweet, tweet! She hopped up and down, twitching her fluffy tail back and forth.

"Missed me, didn't you?"

Tweet, chortle, tweet!

"I missed you, too."

After circling my legs several times to make certain I stayed put, she sat back politely and watched as I arranged her bamboo shoots in her manger.

"This one looks juicy," I said, holding up an especially fat one for her to inspect.

She crept forward, and with a tiny paw, removed the bamboo from my hand. Sniffed it. Stripped it. Munched it. Twitched her little black nose in satisfaction.

I let her forage among the stalks for a few minutes, then produced her reward for being so non-skittish: a large ripe grape.

Tweet, huff, tweet! Her entire body trembled with anticipation.

"Chosen especially for you, Poonya." I held the grape in the palm of my hand, whereupon to my delight, she clambered into my lap and nuzzled the grape into her mouth.

Squish, squish.

Smack, smack, as she licked the grape's juice off her snout.

A grape-eating red panda is a happy red panda.

Tweet, chortle, tweet!

When I produced another grape, she tweet-chortled again,

then settled herself down on my lap, allowing me to stroke her while I hand-fed her the others.

The rest of the day proceeded as happy as usual, with me feeding, raking, and hauling until my back ached. My weeks' long time-out had softened my muscles, and I was paying the price. No matter. I was back to doing what I loved to do.

At break time, I was the first into the staff room, which gave me a few minutes to triple-check the notes I'd made yesterday and now carried in my cargo pants' pocket. If I was right, no one else was going to be murdered. And actually, if Flaherty and Donaldson had played it straight with the staff of *Tippy-Toe & Tinker*, they might not have been murdered, either. But done was done, and now someone had to pay the price.

I was just about to call Joe when a voice behind me said, "What you doing there, Teddy? Writing a book?"

Robin Chase, big cats.

I covered my notes and smiled up at her. She hadn't minded that I'd added a couple of rips to her spare uniform, or that my attempts to mend them were so amateurish. "Nah, I leave the book writing to my mother-in-law."

She poured herself a cup of coffee, then sat down next to me. "How's that going? Her book writing, I mean? *Murder at the Zoo* was soooo good!"

Robin was a longtime mystery aficionado, and was an expert on the genre and its subgenres. And while I wouldn't divulge plot details to anyone, Colleen had given me permission to talk generalities. Such as the number of corpses per book.

"She told me she killed someone else the other day, which brings the current body count to three, I think."

Robin frowned. "Three murders? For a cozy? Isn't that a lot?"

"She said the third one is off-scene, whatever that means."

"No blood, probably," she nodded wisely.

"And she didn't plan that one. It just happened."

"Unplanned murders are the best kind. It means you're so deep into your characters that they begin acting on their own."

Just like real people.

I stuffed my notes back into my pocket, and continued discussing fictional killers with Robin until the other zookeepers filed in and demanded to know how it felt to have a whole week off. Most of them felt like me. A week away from our animals was Hell, unless that week was spent on an African photo safari or a South American birding expedition.

The Honorable Margo Allan Rossiter, governor of the great state of California, didn't arrive at the zoo until three in the afternoon, two hours after she'd originally been scheduled. Dressed in a shell-pink suit with black Chanel trimming, she was trailed by a herd of wealthy supporters, political staffers, reporters, camera and sound people, and the Gunn Zoo's official welcoming committee, which included a gaggle of moneyed contributors, the zoo's director—a harried-looking Zorah Vega—and Aster Edwina, her implacable royal self.

I'd warned Zorah that a big crowd would make Poonya nervous, but she had thrown up her hands in a show of helplessness. "Tell that to Aster Edwina. Maybe she'll listen to you."

To quote the ever-cynical Jocelyn, "As if."

Now here everyone was, crowded around the red panda enclosure.

First off—just so you know—I didn't vote for Rossiter. The fact that she'd been the only female on the ticket meant nothing to me, and her constant harping on the important role stay-at-home moms played in the American social structure reeked of insincerity. Telling me water is wet and the sun is sunny has never swayed me in the voting booth. Life, not to mention a few murder investigations, had taught me to ignore what people *say*, and to pay close attention to what they actually *do*.

Upon the governor's noisy arrival, an alarmed Poonya assumed her *Eeek!* position, standing straight up, furry arms in the air to make herself look as big and dangerous as possible.

"Oh, isn't she just the cutest little thing!" Fine words for a governor who had three times vetoed legislative bills that would have increased funding for wildlife sanctuaries, and had twice vetoed bills guaranteeing jail time for animal abusers.

"All these people are making her nervous," I growled.

It was as if I hadn't spoken.

"So adorable!"

I clenched my teeth. "Maybe if you could step away from…"

"Teddy, let the governor into that enclosure right now," Aster Edwina snapped. "I promised her she could meet Poonya up close and personal."

Zora stepped forward. "I don't think that's a good…" she began, only to be shushed by Aster Edwina.

"Let her in, Teddy!"

Grinding my teeth, I unlocked the staff entrance to the red panda enclosure. Poor Poonya. After all my work calming her down, this would set her back considerably.

Not that Rossiter cared about any of that. She just loved the sound of cameras clicking.

As talking heads extolled Rossiter's "courage," I let the politician into Poonya's enclosure.

Huff, huff, huff!

It wasn't a happy sound. Even a fool would notice. But not Rossiter.

Or Aster Edwina. "Now show the governor how Poonya sits in your lap and lets you pet her."

Feeling like a Judas, I settled onto the dirt. Believing she'd found a sanctuary in the midst of the human swarm,

Poonya jumped into my lap and buried her head underneath my arm.

"It'll be over soon," I whispered, gently hugging her.

Then, too swiftly for me to stop her, Rossiter bent down, snatched Poonya out of my protective arms, and held the terrified panda against her chest.

Huff! Huff! Eeek!!! Poonya wailed.

A flurry of camera clicks, a yelping of reporters.

And Poonya's bowels spoke to the occasion, sending a long dribble of diarrhea down the governor's snazzy pink suit.

I smiled. Zorah smiled.

And somewhere, a sloth was smiling, too.

Chapter Twenty-Three

Poonya, bless her heart, leapt away from the governor and landed in my arms, upon which I whisked her away to her night house and told her what a good girl she was. Then I went back outside to face the music.

Which was considerable.

The governor was gagging, talking heads were yapping, and Aster Edwina was trying to explain away the obvious as nearby zookeepers did their best to hide their snickers.

But after all the apologies and the governor had been dressed in my spare uniform (she was closer in size to me than to Robin Chase), everyone settled down. Aster Edwina, to give the old bat credit, didn't blame Poonya for the disaster, just the too-enthusiastic crowd. As we watched the media chase after the reclothed governor on her way out of the zoo, Aster Edwina simply said to me, "Prepare a press release tendering the Gunn Zoo's formal apologies."

"Will do." This was one press release I'd enjoy writing.

The rest of the day passed quickly, and it was only when I was clocking out that I remembered the final performance of the *Tippy-Toe & Tinker* show was scheduled for this evening. If I didn't hurry, I'd miss driving to the community college with the rest of the gang.

Unfortunately, that's what happened. The beautiful day had turned into a beautiful, star-spangled evening, but by the time I arrived at the house, Lauren's Lexus was gone along with Colleen's red Mustang, and Joe's cruiser was nowhere in sight. The house was silent except for a couple of yipping dogs and a feed-me-or-I-die-right-now cat, but Joe had left me a note on the dining room table. After reading my way through all Xs and Os, I read…

LOVED THE GOVERNOR THING, THREE CHEERS FOR POONYA. SEE YOU AT THE AUDITORIUM—WE'RE SAVING A SEAT FOR YOU. THEN ON TO THE MERILEE FOR A NIGHT OF ROMANCE!
P.S. THE ANIMALS HAVE ALL BEEN FED. DON'T BELIEVE THEIR LIES.

More Xs and Os.

Heart going pitty-pat, I took a three-minute shower, sprayed myself down with Chanel No. 5, and changed into a tight black tee-shirt over the super-tight black jeans Joe had dubbed my Seduction Jeans.

Then I grabbed my keys and headed for the door.

It was a good thing the performance of *Tippy-Toe & Tinker* was taking place at the college instead of the library, because even the school's auditorium was barely big enough to hold the crowd. The off-white walls were bare, and the stage was decorated only by a beige curtain, already pulled to the side. Despite the auditorium's starkness, what looked like the entire town of San Sebastian had turned out to say goodbye to its very own hit TV program. In order to accommodate the late arrivals, some forward-thinking person had rigged up a large video screen behind the small Dino Dell stage so that those sitting in the back rows wouldn't miss any of the action. After all, Tippy-Toe, the largest of the marionettes, stood less than two feet high.

While I was clambering over several people to join my family, I scanned the audience, noticing Gloria Marquand-Donaldson sitting several rows behind us. Next to her was Ethan Ganey, *Tippy-Toe & Tinker's* director. Or, rather, *former* director. Behind them sat Jocelyn Ravel, taking some time away from the machines at Pinball Wizardess. At first, her presence surprised me because I'd heard her Poonya character wouldn't be included in tonight's farewell performance. But remembering Jocelyn's nasty temperament, I decided she probably didn't want to miss the chance to gloat over her former castmates' bad fortune.

Nestor Vanderman, the show's writer, was nowhere in evidence, but I figured he was probably backstage, taking care of last-minute rewrites. As I scooted past an elderly couple, I waved hello to several friends. On the right side of the auditorium sat several harbor liveaboarders, among them Walt MacAdams, with his girlfriend, Annette, and her daughter, Terri. They waved at me with enthusiasm, obviously delighted to be here together. I also spotted Jerome Lukasik, the janitor at the building housing the old *Tippy-Toe & Tinker* offices. When I saw the notebook and pen in his hands, I realized he'd come prepared to do what all smart aspiring writers do—take notes.

"You ready for our big night, and I'm not talking dinosaurs?" Joe whispered, nuzzling me on the neck when I slid into the saved seat next to him.

That's when I was reminded that my Seduction Jeans would ensure an uncomfortable evening. To help loosen the super-tight fit, I'd already left my wallet and phone under the seat of my pickup, but even with only keys taking up space in one of the pockets, the jeans still felt like they were cutting off the circulation to my extremities. Oh, what we women don't go through to look good.

I nuzzled Joe back. "Couldn't be readier. Just you and me and the *Merilee.*"

"Sounds like a hit song."

We nuzzled each other some more until Colleen, who was sitting between me and Lauren and the kids, hissed. "Get a room, you two."

"We are," her son replied. "As soon as this is over."

She nodded approvingly, then leaned toward me, and in a low voice, updated me on the latest family drama. It seemed that just before leaving the house, Dylan had announced that, with Joe's and his grandmother's permission, he planned to stay on in San Sebastian for at least another week. He wanted to learn more about his new family—which, he warned—included his maternal grandparents.

"Lauren's in a mood," Colleen added, her voice still low, "so you might want to give her a wide berth for a while."

Since that was what I'd been doing anyway, I promised to oblige.

But Lauren, who had been talking to Dylan, suddenly turned around and grumped, "I'm surprised so many people have turned up to see some old puppet show."

Immediately forgetting my just-delivered promise, I leaned around Colleen and hissed, "San Sebastian has always been supportive of the arts." I was miffed at Lauren's casual dismissal of the marionettes, since as far as I knew, she'd never seen an episode of *Tippy-Toe & Tinker.* Who was she to judge what was art and what was not?

At my comment, Lauren turned those Valkyrie eyes toward me. "Oh, for Heaven's sake, Teddy. You consider puppet shows 'art'?"

"Why don't you just wait and see?" I snapped.

Joe, always on alert, heard that. "Aw, Teddy, ease up on her, okay? That poor woman's gone through hell these past few days."

While it was difficult for me to see that blinding beauty as "that poor woman," I decided to give it a try because, in a way, Joe was right. Lauren's past had been difficult, and until she made peace with it—just as I had to make peace with the fact that my husband had once impregnated another woman—her heart would remain wounded. Hearts don't always repair themselves; sometimes action must be taken.

Sighing, I leaned back against my seat, and only then noticed Joe's fingers drumming against the armrest.

"I should have taken an aisle seat," he said. "If anything comes up, I'll have to disrupt the whole row getting out."

That was the problem with people in law enforcement. They could never let go of their protect-and-serve attitude, not even during their off-hours.

"No need to be such a worrywart," I reassured Joe. "Lately, everybody's been driving fine on the One, and even those car ninjas over on the west side have been taking a break. They haven't struck in, what, almost a week?"

This didn't work on Mr. Law and Order. His fingers kept drumming away until the lights dimmed. Only then did he stop.

When a recording of "The Teddy Bears' Picnic" began to play, a spotlight lit up the Dino Dell stage and the big monitor behind it came to life. Then the smaller curtain on the Dino Dell stage opened, revealing Tippy-Toe standing next to a pile of suitcases. As on the television show, the puppeteers were already concealed by a backdrop painted to look like a primeval forest.

"This is a happy-sad day," Tippy-Toe/Gordo Walken said, the marionette nodding its bulky head toward the audience. "We're moving to a beautiful new garden with lots more space and lovely flowers to sniff and eat, and we're happy about that. But we're awfully sad to be leaving our friends."

From somewhere down in front, a young child cried, "Please don't go, Tippy!"

The T. rex's small hand brushed away an imaginary tear,

which was the cue for Bev Beaumont, in her persona as the zoo-uniformed Tinker, to enter from offstage.

"Life is full of changes," Tinker said to the weeping dinosaur. "We have to go with the flow or get left behind. But it's all good, because new experiences help us grow."

Then two other inhabitants of Dino Dell came on stage: Karla Dollar's Rosie the Triceratops and Ansel "Bird" Yates's Zip the Stegosaurus. The only puppet missing—besides Jocelyn's Poonya—was Randy the Brachiosaurus, but I was certain Bird would trot him in later, when the small stage was less crowded.

For the next few minutes, the dinosaurs discussed their new home, singing and dancing their way through a medley of cheery, up-tempo children's songs. Then there was a brief intermission, which ended with the small Dino Dell curtain rising on Act Two. Randy Brachiosaurus had joined the group, explaining that Zip Stegosaurus had finally gotten around to packing his suitcase.

"Zip always leaves things to the last minute," Randy complained. "I've been packed for two days."

"That's because you're organized," Tinker said approvingly. "Now you need to learn patience. You can't expect everyone to be just like yourself."

Following this pronouncement, the group sang a song about accepting others, even when they were different. The rest of the play continued on its standard trajectory, a contemporary update of Aesop's stories combined with medieval morality plays. I heard Lauren, still not impressed, murmur to Dylan, "This is just a remake of that old Barney show you used to watch."

Except it wasn't. The beautifully designed marionettes added a mystical element that to my mind the purple-suited Barney had never achieved, making the interplay between the puppets seem more magical, yet at the same time, more realistic. The whole production—the brightly colored characters, the lush jungle backdrop, the sweet-tempered script—transported the audience to an imaginary time when differences with others were settled without harsh words or gunfire.

Five minutes into the second act, and in the middle of a song titled "Moving Day Is a Great Day," I felt Joe's phone vibrate. (Yes, he was sitting that close to me.) After a quick look at the screen, he leaned over and whispered, "Gotta go. They just caught the car ninjas." Excusing himself, he wedged his way past the elderly couple and their grandkids, and vanished up the aisle.

There went our romantic night on the *Merilee*.

But maybe not. Chief Deputy Emilio Gutierrez could help with the paperwork, so all didn't have to be lost. And having driven myself to the college in my truck, I wasn't stuck for a ride. Maybe…

In the midst of my plotting and planning, the dinosaurs romped on, singing songs and shedding tears as they said their last goodbyes. It was so affecting that even Lauren's frosty manner thawed. When the curtain finally came down to the tune of "Goodbye Old Friends, Hello New Friends," even she was crying.

"Got something in my eye," she muttered, as we waited for the rows behind us to make it up the aisle.

"Me, too," I agreed.

"Me, three," Dylan said.

"Crybabies," Colleen, handing out tissues, keeping a few to mop up her own damp cheeks.

The children, however, had interpreted the farewell performance differently.

"I can't wait to see Tippy's new home!" Bridey said. "I'll bet it's great!"

Tonio, old enough to know the difference between a toon and a human-controlled marionette, wasn't as thrilled. He'd be losing his beloved Jocelyn, and that was all he cared about.

The audience being large, it took a while for us to make it

up the aisle, and then to the lobby, where we got separated, with Colleen and the kids far ahead of me. At one point, I found myself briefly shuttled between Ethan Ganey and Gloria Marquand-Donaldson.

"Terrific show," I said to Ganey. "You must be so proud."

He scowled. "Bev blew her lines in the first act." Like many handsome men—PlatoSchmato had said he'd begun his show biz career as a male model—Ganey didn't feel the need to soften his criticism.

"I thought she was great." I felt stung on Bev's behalf, having found no blips at all in her acting.

Haughty mahogany eyes looked down on me from a trim, six-foot-plus height. "You're just a zookeeper, so what do you know?"

My mouth fell open.

Behind me, someone giggled. I turned around to see Jocelyn. "Oops," she squeaked in her cartoon voice. "That just slipped out."

"Hmph," was all I could manage.

With a satisfied smirk, Jocelyn then bullied her way through the crowd, leaving Gloria and Ganey to continue their rumble.

"Ethan!" Gloria hissed. "What the hell's wrong with you?" To my surprise, the widow I'd previously thought was a cold fish turned to me and said, "I'm sorry, Teddy. What he said to you was completely uncalled for."

"Don't you apologize for me, Gloria!" the director shouted, causing some of the exiting crowd to stare at us. "You know damn well what's 'wrong' with me. I should have had that directing job, not that Miyazaki jerk!"

"Shhhh!"

"Don't *shush* me, either! You know what? I'm sick of your nag, nag, nag. Find yourself another ride, if anyone is dumb enough to have you, but as for me, I'm outta here." With that, he pushed himself through the crowd and stormed out the door, leaving Gloria looking stunned, and Jocelyn still giggling.

I finally found my voice. "I've got plenty of room in my truck, Ms. Marquand-Donaldson, and I'd be happy to drive you home."

Teary-eyed, but not from the play, she nodded. "Thank you, Teddy, I appreciate that. And remember, it's Gloria."

Outside, the night had turned even more beautiful, and a soft breeze up from the Pacific fluttered the palms lining the streets. As I drove through this balmy Eden toward the condo Gloria had shared with her murdered husband, I itched with curiosity. If what I had just witnessed hadn't been a lover's spat, my name wasn't Teddy Bentley-Rejas. Good manners kept me from asking her about it until she stopped crying.

As it turned out, I didn't have to ask. When we finally turned on to the road that led to Whispering Willows, she said, "I'll bet you're dying to know what was behind that emotional outburst."

A brief glance proved her eyes were dry. "If there's something you want to tell me..." For delicacy's sake, I let it hang there.

"Marty and I had an arrangement."

"Arrangement?" I asked.

"When you're away from your husband most of the week, every week, you get lonely."

"Ah."

"He didn't mind. Anyway, every Wednesday Ethan would drive up to San Jose and spend the night."

"I see." I wanted to ask why her husband couldn't do the same thing, but there was no point in interrupting.

"Martin had his own arrangement."

What? *What*? "Um, may I ask who...?"

"Jocelyn Ravel. That squeaky-voiced bitch who plays Poonya."

That was one bit of information I hadn't accounted for; did it really matter? The gateway to Whispering Willows lay just ahead, so when I stopped for the guard to make a note of the truck's license number, I was able to give Gloria my full atten-tion. "So you were having an arrangement with Ethan while your husband was having an arrangement with Jocelyn."

"Don't look so shocked, Teddy. Everyone's doing it."

I didn't have time to respond before the guard waved us through.

It being a night filled with shocks, I probably shouldn't have been surprised when on the way back to the house, my cell—which thanks to my Seduction Jeans' tightness, I'd had to leave under the truck's seat—blasted forth with "I'm Too Sexy for My Shirt," Joe's ringtone. I pulled over to the curb, loosened the safety belt, and managed to grab my cell just before the call went to voice mail.

"You sound out of breath," Joe said.

"Long story."

"Good news. I'm already done here. The car ninjas—all teens, the thieving little shits—have been booked and put in a holding cell until their parents arrive. Emilio's handling the paperwork, so we're still on for tonight."

"Just you and me and the *Merilee*!" I bleated, tingling all the way down to my toes.

Joe began singing the chorus of, "Tonight," from *West Side Story*. He had a better voice than mine, so I didn't interrupt.

When his warm tenor delivered the final line, I yelped, "Beat you there!"

I tossed the cell over to the passenger's side, and sped toward Gunn Landing Harbor.

Old Bentley Road can look spooky at night, so it was with relief when, thirty minutes later, I crested the last hill to see the dark Pacific partially obscured by fog. I was still able to catch the outline of my boat, and the sight soothed me. Lately I had become so involved with other people's problems that I'd been neglecting myself, but there was something about the slow, sweet rocking of my *Merilee* that refreshed my soul.

It would feel even more refreshed once Joe arrived.

I coasted down the hill and into the crowded Gunn Landing Harbor parking lot. Apparently not everyone in San Sebastian County had gone to see the last performance of *Tippy-Toe & Tinker*. I'd forgotten that on Saturday nights, the harbor turned into Party Central, where weekend sailors and their invited guests guzzled and danced. Some of them, like the hearty folk along Docks 6 and 7, dressed up like pirates and bellowed old sea chanteys at the tops of their lungs.

I eased my truck into its regular spot a couple hundred yards down from my boat. Off-key sea chanteys may not have been the most romantic of music, but tonight they would provide an element of ribaldry, which was all to the good. As I stepped out of the truck and hurried toward Dock 4, I noticed a car cruising into the parking lot. Joe? No. This was a little compact, not a big police cruiser. Besides, knowing Joe and the way he drove, he was probably already on the *Merilee*, lighting candles and chilling the Gunn Vineyards sauvignon blanc I'd purchased in anticipation of this very evening. I quickened my pace to a fast trot. I couldn't go any faster in my Seduction Jeans, but it didn't matter. They wouldn't be on me for long.

The gate to Dock 4, though, didn't feel like cooperating with my eagerness. When I jammed the keycard into the slot, the green light didn't come on.

I tried again.

Nothing.

Again.

Still nothing.

I kicked the gate in irritation, happily discovering that my foot succeeded where my keycard failed.

The gate swung open.

I made a mental note to tell the harbor master about it in the morning—broken locks being the forerunner of thefts—but as for now...

I hopped aboard, only to discover that Joe hadn't yet arrived. The cabin was still locked, so once I'd let myself in, it was to darkness and silence, the *Merilee*'s tough keel baffling the sea chanteys choruses to a dull roar. After flicking on the galley light, I lay my keys down on the countertop and was about to set the sauvignon blanc into the small refrigerator when the cabin door opened behind me.

"Oh, Joe! Isn't it wonderful that we..."

It wasn't Joe.

It was the killer.

Chapter Twenty-Four

Having run out of tire irons, Jocelyn Ravel stood facing me with a lug wrench.

"Stupid bitch," she squeaked. "You couldn't leave it alone, could you?"

"Apparently not," I said, easing my hand over to my silver key ring, and moving my body slightly so she couldn't see what I was doing. "You led me on a merry chase, didn't you?"

An expression of pride crossed her face. Not surprising, given the fact that most killers are prideful. They'd have to be, wouldn't they, in order to believe that their lives were more important than anyone else's?

"Everybody thinks that with my voice I'm too cutesy to be smart, but I fooled them, didn't I?"

"You sure did." *Keep her talking.* "But why kill so many?"

She sniffed. "They were in my way. Just like you."

"It started with your grandmother, didn't it, Honey Bee?"

She winced at my use of her real name; she'd never liked it, which is why, according to PlatoSchmato, she'd changed it once she'd turned eighteen. The better to cover her murderous tracks, too.

"I don't wanna talk about that old bitch."

"You know what they say; confession is good for the soul." I said, stretching this out enough to give me time to reach my key ring.

It had all begun with a very bad movie titled *Swamp of the Undead*, which was promptly plagiarized by *Zombie Lust*. When Rhonda Estancia, Jocelyn's paternal grandmother, won her court case against the fraudulent firm of Flaherty, Strayle, and Donaldson, Jocelyn probably thought she was set for life. But here we were, years down the line, and the money—wherever it was stashed—was still in some banker's version of dry dock.

"Your poor grandmother," I said. "Years in court, and nothing to show for it. But you killed her for it anyway, didn't you?"

"Poor, my ass! She had *millions*, although in the end she was just another failed actress, then failed producer. How useless can you get? So props to you, Teddy girl. Yeah, I pushed her down the stairs. How was I to know she'd left all her money to those dumb-ass animal charities? It should have come to me, her own flesh and blood! Talk about somebody who deserved killing."

Stalling for time, I asked a question I already knew the answer to. "Did you kill your twin brother, too?"

"I can't take one hundred percent credit for that." Another of her annoying smirks. "Waylon being so big and all."

"Right. You needed a little muscle to help you." I also knew whose muscle it had been. Still, I needed to keep her talking. My beautiful silver key ring, Joe's thoughtful Christmas gift, was now less than an inch away from my fingers. "But geez, Jocelyn, if your attorneys haven't been able to track the money down by now, chances are good they'll never find it. One other thing. Oh, a couple of things, actually. I can understand why you had to, ah, get rid of your grandmother and your brother, the more money for you, right? But what'd you have to gain by killing Flaherty and Donaldson?"

She stuck her lower lip out like a pouty little girl, which she was. "Don't act dumber than you really are. I killed Farthead

Flaherty because he tried to get me scrubbed from the new contract with CFZ Productions just because he didn't like me!"

Which proved that part of the poor man's brain was still
working at the end. "So you killed him for revenge?"

A manic smile. "It's true what they say, that revenge is sweet.
You shoulda heard him squeal when I clocked him."

"How about Donaldson? Why kill him?"

"Because the old creep found out about me and Nestor."

Almost there. I pretended surprise. "Nestor Vanderman?
The scriptwriter?"

She snorted. "You think there's two Nestor Vandermans running around San Sebastian County? As if."

Yeah, as if.

"But why would you care if Marty Donaldson found out you
and Nestor were, uh, dating?"

"'Cause Marty was jealous, dumbass! How do you think I
got my job on that stupid show in the first place? I pretended to
be in love with him, came running every time his wife was out
of town, and he bought it, which shows you how stupid he was.
I mean, did he really think I was doing him because I was into
creepy old men? Then last week he was down here at the harbor
getting some of that clam chowder to take home, and who did
he see leaving *Starvin' Marvin*? Me, that's who! But I didn't see
him, so I didn't know what was up when the next day he called
me down to his office and told me...told me..."

"He told you he was going to pull you from the CFZ contract."

"Yeah."

"The building's security cameras. That was you, dressed up
like a ninja?"

She actually laughed. "What, you think I'm a two penny car
thief? Hell no, it wasn't me, just a couple of friends of mine.
They love pinball as much as I do, and over time, we shared a
few secrets. I knew exactly when I could get into that garage
without being seen."

"Did your ninja friends share their take with you?"

"Of course they did, but it was never enough." Jocelyn's face darkened. "After my bitch roommates threw me out I moved in with Nestor for a couple of days, and problem was, I guess I talked in my sleep, and some of the stuff I said kinda turned him off. Anyway, this afternoon he said that I was losing it, that..." For a moment, the misery lying beneath her viciousness reared its sorrowful head. "He told me...he told me I had to...had to..."

I softened my voice. "Had to what, Jocelyn?"

She gulped. "That I had to get my stuff off his boat and disappear from his life forever, so I..." She raised the lug wrench, and studied the heavy tool as if it contained the answer for all her problems. The dried blood already on it testified that it did.

Nestor Vanderman hadn't been backstage at this evening's performance. Instead, his body was probably stiffening in the galley of *Starvin' Marvin.*

The key ring was in my right hand now, and my fingers were busy finding the right attachment. Finally ready, I turned up my left hand in a beseeching manner. "Why don't you give me that lug wrench, Jocelyn? We can work this out."

She pulled back. "What's that you've got in your other hand?"

"It's empty. Can't you see..."

With a howl of outrage, she lunged forward and brought the lug wrench down, but I'd seen the change in her eyes, so the wrench swept through empty air. Used to working with wilder animals than her, I was all the way up the cabin steps and onto the deck by the time she caught up with me. In the sharp, cool night air, she raised the wrench again.

Too late.

Safe now from asphyxiation in the *Merilee's* tiny cabin, I gave her a long blast in the face with my fully loaded pepper spray canister.

Then, as she shrieked and grabbed at her eyes, I heaved her entitled ass overboard.

Chapter Twenty-Five

Unfortunately, the pepper spray had temporarily impeded Jocelyn's swimming skills, so once I saw her having trouble, I threw her one of the *Merilee*'s life rings. Since she was still half-blind and couldn't see it, I wound up jumping into the dirty harbor water myself to clamp her arm around the ring. While I was doing that, she swung at me again, but in muscle tone a puppeteer is no match for a zookeeper.

I socked her in the nose. Hard.

The blow sent her under the dirty water again, so I had to dive down, grab her by the hair, and haul her back up. Then I left her clutching the life ring, floundering and snorting, while I climbed back onto the *Merilee*.

"You've blinded me!" she sobbed, after hacking water out of her lungs.

"Be grateful I didn't kill you. But if you try to get back on board, I will, and with your own damned lug wrench!" I waved it at her.

She settled down after that, so I set about summoning help, which turned out to be more complicated that it should have been since I'd foolishly left my cell phone in my truck.

Damn Seduction Jeans.

Fortunately, just as I was about to ascend to the *Merilee's* cabin roof and start screaming FIRE!!!—the only certain way to get the attention of partiers who were still singing their way through another verse of "Drunken Sailor"—I saw Walt MacAdams walk toward the dock with Annette and Terri.

"What's going on?" he called.

Before he could attempt to rescue the waif in the water, I gave him a quick rundown on the night's events, whereupon he sent Annette and Terri to take shelter in *Running Wild's* cabin. Then, leaving Jocelyn hissing and screeching in the water, he called 9-1-1.

A few minutes later Joe arrived.

Apparently, Joe had been calling incessantly for the last fifteen minutes to tell me we needed to put off our romantic evening because one of the ninja car thieves had kicked out the side window of a deputy's cruiser. As soon as the kid had managed to weasel his way out, he'd been run down by a golf cart filled with partiers from the San Sebastian Country Club. The kid would be fine, but the paperwork, oh, the paperwork.

"Why the hell didn't you respond to my calls?" he said, furious.

He wasn't happy about my answer.

He was especially unhappy when I handed him my soggy notes—they'd been in the pocket of my Seduction Jeans when I'd gone into the water—detailing how and why Jocelyn Ravel, aka Honey Bee Estancia-Barnes, had murdered five people. Somewhere along the line, more law officers and EMTs arrived, and Jocelyn Ravel was fished out of the drink, handcuffed, and taken away to the hospital to get the harbor water pumped out of her stomach.

Before the ambulance was out of the lot, one of the deputies who'd been sent over to check out *Starvin' Marvin* shouted, "We've got another one down!"

Poor Nestor Vanderman. When one disturbed child meets another, the answer isn't always *Romeo and Juliet*.

Sometimes it's more like *Nightmare on Elm Street*.

Epilogue

FOUR MONTHS LATER

Karma isn't always a bitch. Sometimes she's surprisingly kind.

True, *Tippy-Toe & Tinker* is headed for the big toon screen without any of its original cast, but thanks to CFZ Productions' invocation of the standard "morals" clause in Jocelyn Ravel's contract—can't have a multiple murderer in a kiddie show, can we?—the new producers allowed the rights to the Poonya character to revert back to their original owners: Cliff Flaherty and Martin Donaldson.

Or, rather, their estates.

Speaking of estates, car dealer Big Rick Stevens, in an out-of-court settlement, agreed to drop his long-standing lawsuit against Flaherty and Donaldson in exchange for thirty seconds' airtime during each of the new show's episodes; sales are booming.

And in another surprising act of generosity, CFZ Productions transferred ownership of the dinosaur marionettes to the original cast, with the caveat that the marionettes not be used for public performances again.

Hollywood. All heart.

While the old version of *Tippy-Toe & Tinker* is no more, it has been replaced in the San Sebastian area by *The Case Files of Poonya, Panda Detective*, written by one-time janitor Jerome Lukasik, with an assist by mystery novelist Colleen Rejas. The new show—using the same puppeteers, but with new marionettes modeled after various zoo denizens—is being bankrolled by the former producers' estates. To wit, newly wealthy Dylan Ellis, and old-money veteran Gloria Marquand-Donaldson, who promptly gave each of the puppeteers a big raise.

The additional money has allowed for a certain shift in living arrangements.

Beverly Beaumont and Karla Dollar bought *Scribbler*, and are now learning the delights of liveaboard life in Gunn Landing Harbor. They aren't the only new liveaboarders around. Gordo bought *Starvin' Marvin*, and is busy restoring the boat to its former glory. Meanwhile, Bird and Gloria Marquand-Donaldson are now A Thing, and he's teaching her how to surf.

A few old wounds have been healed, too.

Lauren Ellis Overholdt, under urging by her family-values son, finally visited her parents. Angry words were spoken and tears were shed, but in the end, they hugged it out.

Justice was served in the case of the State of California against Jocelyn Ravel/Honey Bee Estancia-Barnes, the confessed killer of four people. In case you haven't been keeping score, they were, in order: her grandmother, Rhonda Estancia; Jocelyn's twin brother, Waylon; and producers Cliff Flaherty and Martin Donaldson.

That's four people, not five, because Jocelyn only thought she'd successfully killed her sometimes-lover, Nestor Vanderman. But Nestor survived the blow on his head, and took his revenge by testifying against her at the trial. His loquaciousness lightened his own sentence for helping kill Jocelyn's twin brother to a measly fifty-five years in San Quentin.

The judge wasn't as lenient with Jocelyn/Honey Bee. She is

now serving a sentence of Life without Parole at the California Institution for Women.

From what I hear, she's having trouble with her roommates.

As for me, I promised Joe I would never again involve myself in a murder investigation. What I didn't tell him was that I'd begun taking shooting lessons at Sharp Shooters International Firing Range, over in Salinas.

Just in case.

The End

(for now)

ACKNOWLEDGMENTS

Much fiction is based on truth, and the DNA surprise in this book actually happened to me. My "new" brother Ron and his wonderful family have brought me great joy, and I believe much of that joy has been transferred to these pages.

On that note, I guess it is only fair to thank our rather naughty father, Jacob Gaston Webb, for acting on the Biblical advice to "go forth and multiply." Dad, it's too bad you didn't live long enough to know about all of us, because I think you would have been delighted.

Also helping to make writing this book a joyful process are my human and animal friends at the Phoenix Zoo; the plot hole-conscious Sheridan Street Irregulars; my patient husband, Paul Howell; and my trusty readers, Delpha Wright, Judy Par, Marge Purcell, and Debra McCarthy. Thanks a million, guys!

Any mistakes that made it into these pages are down to me, not them.

ABOUT THE AUTHOR

Before writing mysteries, Betty Webb was a journalist and interviewed U.S. presidents, Nobel Prize winners, astronauts who walked on the moon, as well as the homeless, dying, and polygamy runaways. Now she is best known for her prize-winning Lena Jones mysteries based on stories she covered as a reporter *(Desert Noir, Desert Wives, Desert Shadows, Desert Run, Desert Lost, Desert Cut, Desert Wind, Desert Rage, Desert Vengeance,* and *Desert Redemption)*, and the humorous Gunn Zoo mysteries (*The Anteater of Death, The Koala of Death, The Llama of Death, The Puffin of Death,* and *The Otter of* Death). Betty is a member of the National Federation of Press Women, the Mystery Writers of America, and the National Organization of Zoo Keepers. For more, see bettywebb-mystery.com.